NO HIDING PLACE

ROBERT MCNEIL

BLOODHOUND
— BOOKS —

First published in 2023 by Bloodhound Books.

www.bloodhoundbooks.com

Print ISBN: 978-1-5040-8523-6

ALSO BY ROBERT MCNEIL

1

OXFORD

Oliver Upton thought he glimpsed a movement in the trees up ahead. Feeling a sudden pang of anxiety, he shielded his eyes from the sun and looked again. He couldn't see anything. Taking a deep breath to calm his racing pulse, he decided it was nothing.

Although memories of the past were well behind him, there were still times when Upton felt the urge to look over his shoulder. He had to stay alert, could never let his guard down, and was always wary of strangers. It was five years since they'd changed his life. He felt safe, at least most of the time. But it was small things like this that triggered unease. This was the second time today his heart had raced.

Having taken the day off from his taxi-driving job in Oxford, he'd decided to enjoy a round of golf. It was late spring and there was hardly a cloud in the sky. He'd packed his clubs and trolley into his Volvo XC40 and set off first thing in the morning. Despite the early start, traffic had already begun to build up on his way out of town.

Glancing in his rear-view mirror several times, he'd seen the same black car. Was it following him? He'd tried to stay calm, but without realising it, his hands had gripped the steering wheel tighter showing the whites of his knuckles. Upton cursed the nervous knot forming in his stomach. The roads were busy. Why wouldn't other cars be going in the same direction? He didn't have an exclusive right of way. Taking a couple of deep breaths, he'd carried on, keeping a wary eye on the mirror.

The black car had followed Upton to the golf course on the outskirts of Oxford. But much to Upton's relief, it had driven past as Upton turned into the driveway. He'd changed into his golf shoes, watching the entrance to the car park while setting up his trolley and clubs. The black car hadn't appeared and Upton was beginning to feel paranoid as he made his way to the golf shop to check in.

The strong aroma of frying bacon wafted through from the clubhouse café as he'd entered the building. He'd wished then he'd had a bigger breakfast.

Although Upton had a few golfing friends, he'd decided to have a little practice on his own. His game had gone downhill of late and he felt he needed a round without the pressure of others watching him. It was midweek and Upton guessed the course wouldn't be busy this early in the morning. He was right.

A young man had been serving behind the desk in the golf shop. 'Morning,' he'd said. 'Mr Upton, is it?'

'Yeah. Tee time booked for eight.'

'Got you,' the young man had confirmed. 'You should be all clear. No one else has teed off before you, and there's no one behind for half an hour.'

Upton had played the first four holes well and was beginning to relax. His score was reasonable so far. The sun had picked up some heat and the leaves in nearby trees rustled in the faint breeze. Things were looking up as Upton pulled his baseball cap further down over his eyes against the glare of the sun. He placed his ball on a tee and then walked behind it to point his club up the fairway. It was when he was checking the intended flight of the ball that he thought he'd glimpsed the movement in the trees up ahead. He frowned. *No one else has teed off before you,* the man in the golf shop had said.

Upton shrugged. *Could be a dog walker.*

Standing to one side of the tee, he took three practice swings. He was about to move closer to the ball to take the shot when something glinted in the sunlight up ahead. He frowned. *There is someone up there.*

Upton turned to take one more look up the fairway. It was then that the first bullet thudded into his chest. The second ripped into him before he hit the ground.

The man hiding in the trees looked through the telescopic sights of his rifle for any sign of other golfers. There was no one around. He made his way down through the saplings on the edge of the fairway, checking all the time that no one appeared.

When he reached a clearing opposite Upton's body, he scanned the course again. There was still no one in sight. He strode across to the body and bent down to check for a pulse. There was nothing.

The assassin ran back to the tree line and made his way to where he'd parked his car in a clearing by the side of the course. Throwing the rifle into the boot, he climbed into the driving seat.

Smiling, he turned on the ignition, put the car into gear, and eased out onto the road.

2

LONDON

A grey blanket of cloud had descended over London blotting out the sun. Wisps of black vapour raced underneath, driven by gusts of high wind. Lightning flashed over the city and thunder rumbled in the distance.

Toby Enderby sat in his car outside his mother's house waiting for a break in the rain which didn't come. Having no option, he grabbed a bag of groceries and prepared for a mad dash to the front door. A gust of wind wrenched the car door out of his hands and threw it wide open. Shards of icy rain pelted his face as he struggled out of the car. He slammed the door shut and ran for the house; the bag of groceries in one hand and the other pointing his key fob back towards the car.

Enderby cursed as he fumbled for the front door key. The rain had plastered his brown curly hair to his head and his breath came in wheezing fits as he opened the door. He stepped inside and pushed the door shut against the whistling wind. He leant his slender frame back against the door and took several deep breaths.

There was no sound from the sitting room. His mother

usually had the TV on full blast. 'Mother, it's me, Toby,' he called out.

There was no answer.

'Mother!'

After a few seconds silence, the sitting room door opened and Doreen Enderby stood there, her frail body hunched over her walking stick. 'Oh, for goodness' sake! Don't shout, Toby. I must have fallen asleep.'

'Sorry.'

'Did you get everything?' Doreen asked in a croaky voice.

'Yes.'

Doreen examined Toby through watery blue eyes, sunk deep into a wrinkled face. 'My cigarettes?'

Toby shook his head. 'They weren't on the list.'

Doreen tugged at the red bead necklace round her scrawny neck. 'Oh, you're useless. You know I always have cigarettes.'

'You smoke too much.'

'Makes no difference at my age. I happen to enjoy a cigarette. Helps calm me down.'

'Hmm. Let's get your shopping into the kitchen.'

Doreen shuffled in after him. 'You sound a bit wheezy. Have you been using your inhaler?'

'Of course. Look... there's some–'

'My prescription. Did you remember to get it?' Doreen interrupted.

'Yes, Mother. It's in the bag. Listen–'

'And the library books. Did you return them?'

'Yes! I'm trying to tell you something, Mo–'

'Toby! Why are you shouting? You sound irritable. What's the matter? It's not that woman again, is it? She's been back in touch and it's made you cross. Is that it?'

'No, it's not *that* woman. Her name was Hanah, and she

hasn't been in touch. There's not much chance of that since you put paid to our relationship.'

'Don't be ridiculous, Toby. She wasn't right for you. I could see that. Anyway... she was the one who broke off the engagement.'

'Yes, because she couldn't stand your continual interference. And... you told her she wasn't good enough for me.'

'I did not!'

'Yes, you did.'

'I'm sure I didn't. She never liked me, you know. It wouldn't have worked.'

Toby sighed. 'Can we *not* get into this again. I'm trying to tell you something important.'

Doreen tapped her walking stick on the floor. 'Well, get on with it. You do beat about the bush.'

'I saw the doctor last week and–'

'Whatever for? There's nothing wrong with you! I'm the one who suffers from aches and pains. You're always complaining about something. You need to give yourself a good shake.'

Toby ignored the outburst. 'He reckons I'm suffering from stress-related anxiety, and cycling to work every day in heavy traffic isn't helping my asthma. He said London wasn't the best place to live and work in my condition.'

'Don't be silly. You love it here. Is that all you wanted to tell me?'

'No. I saw an advert for an interesting job and, because of what the doctor was saying, I'm thinking of applying for it.'

'A job? But you've got a good job here in London. Your school is only a twenty-minute bike ride from your flat. Whatever possessed you to look for another job?'

'It's becoming too stressful. Too much paperwork, classes are too big, the children are disruptive, and the headmaster's a bully.'

'Oh, for goodness' sake. Get a grip of yourself. You've no idea what stress is. Think about me left on my own after your father died. I'm the one suffering from stress. As for your schoolchildren, they just need a bit of discipline. And... you need to stand up for yourself against the headmaster. He'll soon back down if you challenge him.'

Like you do, Toby thought. 'London's not exactly a relaxing place to live. It's bad for my health and this job sounds perfect.'

'I hope you're not going to tell me it's out of town. I need you here to look after me.'

'I'm afraid it is. It's up in Scotland. A small village called Balcorie... near Lochinver.'

'Scotland! Lochinver! Where about in Scotland is that?'

'Up in the Highlands, on the west coast.'

'What's the job?'

'Teaching. It's a tiny primary school. There are only ten pupils and the teacher there is retiring.'

'Have you gone out of your mind? A school with only ten pupils in the middle of nowhere, and hundreds of miles away from me. You can't apply for it.'

'Don't worry, Mother. If I do apply and get it, Quentin will still be here. He can look after you.'

'Toby, your brother's a married man with two young children. He hasn't got the time. You can't possibly think about moving out of London. I won't cope on my own.'

'You'd be fine. I'd be able to come down some weekends, and there's the school holidays as well.'

'Weekends! School holidays! I need you here all the time! What if there's a crisis? You're only half an hour away now. It would take you all day to get back from this Balcorie!'

'I'm thirty-five! I need to get out of the rut I'm in and make a new life for myself. This school in Scotland seems perfect. And it'll be better for my health.'

'Oh, I see. It's come to that, has it? I'm just a rut, a hindrance to you, and you want to leave me here all on my own. Some thanks for everything I've done for you. It'll all end in tears you know. Mark my words.' Doreen sniffed. 'You wouldn't get an interview anyway.'

'I'll sleep on it.'

Toby finished unpacking the shopping and left saying he needed to prepare some lessons. He'd already made up his mind about what he was going to do.

3

OXFORD

DS Logan and DC Anderson were sitting at a table in the archives room at Thames Valley Police HQ. It was hot and stuffy and dust floated in the air under the strip lighting. The bulb above the table flickered and buzzed as though it were about to emit its last glimmer of light. In front of them, piled high on the table, were the files from their previous case.

Logan was about to make a comment when DCI Fleming walked in. 'How's it going?'

'We need a cup of tea working in all this dust,' Logan complained.

'As it happens...' Fleming said, putting down a tray with three mugs on the table.

'No biscuits?' Logan queried.

'Think yourself lucky you've got tea,' Anderson said.

'True. Didn't hear you offering to go and get some.'

'Far too busy with this lot.'

'Still a bit of archiving to do,' Fleming noted, looking at the pile of documents and box files on the table.

Logan took a grateful sip of his tea then looked up at the

blackened ends of the guilty strip light. 'About time they did something about these. Not good for your eyesight.'

Anderson sighed. 'Here we go. He'll have the health and safety rep in here next.'

Logan nodded. 'Good idea. They ought to do something about the dust in here as well.'

'Sarge is in a grumpy mood today, sir,' Anderson said, looking at Fleming after blowing on her tea to cool it.

'For good reason. Scam phone calls and emails are getting on my wife's nerves. Had a go at me over it. Reckons we ought to be doing something.'

'Like what?' Anderson asked.

'Like tracking them down, locking them up, and throwing the keys away.'

'Not so easy,' Fleming said. 'They're often from overseas and use burner phones.'

'What calls has she been getting?' Anderson asked.

'Loads of them,' Logan said. 'One of them said they were from HMRC saying she had a refund due. Asked for her bank details. Another claimed to be from Amazon saying someone was trying to hack into her account to place an order worth over a thousand quid. Then she got a call to say someone had accessed her bank account and she needed to transfer her money to another account.'

'Bloody hell!... Sorry,' Anderson added.

'There's more. She had one caller who said he was from the National Crime Agency and that someone was trying to steal her identity. He suggested she transfer her bank account to be on the safe side.'

'How do these people target you?' Anderson asked.

'Random calls, I guess,' Logan said. 'Hoping they get someone who'll fall for the scam and give them their details. She had one claiming to be our internet service provider. Reckoned they'd found criminal activity on our account and were about to close it. They wanted her to click on a link to keep it open.'

'Best bet is to hang up on all cold calls from people you don't know,' Fleming said.

'Sad state of affairs,' Logan said. 'Can't trust anyone these days.'

'I delete all emails from people I don't know, especially if it asks you to open a link,' Anderson added.

'We could get rid of our mobiles and computer and we'll be free of the scheming bastards,' Logan muttered.

Anderson smiled. 'Still get you on your landline though.'

'Your optimism never ceases to amaze me, Naomi.'

'Just stating a fact, Sarge.'

'Hmm. Here's a fact. I'm bloody starving. Break for some lunch?'

'Tell you what. How about I pop out to the local chippy and get us some fish and chips,' Fleming suggested.

'Best thing I've heard all morning,' Logan said.

Fleming was about to go when his mobile vibrated, indicating an incoming call. He looked at the screen: *Superintendent Temple.*

Fleming sighed. 'Super, need to take this.' He listened for a minute, then ended the call.

Logan looked at the frown on Fleming's face. 'Problem?'

'Chips will have to wait, I'm afraid. There's been a murder on one of the local golf courses. Someone's shot a golfer. I need to get over there.'

4

OXFORD

Fleming had finally accepted his old Porsche had seen better days and had traded it in to buy a new silver Audi Q5. He pulled off the road and drove up the narrow lane leading to the golf club car park. Up ahead, a uniformed officer stood in front of blue and white tape stretched across the lane. Fleming stopped and lowered his window.

'Sorry, sir. There's been an incident. They've closed the golf course for the day,' the uniformed officer explained.

Fleming flashed his warrant card. 'DCI Fleming. I'm the on-call SIO.'

'Oh, right. Pull your car over to the side and you can make your way on foot up to the car park.'

Fleming parked the Audi and opened the boot to get his scene-of-crime protective clothing out. Once kitted out in white overalls and elasticated overshoes, he nodded to the uniform and ducked under the tape. A canopy of tall trees shaded the driveway from the sun, but then it opened out into a large car park. There were a few cars there and two SOCOs in white overalls were searching through a blue Volvo XC40 up near the entrance to the clubhouse.

Fleming wandered over. 'Victim's?'

There was an enquiring look from one of the men.

Fleming showed his warrant card again. 'DCI Fleming... on-call SIO.'

The man nodded. 'Yeah. Not found anything. There were a few business cards for an Oxford taxi firm in the glove compartment... Andy Cabs.'

'Right. Where's the body?'

'He was about to tee off for the fifth hole,' the same SOCO said. 'I'm done here. I'll take you.'

More SOCOs were searching the ground round the tee-off green for the fifth hole. A tall thin man was standing a few yards in front of the body, scratching his short grey hair as he looked up the fairway. He was shielding his eyes against the sun, which seemed unnecessary as he was wearing sunglasses.

'If it isn't the Lone Ranger,' Fleming said, coming up behind the man. He knew straight away from the long gangly legs who the man was. Fleming had come across DI Vincent Rainger of Oxford local CID several times. One of Rainger's colleagues, who happened to be a big western fan, hadn't been able to resist the temptation to give Rainger the nickname.

Rainger turned and gave Fleming one of his rare smiles. His face was showing signs of deep wrinkles and his Adam's apple looked as big as Upton's golf ball. 'Hi, Alex. See they've called in the big boots DCI from the Major Crime Unit.'

'You know the drill. Local CID assist with enquiries, but we take charge of major crimes. Murder is one of them.'

'I know, only teasing. Come in that old Porsche of yours?'

'No, traded it in for a new silver Audi.'

Rainger's response brought a smile to Fleming's lips as Rainger's colleagues knew him to be a dour character with little sense of humour. 'You came in your silver bullet then, eh?'

The SOCO who had guided Fleming to the body shook his

head and smiled. 'We have a dead body here and all you two want to do is talk about The Lone Ranger and his silver bullet.'

Fleming returned the smile. 'Suitably chastised.' He turned to Rainger. 'Anyone touch the body?'

'No. We know who he is though. Man called Upton... Oliver Upton. One of the golfers who found him knew who he was. Local taxi driver.'

'Andy Cabs,' Fleming said.

'How'd you know that?'

'Business cards in his car,' the SOCO said.

Fleming glanced at Rainger. 'What time was he found?'

'About nine thirty.'

'So we know the time of death is between when the golf shop opened and nine thirty.'

'Right.'

'Any witnesses?'

'None that we know of.'

Fleming bent down and felt in Upton's pockets. All he found was a mobile phone, house keys, a wallet, and Upton's driving licence confirming Upton's name and address. He looked up at Rainger. 'Any close relatives we know of?'

'One of the men who found the body reckons he lived with a partner, Jamila Kazan. Want me to send a couple of officers round?'

Fleming thought for a moment. 'Please. Best let her know straight away. Tell them to let her know I'll be calling in to speak to her.'

'Right.'

Fleming handed Upton's mobile to Rainger. 'Get one of your telephone whizz kids from your technical department to check this out. All the usual stuff; contacts, memory, messages, calls, social media, and anything else they can find.'

'First thoughts?' Rainger asked.

'Not a robbery. Unlikely he would have anything of value on him. His wallet's still full of cash.'

Rainger scratched his head again. 'Whoever shot him must have known he was coming here.'

'Or followed him,' Fleming added.

'Hate crime, revenge, professional hitman, serial killer. Take your pick,' Rainger muttered.

'Or maybe someone wanted him silenced,' Fleming offered.

'That too. Think it was a handgun or rifle.'

'Ballistics will confirm, but my guess is it was a rifle.'

Rainger rubbed his chin. 'How'd you work that out?'

'The killer would've been close to him if he used a handgun. Upton would have seen him coming. He'd put his ball on the tee which would suggest he didn't.'

'Could have appeared after Upton had placed his ball.'

Fleming looked around. 'Quite a few yards from the nearest trees. If Upton did see someone approaching with a gun, he'd have turned and run, in which case the killer would have shot him from behind.'

Rainger looked down at Upton's blood-stained T-shirt and the two neat bullet holes in his chest. 'Fair point. Maybe he was in shock and couldn't move.'

'As I said; it's just a guess. Let's wait for the ballistics report.'

'Alex!' a man called out, approaching from behind. 'Got here as quick as I could. Traffic.'

Fleming turned. 'Nathan, good to see you.' He nodded towards Rainger. 'This is DI Rainger, local CID. Vincent this is Dr Nathan Kumar, Home Office pathologist.'

Rainger held out a hand. 'Good to meet you. You two obviously know each other.'

'We keep turning up in the same place where there're dead bodies,' Kumar said. 'Okay to have a look?'

'Sure, go ahead,' Fleming said. He turned to face Rainger. 'Got your notebook handy?'

Rainger fished inside his overalls and pulled it out of his jacket pocket.

Fleming continued. 'Get everyone who was on the golf course or in the clubhouse questioned, including staff. I'll have a word with whoever was in the shop on my way out. Check for any CCTV cameras at the clubhouse and surrounding roads. Trace drivers of all vehicles logged this morning and arrange for them to be questioned.'

Rainger tapped his pencil against his notebook. 'Got it. As a firearm was involved, should we get a TV bulletin out to reassure the public; appeal for any witnesses, that sort of thing?'

'Good idea. Can you arrange it?'

'On my list.'

Kumar had finished his preliminary checks on Upton. He stood and faced Fleming.

'I'll get the body off to the local mortuary and let you have a full report when I'm done. From an initial examination of the gunshot entry points though, I'd guess the killer used a rifle and shot him from some distance.'

'Thanks, Kumar.' Fleming turned to Rainger. 'Think I'm done here. Get the SOCOs to check up in the woods where the gunman may have been hiding. I'll be in touch.'

5

OXFORD

Fleming watched as they loaded the blue Volvo XC40 onto a trailer ready to be taken away for more detailed forensic checks. Under the circumstances, he wasn't sure they'd find anything, but then a thought occurred to him. He walked over to the SOCO who was supervising procedures. 'Forgot to ask, was the car locked when you found it?'

'Yes. No sign of anyone breaking in to it, sir.'

'Okay, thanks.' Fleming made his way into the clubhouse, a question in his mind resolved. *The killer couldn't have been looking for something.*

The attendant had closed the shop so Fleming went into the café and bar. It was empty apart from a woman tidying up behind the counter and a young man sitting at a table looking out over the golf course. He looked pale and was cradling a glass of what looked like whisky or brandy in both hands. His legs twitched up and down and the heels of his shoes tapped the floor under his seat.

The aroma of frying bacon Upton had smelt when he arrived still lingered in the air. Those who had been enjoying breakfast before a round of golf had long since gone. Rainger's men had taken statements and contact details from everyone in the clubhouse before they'd allowed them to leave.

Fleming walked over to the man by the window. He was wearing golfing trousers and a black T-shirt with a logo design of two crossed golf clubs on the left of his chest. The man looked up as Fleming approached. Fleming noted the red eyes and saw a flicker of unease. 'I guess you're the guy who was working in the shop this morning.'

'Yeah.' The man looked at Fleming's white overalls. 'I see your lot are taking Mr Upton's car away. That for forensic checks?'

'Yes, but I'm not one of the forensics team.' For the third time that morning, he fished out his warrant card. 'DCI Fleming. I'm in charge of the investigation.'

'Ah.' The man pointed at Fleming's overalls. 'Everyone seems to be dressed in those.'

'Easy mistake. We all have to wear scene-of-crime protective clothing once we cross the cordon marked by the blue and white tape draped across the driveway.'

The man looked confused. 'Oh. How come they never gave me any?'

'Because you were already here. It's for people arriving at the scene. Aims to avoid any cross contamination of evidence. Police procedure.'

The man nodded his understanding. 'Two uniformed officers questioned me before you arrived. They took statements from all the golfers who were having a bite to eat before going onto the golf course.'

'Fine, but if you're up to it I'd like to go through things with you. Save me waiting to get all the statements sent over to me.'

The man's hands shook as he took a sip of his drink. 'Okay.'

'What's your name?'

'Sam... Sam Galland.'

Fleming could see the young man was distraught. 'Play yourself?'

Galland attempted a smile. 'Yeah. Got my handicap down to fourteen.'

'Impressive.'

Galland shrugged. 'Practise.'

'You mentioned Mr Upton by name. Did you know him?'

'He was a member.'

'Not personally?'

'No.'

'How long had he been a member for?'

'About two years.'

'He presumably had golfing friends... I mean fellow members?'

'He sometimes played with other members, yeah.'

'But today he was on his own. Did he say why?'

'He said something about needing the practise. Thought one or two aspects of his game needed sorting out. Best to do that on your own.'

'What time did you open the shop?'

'About seven forty-five. Mr Upton's tee time was eight. Booked it the night before. The café was open from about seven thirty. Members sometimes just come here for a social breakfast. Others like to eat before they set out on the course.'

'Anyone else out on the course before Mr Upton?'

'No, I remember telling him it wasn't busy. No one teed off before him.'

'And after him?'

'No one for half an hour.'

'So he paid for his round just before eight and then went straight out?'

'He was a member, so didn't need to pay. We like members to

check in though, so we know who is out there on the course at any one time.'

'So if no one teed off before Mr Upton, and no one else teed off for half an hour, he should have been the only one on the course between eight and half past?'

'Except for grounds staff.'

'Have you given their names to the officers who questioned you?'

'Yes. We pulled them off the course as soon as we found out what had happened. Officers questioned them and took statements.'

'You said he sometimes played with other members. Would they be more or less the same people?'

'I think so, apart from competitions when you get drawn with partners.'

'But otherwise, the same guys?'

'I guess so.'

'Did he get on with other members, do you know?'

'As far as I know... except...'

'Go on.'

'A few weeks ago, there was a big commotion in the clubhouse. Guy called Ian Hunter had a big row with Mr Upton. Accused him of stealing an expensive golf club.'

'And had he?'

'Never found out. It all died down.'

'Were the police involved?'

'No.'

Fleming watched Galland sip the last of whatever it was he was drinking. 'The golfers who found the body told my colleague they found Mr Upton around nine thirty. How long would it take for them to reach the fifth hole?'

'Depends how well they were playing. Four guys had a tee time of eight thirty, half an hour after Mr Upton. On average, they would play the first four in about fifty minutes. Maybe just over.'

'So they must have been the men who found the body.'

'They were. They came back here and asked me to call the police.'

'Had other golfers teed off after them?'

'Yes, but the guys told them what had happened on their way to the clubhouse. They all returned.'

'Why didn't one of the men ring the police on a mobile?'

'They were playing in a group and it's protocol not to have your phone on. I guess they'd left their phones in their cars.'

'You've been really helpful, Sam. Thank you. Are you going to be all right? It must have been a bit of a shock.'

Galland gave a weak smile. 'Thanks. I'm fine.'

'Okay.' Fleming got up to go. 'You take care.'

Fleming made his way back to his car making a mental note to make sure DI Rainger's officers questioned Ian Hunter. *Maybe there was more to the row than a stolen golf club.*

6

LONDON

Toby's apartment was in a new block of flats near Croydon. It was all he could afford on his salary but it suited him. It was near enough for him to be able to cycle to the primary school where he taught. His elder brother, Quentin, used to work in a bank. He was now the managing director for a financial services company and had helped Toby to get a mortgage. The monthly payments were crippling but Toby was able to make ends meet.

The apartment had a long rectangular lounge, a dining area, a small kitchen, a bathroom and one bedroom. Toby had decided on grey walls in the lounge which he'd adorned with paintings, some of which he'd done himself. A TV sat in the far corner, but Toby seldom watched it. He spent most of his spare time listening to music, reading and painting. That was when he wasn't running errands for his mother or sorting out her problems.

Toby was standing at the large window at the end of the lounge, looking down on the communal car park below. He was waiting for his brother to arrive. Quentin had phoned to say he would be round as soon as he could after work, about six. Toby had expected the call after his recent visit to drop their mother's shopping off. He knew their mother would have wasted no time in enlisting Quentin's help to try to dissuade him from applying for the teaching job in Scotland.

Someone in the block of flats opposite waved. Toby had no idea who it was, but returned the wave anyway.

A few minutes later, Quentin's black Alfa Romeo Giulietta pulled into the car park. The car was a company car, a perk that came with his recent promotion to managing director of Able James Financial Services. That said, with the salary Quentin enjoyed, he could afford to buy one.

Toby watched him climb out of the car. He was on his own, having left Margo, his wife, and the two children behind. It confirmed Toby's expectation that he and Quentin were about to have an awkward conversation. On visits to Toby, Quentin would normally dress in his casual clothes: white polo neck, brown leather jacket, and blue jeans. The urgency of today's visit was obvious. Quentin still wore his typical city financier dark suit and white shirt.

The doorbell rang a few moments later and Toby opened the door to see Quentin had at least removed his tie. 'Hello, Quentin. Busy day?'

Quentin was a bit taller than Toby and five years older. His short brown hair was showing early signs of greying and the tightness of his shirt round the waist told a story of lavish hospitality dinners. He unbuttoned the suit jacket and pulled it off as he came through the door. 'As always, Toby. Pressure is relentless.'

'Well, come in and put your feet up. Want a tea or coffee?'

'Got any beer in your fridge?'

'As it happens, I have. In a glass or straight out the bottle?'

Quentin smiled. 'Margo's not here, so let's dispense with niceties. The bottle will do fine... as long as the beer's cold.'

Toby retired to the kitchen and called over his shoulder. 'How are Margo and the boys? Haven't seen them for a while.'

'They're fine. Must bring them round soon. Maybe have dinner.'

'That would be nice,' Toby said, coming back into the lounge.

Quentin had sprawled himself out on the brown leather sofa. He took the beer from Toby. 'Cheers.'

'So why the visit?' Toby asked, as though he didn't know.

'You seen Mother lately?'

'Yes. Only yesterday. I took her shopping round.'

'Bit of a grim day, yesterday. Complete opposite today. Sweltering. How was she?'

'Oh... her usual. All complaints and everything a problem.'

'Hmm. I'm worried about her. She's getting rather frail, don't you think?'

'It's what happens when people get older.'

'Right.' Quentin took a long swig of his beer and examined the bottle as though trying to decipher what it was. 'I guess that's why she needs you to look after things. I'd do more if I could, but I'm so busy with the job. I hardly have enough time to spend with Margo and the boys, let alone run around after Mother.'

'You should make time.'

'What? To see Mother, or spend time with Margo and the boys?'

'Both.'

'It's difficult, with being an MD. So many demands on the job.'

'You could change jobs.'

'Nah, we like the lifestyle too much.'

'So much that you don't have time to spend with your own family.'

'Fair point, Toby. But the money's so good.'

'It isn't everything.'

Quentin took another sip of beer. 'Thing is, Mother rang me last night. She was a bit upset.'

Toby feigned surprise. 'Oh?'

'She said you told her you were thinking of applying for another job. That right?'

'Yes. Did she tell you why I was thinking of it?'

'Said something about you'd seen a doctor who suggested living in London wasn't doing your asthma any good.'

'It happened to coincide with me seeing an advert for a teaching job.'

'But you're already a teacher.'

'Yes, but this is different. It's a tiny primary school in a remote part of the Scottish Highlands. There're only ten pupils. Sounds ideal. Less pressure, cleaner air. Away from crowds. No stress.'

'Sounds like you've made up your mind. Have you?'

'Not yet,' Toby lied.

'Where is this place?'

'Small village called Balcorie, a few miles north of Lochinver.'

'What about Mother?'

'I can't be her carer for life, Quentin. As I said to her, you're here in London. It's not as though she'll be completely on her own.'

'I haven't the time, Toby. You're a primary school teacher. You get loads of time off. Better position than me to look after her.'

'It's becoming a... a chore. I get no thanks and, to be honest, she's ruling my life. I need to break free. Do something for me.'

'Sounds like you *have* made up your mind.'

'Still considering. All I'm saying is there're good reasons why I should apply for the job.'

Quentin downed the rest of his beer and rose to go. 'Mother will be bereft if you do. So will the boys. Think hard about it, Toby.'

7

OXFORD

Parking was for permit holders only, but Fleming had found a space near Oliver Upton's mid-terrace house. It was in a small street off the Cowley Road. He knew parking might be an issue and had opted to use a marked squad car.

Fleming and Anderson climbed out and made their way along the pavement looking for number twenty-nine. It was a bay-fronted house with a small front garden, shielded from the pavement by a low brick wall with iron railings on top. Broken paving slabs covered the entire frontage apart from a small square area in the middle where there was a solitary fuchsia bush. Two wheelie bins sat to one side of the bay window in front of a black drainpipe.

Fleming pushed a metal gate open and was at the front door in three strides. He rang the doorbell and waited. A minute later, a woman who looked to be of African-Caribbean descent opened the door. She was tall, slim, possibly in her forties, and had shoulder-length jet-black hair. Her eyes were red as though she'd been crying. The white T-shirt she was wearing was crumpled, as though she'd been asleep in it. A rip in one of the knees of her faded blue jeans was either a sign of wear and tear or a fashion statement.

'Are you...?'

'DCI Fleming and DC Anderson. I phoned,' Fleming said.

There was a flicker of a smile. 'You'd better come in. I'm afraid the place is a bit of a mess. Haven't had the motivation to tidy.'

'Don't worry. We won't take much of your time. Just a few questions we need to ask.'

'Sure.' Jamila turned, walked down a small hallway, and pointed through a door that led into a small square sitting room. 'Kitchen is tiny, so we can talk in here.'

The room contained a two-seater settee and two small single chairs. There was a TV in one corner, and an empty cup, a packet of cigarettes and full ashtray sat on a small coffee table next to the settee.

Jamila pointed to the settee. 'Have a seat.'

'Local CID said they would get someone to stay with you yesterday. Have they gone now?' Fleming asked.

'Two officers came to see me... to tell me...' Jamila stopped and fought back tears. 'They phoned for a doctor. I was in shock. He gave me some sedatives. One of the officers stayed all night. She left about half an hour ago and said she could get someone else to call round.'

'I'm sure you're not at risk, but good to know they're watching out for you.'

'I told them it wasn't necessary. I've got time off work. They've been very good. Said to take as much time as I needed. I'm going to stay with my older sister.'

'Where does she live?'

'London. She's a solicitor there.'

'I'll need contact details so we can get in touch if there're any developments.'

Jamila reached under the coffee table and pulled out an address book. 'Zaina Mwangi.'

Anderson held out a hand. 'Mind if we borrow this to make a note of all Mr Upton's contacts?'

'Yeah, sure. The officer who stayed with me yesterday phoned everyone to let them know, so I don't need it for now.'

'Where do you work?' Fleming asked.

'I'm a researcher at Oxford University... Humanities Division, Faculty of History.'

'Must be interesting. How long have you been working there?'

'About twenty-five years. It's where I met my husband... Atticus Kazan.'

'Unusual surname.'

'His father was from Greece and married an English woman.'

'When did you move in with Mr Upton?'

'About six months ago. He'd recently divorced. I had an affair with him. Atticus had become dull... obsessed with his work. It was all he was interested in.'

'How long had you been married?'

'Twenty-two years.'

'Children?'

'No.'

'Are you divorced or separated?'

'Separated, but getting divorced.'

'You met your husband at the university. Is that where he works?'

'Yes.'

'What does he do?'

'He's a lecturer. Teaches mathematics and computer science.'

'How did you meet Mr Upton?'

'Oliver drives taxis for Andy Cabs. He picked me up one day

to take me to a restaurant where I was having a meal with work colleagues, then picked me up again at the end of the night. We got chatting. Met him again when I was shopping in Oxford and I said hello. We chatted for a while and he asked me out. He seemed a nice guy so I agreed. Things developed from there and I moved in with him.'

'How had Oliver been lately?'

'What do you mean?'

'Was he his normal self? Did he seem worried... distracted?'

'No. He seemed fine.'

'Any post or phone calls which seemed to worry him. Did he talk about problems at work or mention any altercations with customers?'

'No.'

'Did Oliver tell anyone else he was going to play golf yesterday?'

'No. It was a spur-of-the-moment thing. He had the day off. Phoned the golf course the night before to check there was an early tee time available, packed his clubs in the morning, and set off.'

'You didn't mention to anyone that he was going to play golf?'

'No.'

'Can you think of anyone who might have had a grudge against him?'

Jamila shook her head and dabbed her eyes with a handkerchief she'd pulled out from under the sleeve of her T-shirt.

'Did you and Oliver talk about your lives: where you'd both been, what you'd done, what you liked and disliked... that sort of thing?'

Jamila frowned. 'No. Come to think of it, Oliver never spoke about the past.' She looked perplexed. 'I don't know anything about him, where he was born and brought up, how he came to drive taxis here... nothing.'

'Did he speak about his divorce?'

'He did talk a little about it, but not much.'

'Where's his ex-wife now?'

'She met another man and lives with him in Spain, he's an actor I think.'

'Do you have contact details for her?'

'It's in the address book, Vivian Upton.'

'How long had Oliver worked for Andy Cabs?'

Jamila shrugged. 'I don't know.'

'Does he have a computer?'

'A laptop.'

'Mind if we take it for examination?'

'It's upstairs. I'll go and get it.'

Fleming looked at Anderson. 'I think we're done here,' he said when Jamila had left the room, 'unless there's anything else you can think we need to ask.'

'No, I don't think so.'

Jamila returned with the laptop and handed it to Anderson. 'No rush to bring it back.'

Fleming and Anderson rose to go. 'I'm sorry about your loss,' Fleming said. 'We'll be in touch. You take care.'

'Someone must have followed him,' Fleming said, back in the car with Anderson. 'No one knew he would be on the golf course.'

'Except Jamila and the man who took Upton's call to book his round.'

'Which would mean he was an accomplice if he told the killer. I think we can discount Jamila as an accomplice, but best check that Sam Galland didn't make any calls before Upton's tee time.'

'Sam Galland?'

'He works in the golf shop.'

8

OXFORD

The sun was shining. Only a few white clouds drifted across the blue sky as Anderson parked the squad car in the golf course car park. It was two days after Upton's murder and the course was open. A few golfers were there: some packing their clubs away, others getting them out of their car boots ready for a round. Ignoring curious glances, she made her way into the golf shop.

Anderson had checked that Sam Galland would be there before leaving Long Hanborough. He smiled as she entered the shop. 'Be with you in a sec,' he said, handing scorecards to a couple of golfers.

The two men left and Anderson introduced herself. 'DC Anderson. I phoned.'

'Oh, right.' Galland looked perplexed. 'I've already given a statement and spoke to DCI Fleming. What can I do for you?'

'I need to follow up on a couple of things if you don't mind.'

'Sure, go ahead.'

'Presumably it was you who took the call from Mr Upton to book his round?'

'Yes, the night before. He phoned to ask if there was an early tee time free.'

'Did anyone else know he'd booked?'

'Not that I know of.'

'You didn't tell anyone?'

'No, why would I?'

'I need to make sure nobody else knew Mr Upton would be on the course.'

'It was in the booking log on the computer. Anyone here could have seen it, I suppose.'

'Would there be any reason for anyone else to look at the log?'

'Not really. I was the only one taking bookings.'

Anderson thought for a moment. 'Did you make any calls to anybody on the landline or your mobile phone between accepting Mr Upton's booking and when he arrived here the next day?'

Galland thought for a moment. 'No, I don't think I did. Why?'

'Just checking.'

'Anyone else have access to your phone during that time?'

'No.'

'Thanks for your time, Mr Galland. You've been very helpful.' Anderson asked for Galland's mobile phone and BT landline accounts then left.

'How'd you get on?' Logan asked when Anderson returned to HQ.

'Seems the boss was right. Someone must have followed Upton from his house. Chap in the golf shop says no one else at the club would have had any reason to know Upton had booked a round. Claims he didn't make any calls on his mobile between taking Upton's booking and when he teed off.'

'You should check with BT for any calls made from the club landline the night before the murder and when Upton teed off. We need to see who made the calls and to whom. Best check with Galland's mobile service provider as well.'

'On it,' Anderson said, turning to her computer screen.

Anderson was at home in her flat after checking with BT and Galland's mobile phone provider. She'd obtained a list of numbers called from the golf course landline from the night before the murder until Upton's booking time. There were only a few, and she and Logan had checked them. All the calls were from the club secretary. One to his wife to say he would be home a little later. Another to return a call to someone who had phoned about golf membership.

All the other calls were to members about a tournament that he was arranging. There were no outgoing calls before 8am on the morning the killer shot Upton. A check on Galland's mobile phone confirmed his claim he made no calls the night before Upton's murder. Nor had he made any the following morning before 8am.

Feeling hungry, Anderson had a look in the fridge. There was a bottle of white wine and some eggs. 'Trip to the supermarket then,' she muttered. She walked over to the window where the first few drops of rain had started to run down the glass. A few people were walking along the street below. Lightning flashed on the horizon above the rooftops, followed by a long low rumble of thunder.

Anderson changed her mind about the trip to the supermarket and returned to the fridge. She found an open bag of frozen chips in the freezer compartment and decided egg and chips with a glass of wine would have to do.

After eating, she settled into her favourite chair with another glass of wine and put the TV on. She caught the back end of the news which was covering the golf course shooting. Public concern was mounting and there was speculation about a possible serial killer on the loose. There appeared to be little information about the victim apart from the fact he worked for Andy Cabs. One newspaper had put forward the theory that the killer could have been a hitman.

Anderson took a sip of wine and recalled Jamila Kazan's words, *Oliver never spoke about the past. I don't know anything about him.* Anderson started to doze off, wondering why Jamila knew so little of her partner.

9

OXFORD

The day after Anderson's visit to the golf course, the weather had changed. The thunderstorm the night before had passed over but dark clouds still lingered in the sky. Rain pelted in gusts against Fleming's Audi Q5 as he parked in the Major Crime Unit car park. He ran across to the entrance and made his way upstairs to find Logan and Anderson debating who should get the coffee.

'No work to do then?' Fleming quipped.

'Just got in,' Logan said. 'Naomi was about to get coffees. Want one?'

Anderson thumped Logan on the arm. 'Sarge, I thought we'd agreed I got them in last.'

'We did indeed, but now the boss is here, I need to update him on where we are with the archiving of the previous case files.'

'I could do that,' Anderson insisted.

'You could, but you make better coffee than me.'

Anderson raised her eyes to the ceiling. 'You're such a flatterer. Anyway, I need to update the boss on how I got on at the golf course yesterday.'

'Okay, you win, Naomi. I suppose that's more important than the state of play on archiving.'

Anderson smiled. 'Knew you'd see sense, Sarge.'

'You get the next ones though,' Logan called over his shoulder.

'Glad you both got that sorted out,' Fleming said. 'So how did you get on?'

'I think someone must have followed Upton from his house. I spoke to Sam Galland at the golf course. He said he didn't tell anyone about Upton's golf booking. Harry and I checked all the calls made from the clubhouse after Upton rang to book a round until he teed off. They were all accounted for and no one mentioned Upton.'

'So you're sure no one apart from Galland could have known Upton would be at the course?'

'Sure as I can be, sir. Galland logged Upton's reserved tee time on the computer booking system, but he reckoned no one would have any need to see it as he was the only person taking bookings.'

'Hmm. No one had the need but someone could have looked at it. And Jamila Kazan and Galland both knew Upton would be there.'

'Jamila told us she didn't tell anyone Upton was going to play golf.'

'That's what she told us. Doesn't mean she didn't tell anyone.'

'You don't think...?'

'No, I believe her. I'm sure we can discount her as an accomplice.'

'Galland? He could have told someone when he was at home or in a pub.'

'True, but why would he do that? I'm sure we can discount him as well.'

Anderson was about to say something when Logan returned with the coffees, managing to spill some as he struggled with three mugs in his hands. He put one in front of Fleming. 'By the way, the super wants to see you.'

∼

Fleming wandered up to Temple's office and found her sitting at her desk, peering at her computer screen. She pulled off her rimless reading glasses and placed them in front of her. 'Chief constable's been emailing me. She's worried about public reaction to the shooting on the golf course. Or, should I say, pressure from golf club secretaries from round the region. They're all concerned it might affect business. We can't have someone on the loose with a rifle.'

'DI Rainger from local CID arranged for a TV bulletin to go out. Thought it would be a good idea to reassure people that we were doing everything possible to ensure the safety of the public since the killer used a gun.'

'The only thing that'll reassure the public is an arrest, and pretty damn quick. Dare I ask how it's going?'

'I'm waiting for Dr Kumar's autopsy report, and forensics and ballistics. DI Rainger is arranging for his people to question everyone who was on or at the golf course, including grounds and clubhouse staff. Logan and Anderson have been doing some checking, but we're pretty sure no one other than Upton's partner and the guy in the golf shop knew he had a round booked.'

'Suggesting the killer must have been watching his home and followed him.'

'That's what I'm thinking,' Fleming agreed. 'I've questioned Upton's partner, Jamila Kazan. She has no idea who might have wanted to kill Upton. They had an affair and she moved in with him about six months ago.'

'You'll be questioning her husband, assuming he is still her husband?'

'They're separated getting divorced.'

'Who is he?'

'Atticus Kazan. He teaches mathematics and computer science at Oxford University. He's on my list of people to question.'

'Was Mr Upton married?'

'Divorced. Not sure if it was due to the affair with Jamila or other reasons. I need to go and speak to his ex-wife. She lives in Spain.'

'You see her as a suspect?'

'I spoke to local police in Spain and they confirm she was in Spain at the time of Upton's murder and there's no record of her booking a flight to England recently.'

'So why the need to go over there to speak to her?'

'Jamila Kazan told me Vivian Upton lives with another man.'

'So get the local police to question him. Keep expenses down.'

'I could but they weren't exactly enthusiastic about checking up on Mrs Upton. And, I'd prefer to speak to him in person. I'd also like to ask Mrs Upton about him first.'

'You could do that over the phone.'

'I always prefer to question people face to face. You lose opportunities to observe body language and miss eye contact with telephone calls. And... the person you're questioning could hang up. Anyway, I can get cheap flights for less than thirty quid. Costs more to get a train to London.'

Temple sighed. 'Okay, just make sure you do keep costs to the minimum.'

'I will. By the way, Jamila Kazan did say something

interesting. She knew nothing about Upton's past. He never spoke about it. Almost as though he had to keep it secret.'

'I take it finding out is on your list of things to do?'

'It is. He worked for Andy Cabs in Oxford as a taxi driver. They may be able to throw some light on it.'

'Anything else?'

'Yes. Seems Upton had a bit of an altercation with someone at the golf course. Guy called Ian Hunter accused Upton of stealing one of his expensive clubs.'

'Would you murder someone over a golf club?'

'I've known people to kill for less. There's always the chance there was a deeper feud between the two of them and the golf club was the last straw. I need to question him.'

'Okay, sounds like you have a few leads to go on. That it?'

'We have Upton's laptop and address book. We'll be checking all contacts and any leads they provide. DI Rainger is also checking out all the CCTV and ANPR cameras in the area. He's going to arrange questioning of drivers of all the cars seen on the morning of the murder. Oh, and I've got DI Rainger's technical department doing a data extraction from Upton's mobile phone.'

'Thanks, Alex. Keep me informed.'

'Of course.' Fleming left Temple putting her glasses back on to study her computer screen once more.

Thinking about Upton's secretive past, Fleming made a mental note. He would get DI Rainger to arrange for his people to question all the golf club members and Upton's neighbours. Someone ought to be able to throw some light on Upton's background.

10

EDINBURGH

Fleming's old Edinburgh University friend, DI Gordon Aitken, sat behind his desk in his Gayfield Square office. He'd joined Lothian and Borders Police as a uniformed constable and became a detective constable two years later. Four years after that, he was a detective sergeant. A year later, Lothian and Borders Police became part of Police Scotland and Aitken moved to Gayfield Square. Three years after that, they promoted Aitken to detective inspector.

'Do anything special for your fortieth last week?' DS Jock Quigley asked.

'Nah. My wife wanted to arrange a big party, but why would I want to celebrate getting older?'

Quigley laughed. 'It's not as though you're coming up to retirement. You've a long way to go yet. Still got all your hair. Mind you... it is receding. Bit greyer these days as well.'

Aitken hauled his lean six-foot frame out of his chair and gave Quigley a playful clip over the head as he went to go to his coffee machine. 'Want one?'

'Thanks, boss. Don't mind if I do.'

Aitken returned and put the two coffees on his desk. He

tapped the file in front of him. 'The thing on the top of my list of things to do before I do retire is to put Big Col Calhoun behind bars.'

'Others before you have tried and failed.'

'He's a slippery customer, for sure. There never seems to be enough evidence to bring charges against him. He's too smart. Reckons he runs a legitimate nightclub, but we all know he controls the Edinburgh crime scene. He'll slip up at some point. It's just a matter of time.'

'Nobody dares testify against him though.'

'That's what gangland bosses do. Rule by fear.'

'So what's in the file?' Quigley asked.

'Super wants us to look into a suspected drugs and gun smuggling operation.'

'Let me guess. You reckon Calhoun's fingerprints are all over it.'

'Correct. I want to pay him a courtesy visit at his club. Let him know we're watching him.'

Quigley took a sip of his coffee and the hit of caffeine seemed to jolt his memory. 'Calhoun walked free five years ago. There was a DI Taylor who suspected him of being the mastermind behind a jewellery shop robbery here in Edinburgh.'

Aitken nodded. 'I remember the case.'

'Yeah,' Quigley said. 'Calhoun's younger brother was one of the robbers. The whole thing went pear-shaped when they were trying to escape. A cop on the beat happened to turn up on the scene and tried to stop them. Calhoun's brother shot him but the copper survived.'

Aitken clicked his fingers. 'That's right. There were three of them. They all went down. Calhoun's brother got life.'

'And there was never enough evidence to link Big Col to the crime,' Quigley added.

'You never know. We might come across something once we start digging into the drugs and gun smuggling case.'

'Speaking of Big Col,' Quigley said, 'DI Taylor was looking into a haulier company... Jenner Transport. He suspected the owner, Doug Jenner, had links to Big Col. Nothing came of it and he put the file in mothballs. Taylor's retired now, but he had a sergeant working with him, DS Liam McCabe. I know of him. Good cop by all accounts. Might be worth having a word with him.'

11

OXFORD

Traffic was heavy first thing in the morning as Fleming drove down from his flat in Summertown to St Aldates police station. He'd arranged to meet DI Rainger there.

Rainger's office was on the third floor at the end of an open-plan area. Officers were already busy on the phones. Those who were not on the phone stared at computer screens and thumped furiously on their keyboards. Fleming walked up the aisle between the desks to Rainger's office. He tapped on the glass door and Rainger waved him in. As Fleming closed the door, the noise of telephones ringing and chatter became a muted hum.

Rainger stood from behind a desk covered in files and sheets of paper. 'Morning, Alex. Can I get you a coffee?'

'No, thanks. Not long since I had some with breakfast.'

'Okay. Come in and have a seat.' Rainger pointed to two chairs tucked under a small side table in a corner of the office. 'Short staffed this week,' he moaned. 'Sickness, annual leave... bloody nightmare.'

'Cheery as ever, eh?'

Rainger forced the corners of his mouth into a rare smile.

'Was a time when you could retire at fifty-five. I need to work a few more years yet to rack up my pension.'

'You'll be missed when you do go.'

'Try telling my super that. Anyway, I guess you'll want to know where we're at with my to-do list?'

Fleming was about to speak when there was a knock on Rainger's door. 'Some of the results about to appear by the look of it,' Rainger said, waving a young officer in holding a pile of papers.

'These are all the statements taken from people who were on the golf course or in the clubhouse on the morning of the murder, boss,' the officer said.

'Thanks, Yorkie. Dump them on my desk.'

Fleming watched as Yorkie deposited the papers and made his exit. 'Get the nickname because he likes chocolate bars?' Fleming asked with a smile.

Rainger's face showed no sign of breaking into amusement. 'His name's York.'

'Right.' Fleming pointed to the papers Yorkie had dumped on the desk. 'Know if there's one there for a man called Ian Hunter?'

Rainger narrowed his eyes. 'Any particular reason?'

'Guy in the golf shop reckoned there was an altercation between him and Upton a few weeks ago.'

'Oh?'

'Hunter accused Upton of stealing one of his expensive clubs.'

'Seriously? You can't think he's a suspect because of a dispute over a golf driver. And shooting Upton? He's more likely to have clubbed him to death.'

Fleming smiled. 'That your attempt at humour?'

Rainger raised an eyebrow and got up to rifle through the

statements. He picked one out. 'Here we are... club member for ten years. Want to see it?'

Fleming held out a hand. 'I'll have a quick look but I'll want to speak to him.'

Rainger handed over the statement and shook his head. 'Think you'll be wasting your time.'

Fleming scanned through the statement. There wasn't much there. All Hunter had said was that he turned up to have a round of golf and went into the clubhouse to have breakfast first. He was still there when four golfers came back shouting someone had been shot. Fleming handed the statement back to Rainger who returned it to the pile on his desk. He was about to go back to sit with Fleming when his phone rang.

'Rainger!' He took a deep breath and listened. His eyes looked to the ceiling. 'He knows I've got a meeting. Tell him I'll see him in twenty minutes,' he shouted into the phone, then slammed it down in its cradle. 'Bloody man! He's a demanding pain in the arse.'

'Let me guess. Your super?'

Rainger was about to answer when Yorkie appeared at the door again. 'Sorry, boss, there's been a break-in at a shop in Cowley.'

'Christ! What next! I'm up to my ears in it. Get over there with whoever's not on a bloody phone!'

Yorkie looked suitably chastised. 'Okay,' he muttered and beat a hasty retreat.

'Listen, if this is a bad time, I can always come back,' Fleming said, seeing the anger beginning to show in Rainger's eyes.

'No, it's okay. Let's carry on before I go to see the super.'

'Right. Anything turn up on CCTV or ANPR cameras on the roads nearby?'

'There's bloody hundreds of them. Early in the morning.

Rush hour. It's going to take a hell of a time to trace and question all the drivers.'

'Hmm, might have guessed. Do what you can. Give me a shout if anything turns up.'

'Might be Christmas at this rate,' Rainger grumbled.

'Sorry. One of those painstaking lines of enquiry you have to follow. You never know what it might throw up.'

'I might throw up if pressure of work keeps getting to me.'

Fleming smiled. 'Did the SOCOs find anything up in the woods?'

'Nothing.'

'There you are. One line of enquiry that's not going to lead to more work.'

'I'm so grateful.'

'How about Upton's mobile phone? Has your technical whizz kid managed to find anything of interest?'

'There's nothing on social media. Seems our Mr Upton steered well clear of using any of that stuff.'

'Contacts, calls, messages?'

'I've got my people tracking his contacts to question. They're checking out the numbers of all calls made and received. There aren't any text messages.'

'Something interesting came up when I went to speak to Upton's partner, Jamila Kazan. It seems Upton never spoke about his past, where he'd been, what he'd done, and so on. She had no idea how or why he ended up driving taxis in Oxford. In fact, by her admission, she knew nothing about him.'

'Stayed clear of social media. The man obviously liked to keep things to himself.'

'Secretive more like. When your lot question Upton's contacts, neighbours and golf club members who weren't on the course the day of the murder, get them to ask about Upton's background.'

'Okay. That it?'

'Yes. Thanks for your help on this. Don't let the super get you down,' Fleming said, rising to leave.

'Don't forget the statements,' Rainger said, at which point his phone rang again.

12

EDINBURGH

Only a few lights remained on when DI Aitken and DS Quigley left the office at Gayfield Square. Rather than use a squad car, they took a taxi down to Cowgate to pay a visit to Big Col Calhoun's nightclub. There was no particular aim other than to try to unnerve the gangster.

The club was in a rabbit warren of streets off the Cowgate. It was well past opening time and the queues outside had long since disappeared down the stone staircase into the bowels of the club. On top of the entrance, there was a large purple neon sign announcing they had arrived at Calhoun's Cave. Two bulky bouncers stood at the entrance and gave the detectives a wary look.

'There a reason for a police visit?' one of the men drawled. The other was staring the detectives out.

Aitken feigned surprise. 'You can tell we're police?'

'A mile off.'

'So much for the disguise, eh? Mind if we come in for a drink. Like a chat with Big Col if he's here.'

The two men stood aside to let the detectives inside. The bouncer doing the talking grabbed Aitken's arm and smiled.

'Don't overstay your welcome. Come to think of it, welcome isn't the right word.'

Aitken looked at the man's hand, then his eyes locked onto the bouncer's. 'I'd remove your hand before I slap cuffs on it.'

The bouncer hesitated for a second, smiled again, and withdrew his hand. 'Just making sure you don't fall down the stairs.'

'Very thoughtful of you,' Aitken growled and pushed past the man.

Halfway down the stone steps, they turned to the left. A few more steps down and they were in a cavernous room. The lighting was diffused, and loud music throbbed against the stone walls. There were a few tables and chairs, most of them occupied. A purple carpet stretched across the floor to a long bar. Over to the left was a small raised stage with a wooden dance floor in front.

There was an entrance to the side of the dance floor which led into an area that could have once been a wine cellar. It had low brick walls and a curved brick ceiling. Clubbers sat on stools lining the walls, enjoying their drinks.

'Drink?' Aitken asked Quigley.

'Are we on or off duty?'

'For the purposes of this exercise, we're off duty... and we're not driving.'

'In that case, I'll have a pint.'

Aitken walked over to the bar. The front glowed with purple neon lights with the odd strip of vertical white light. Soft orange lighting bathed the bottles lined on shelves behind the bar. He surveyed the beers on offer on tap. 'Which one?' he asked Quigley.

'Let's play safe. Tennent's.'

A barman wearing black trousers, a white shirt, a tartan bow tie and a tartan waistcoat came over to them. He eyed them suspiciously. 'What can I get you?'

'Two pints of Tennent's please,' Aitken said. 'Big Col here?'

'In his office. Is he expecting you?'

'No, I'm not,' came a hoarse voice from behind Aitken. 'But always a pleasure to see my best detective friend.'

Aitken and Quigley turned to see the tall stocky figure of Big Col Calhoun limping towards them. In his sixties, he still sported thick shoulder-length grey hair and had a goatee beard. He was wearing a black suit, white shirt and black bow tie. The white carnation pinned to his suit was in stark contrast to the suit.

'I'm not your friend,' Aitken retorted. 'Dressed to kill, I see. No tartan tonight?'

Calhoun gave out a loud guffaw. 'One-track mind as always, Aitken. Want to pat me down to see if I have a gun hidden away?'

Aitken smiled. 'That won't be necessary. I meant it in the sense you're dressed to create a striking impression, not to kill someone.'

Calhoun laughed again. 'Been to a black-tie dinner. Assistant chief constable, Ramsay Irvin, was there.'

'Didn't know you had friends in high places in Edinburgh.'

'Friend of mine arranged it. He mixes with the great and the good.'

'Surprised you were there then.'

Calhoun glared at Aitken as the barman put two pints on the bar.

Aitken was reaching for his wallet when Calhoun, who had recovered his composure, put a hand on his arm and smiled. 'On the house. Put your money away.'

Aitken shrugged off the hand and thumped a twenty-pound

note on the bar. 'Thanks, but no thanks. Can't be seen taking backhanders from a suspected gangland boss.'

Calhoun fixed his steely blue eyes on Aitken. 'Ah, you upset me. I run a legitimate club here.'

Aitken took a sip of his beer. 'And how *is* business?'

'It's going very well. Can't complain.'

'Visit your brother in the nick?'

'Sometimes. We're not very close.'

'Is that since he shot and wounded a policeman trying to escape after the jewellery shop robbery?'

'Your lot tried to pin that one on me. They failed of course. I had nothing to do with it. Scottie was always a hothead. He chose a life of crime. I went into business.'

Aitken took another sip of beer and thought for a moment. 'Does your business have anything to do with Jenner Transport?'

Calhoun frowned. 'I know of Doug Jenner and his haulage business. Don't have any business dealings with him though.'

'Know him on a personal basis?'

Calhoun's eyes narrowed. 'No. Why the interest?'

Aitken fixed his eyes on Calhoun. 'Just curious. We're starting an enquiry into drugs and gun smuggling.'

'And you think he's involved?'

'Police questioned him some time ago over some other enquiry. Nothing came of it, but there was a suggestion he had links to you.'

'Really?'

'Must have been some mistake, eh?'

'The police make mistakes?' Calhoun gave one of his raucous laughs. 'I'd never have thought it.'

Aitken nodded at Quigley and they made to leave. 'Be seeing you,' Aitken said.

'Have a nice evening,' Calhoun drawled.

13

OXFORD

The house was a detached red-brick property on the outskirts of Headington. Fleming drove into the cul-de-sac and found the house at the end. He turned and parked the car in a gravelled area bordered by a small box hedge in front of the house.

'Missing the old Porsche, boss?' Logan asked.

'A bit. It was a good old car. Served me well, but it was time to change.' Fleming patted the steering wheel. 'Pleased so far with this.'

'What made you go for an Audi Q5?'

Fleming shrugged. 'Not sure. I did some research into SUVs and got a good deal on part exchange.'

'Looks smart, I have to say,' Logan said. 'Anyway, Kazan should be in. I phoned. Promised he would be here.'

'Okay, let's go and see what he has to say,' Fleming said, getting out of the car.

A paved path led up to a wooden porch with a tiled roof. Fleming rang the bell and waited. A minute passed but no one answered. Fleming rang again and kept his finger on the buzzer a bit longer this time.

After a few more seconds, the porch door opened to reveal Atticus Kazan, dressed in cream trousers, brown suede shoes, and a pink shirt. Early fifties, Fleming guessed. His hair was thick, greying, shoulder-length, and swept back from his forehead. 'Sorry for the delay. I was upstairs on the computer preparing a lecture. I take it you're DCI Fleming and DS Logan?' The voice was soft and smooth. Fleming's first impression was of an oily, smarmy character, reminiscent of a politician he had once come across.

'Yes,' Fleming confirmed, showing his warrant card. 'May we come in?'

'Of course, please do.' Kazan turned and showed the two detectives through a door into a hallway, then right into the living room. The sun shone through a large bay window, casting shadows behind a settee and two armchairs. A silver patterned wallpaper adorned the walls. The floor comprised stained and polished floorboards with a grey carpet in the middle. There was a TV in one corner and a drinks cabinet to the side of the window.

Kazan waved towards the settee and chairs. 'Please, take a seat,' he said, lowering his tall thin body into one of the armchairs.

Fleming took the other chair, leaving Logan to sit on the settee. 'We just wanted to ask a few questions about Oliver Upton,' Fleming said.

'I've been expecting you to call round, but I'm afraid I won't be much help.'

'Any reason you were expecting a visit?' Fleming asked.

'Husband of the woman who left him to move in with a man who turns up dead. Stands to reason I'd be a suspect.'

'Mr Kazan, we're here because we need to question everyone who had links to Mr Upton, not necessarily because you're a suspect.'

'In which case you've wasted a visit. I had no links to him.'

'The link is your wife,' Logan reminded him.

Kazan smiled. 'Of course, but I know nothing about Mr Upton other than he was a taxi driver and Jamila moved in with him.'

'You met your wife at the university I gather.'

'I did.'

'And you got married about twenty-two years ago?'

'Yes, listen, inspector, I don–'

'It's detective *chief* inspector,' Fleming reminded him. 'I'm just trying to get as much background information as I can.'

Kazan's face broke into an ingratiating smile. He held up his hands as though in surrender. 'Yes, of course, but what has my background got to do with Mr Upton?'

Fleming ignored the question. 'Jamila works at the university. Do you still see her there?'

'Sometimes.'

'Do you speak?'

'Not if I can help it.'

'And otherwise... outside of work I mean?'

'She came to the house once to pick up more of her things.'

'She moved in with Upton about six months ago. How long after that was it when she came back to the house?'

Kazan shook his head. 'I'm not at all sure where your line of questioning is going... *Chief* Inspector.' There was no mistaking the sarcasm in his voice.

'Just answer the questions, sir,' Logan said.

'A couple of weeks ago.'

'Did you talk to her?'

'We had a row... if you must know the details of my personal life.'

'About Upton?'

'What else? I wasn't exactly happy with the situation.'

'Did she talk about Upton?'

Kazan ran a hand through his well-groomed short beard. 'Only to rub my nose in it. She gloated how things were so much better with him. How happy she was.'

'That must have made you angry.'

'Of course.'

'More with her... or with him?'

'Ah, so you *are* now seeing me as a suspect, are you not?'

'Just trying to get a picture of the situation between you and your wife.'

Kazan sighed. 'Look, I can't pretend I wasn't angry, who wouldn't be? I'm a university lecturer, not a murderer.'

'Do you ever use taxis?'

'Sometimes.'

'Ever get one driven by Upton?'

'Can't say I did, no.'

'You've never met him?'

'Not formally. I've seen him with Jamila in town a few times.'

'Do you play golf, Mr Kazan?'

'As a matter of fact I do. But not very often.'

'Have you ever played on the course where they found Mr Upton's body?'

'Yes, but before you ask... a long time ago.'

'How long?'

Kazan hunched his shoulders. The smarmy smile had returned to his face. 'Must be three, four months ago.'

'One final question, Mr Kazan. Where were you on the morning Mr Upton was shot?'

The smile hadn't left Kazan's face. 'Lecturing at the university.'

14

LONDON

All the way through school lessons, Toby had worried about going to see his mother. He'd tried to put it off, but knew it was something he had to do. Leaving school that afternoon, he drove over to his mother's house, dreading the reaction he was sure to get.

He let himself in and heard the TV going on at full blast in the sitting room. He hung his coat in the hallway and shouted, 'Mother, it's me, I'm here.'

There was no answer. Toby opened the sitting room door. His mother was asleep in the armchair, despite the noise emitting from the TV. Toby walked over and switched it off.

'Toby! What are you doing? I was watching that.'

It was odd the noise had failed to keep Doreen awake, but the sudden silence had woken her from the depths of oblivion.

'I told you I was coming to see you. Can't have a conversation with that thing on.'

'It was interesting.'

'So much so that you fell asleep.'

'I did not!' Doreen sniffed. 'May have closed my eyes for a

second. Did you remember to bring some eggs? Forgot to put them on my last list.'

Toby held them up. 'I'll put them in the fridge.' He walked through to the kitchen and opened the fridge door. Inside the door rack was a dozen eggs. Toby shook his head and went back into the sitting room.

'You had eggs. Where did you get them from?'

'Oh, forgot. Neighbour brought them round.'

'Good to know you have thoughtful neighbours.'

'I suppose so. But they'll never provide the same support I get from you. I do depend on you, Toby.'

Toby felt a sudden pang of guilt and delayed the pain of what he'd come to tell her. 'How have you been since I brought your shopping the other day?'

'Not good. Aches and pains are getting the better of me. I'm sure I'm not well.'

'Have you seen a doctor?'

'No. Last time I went, he said there was nothing wrong with me.'

'Have you ever thought he might be right? You're just getting older, not ill.'

'Easy for you to say.'

Toby sighed. 'Quentin came to see me.'

'Oh?'

'Said you phoned him sounding a bit upset.'

'That was after you came round with my shopping and told me about this ridiculous idea of applying for a teaching job up in Scotland.'

'He tried to convince me not to apply.'

'Quite right! I need you here. I hope he managed to talk sense into you.'

Toby decided he couldn't delay matters any longer. 'I made enquiries about the job.'

'You did what! I can't believe you even gave it another thought. I told you why you couldn't apply for it.'

'I spoke to a very nice lady, Ailsa Brodie.'

'Who's she?' There was an edge to Doreen's voice. There was always an instant suspicion when there was any mention of Toby even speaking to a woman.

'Works for Highlands Council. She's handling the recruitment process.'

'I hope what she had to tell you put you off applying.'

Toby couldn't delay any longer. 'It sounds interesting. I've asked for an application form.'

'Toby! After all I've said. I can't believe you ignored what I told you!'

'Mother, it's only an application form at this stage. I may not get it.'

'May not get it? You'd better not. What would I do? I can't go moving house up to some remote part of Scotland at my age.'

'I wouldn't expect you to. As I told you, there'll be plenty of opportunities for me to come and see you if I get the job.'

'Weekends and school holidays you said. That's not enough.'

'I need a change.'

'That's the trouble with you. It's all about you. No thought for anyone else.'

Toby's mouth dropped open. *I don't believe what I just heard.* 'That's not exactly fair. I've looked after you for years and never complained.'

'Hmph. You won't get an interview. Stands to reason they won't want an outsider. They'll only want to see local people.'

'That may be so. But I'm applying anyway. It's too good a chance to miss.'

'The cooler climate up there won't do your asthma any good.'

'It'll be much better than here in London. I checked with the doctor and he says it won't be a problem if it's well controlled. The cleaner air quality will be beneficial he says. Do me good to get out of London.'

'And what about *me*? Who'll do the shopping?'

'What about your nice neighbour?'

'I couldn't possibly ask her.'

'There's always Quentin.'

'I told you before; Quentin is a busy man with a responsible job. He has a wife and two young boys and won't have the time.'

'He needs to make more time to spend with his family. Margo could always help.'

'She has the boys.'

'Mother, they're hardly babies. They're nine and eleven. They could go shopping with her.'

'It's much easier for you to do it.'

'She could do an online shop and get it delivered.'

'You don't want to do it anymore, do you?'

'That's not why I'm going to apply for the job. I'm doing it to get out of the rat race and because it'll be better for my health.'

'On the off-chance you do get the job, you won't fit in there. It'll be a close-knit community, I'll bet. You won't make friends and you'll wish you'd never gone. Mark my words.'

'I'll take that chance.'

'The house needs decorating. I was going to get you to do it. Who'll do it if you go up to Scotland?'

Toby sighed. 'Pay someone.'

Doreen pulled out a handkerchief and dabbed her eyes. 'You can't go, Toby. I won't be able to cope without you here.'

'Let's see if I get an interview first, shall we? I must go. I need to do some shopping.'

Toby left with mixed feelings. He needed to make a new life for himself but worried about his mother.

15

OXFORD

'Want to have a look at the autopsy, forensics and ballistics reports before we go?' Logan asked.

'I'll read them later,' Fleming said. 'Give me a summarised version for now.'

'Kumar's autopsy confirms Upton died from two gunshot wounds to the chest. Caused major bleeding and catastrophic injury to the heart and major blood vessels. There's loads of technical medical stuff but that's about the gist of it.'

'Ballistics?'

'Confirms the weapon used was a Remington Model 700 bolt-action sniper rifle. The estimated distance from the target was 200 yards.'

'Looks like the killer's an expert marksman. Not the most common murder weapon. Anything from forensics?'

Logan rubbed his chin. 'Nothing. No clothing fibres, no hair, no blood... other than Upton's. They did find some broken tees with fingerprints on them, but they're not going to be the killers. He wasn't playing golf.'

'That's it?'

'There were loads of footprints around, but could be golfers or groundsmen. They did a further search up in the woods once they knew where the shots came from, but found nothing.'

'Not only a professional marksman, but someone with enough savvy to ensure they left no forensic evidence,' Fleming said. 'I don't suppose there was anything in Upton's car? SOCOs said it was locked and there was no sign anyone had broken into it.'

'Nothing to suggest the killer had been in it.'

'Thought so. Let's go and speak to Andy Cabs.'

The shooting on the golf course was still a topic of conversation in the pubs and cafés in Oxford. It was crazy that such a thing could happen there. People questioned the mystery surrounding the murdered man. No one seemed to know anything about him.

People had stopped talking about the weather, at least for now. That said, it was late spring and the weather was changeable. The golf course was open, but they'd moved the tee-off point for the fifth hole to another location. Someone had thought to sprinkle sand over the patch where Upton's blood had soaked into the ground.

'Andy Cabs can't be one of the bigger companies,' Logan observed. He was looking at the terraced house off the Cowley Road through the squad car's rain-splattered windscreen.

'It's the address Jamila Kazan gave me,' Fleming said, parking the car. 'Let's see what Andy, assuming that's his name, knows about Upton.'

The door opened and a short balding man with a cigarette dangling out the corner of his mouth stood there. By the look of the tightness of the shirt across an ample stomach, Fleming guessed he liked his food and drink, more than any form of exercise.

Fleming showed his warrant card. 'Hello. DCI Fleming and DS Logan. The owner is expecting us.'

'I am indeed,' the man said. 'That's me, Andy Wade.' He thrust a podgy hand towards Fleming.

Fleming shook the offered hand. 'Right. May we come in?'

'Yeah, of course,' Andy said. 'Come into my office.'

The office was a small room off the hallway, beyond the sitting room. Drops of rain pelted against a tiny window with no curtains. The cream carpet had seen better days. It was threadbare in places and had the odd burn mark where ash from Andy's cigarettes had no doubt fallen. The evidence lay in a full ashtray of cigarette butts sitting on a desk pushed up against one wall. A computer screen, telephone and a stack of wire trays filled with papers occupied the rest of the desk. Box files littered a bookshelf on the wall opposite.

There were three chairs. One in front of the desk and the other two under the window. Andy waved at the two chairs. 'Take a seat.'

'Thanks. I'd like to ask a few questions about Oliver Upton,' Fleming said as Logan fished out his notebook.

Andy pulled the cigarette from his mouth and stubbed it out on top of the other butts in the ashtray. 'Sure, go ahead.'

'How many taxis have you got?' Fleming asked. 'Seems a small operation if you're running it from home.'

'It is. I'm a small business, trying to compete with the big boys. I have five taxis in total, but now only four drivers.'

'Where do you keep the cars?'

'There's a tyre company nearby. A friend of mine runs it. He lets me use a bit of the car park for a small annual rental.'

'When did Mr Upton start work for you?'

'About four years ago... maybe five.'

'How did you find him?'

'I had a vacancy for a driver. Put out a small advert in a local paper and he rang up about the job.'

'Was there an application form?'

Andy laughed. 'You're joking, right? Small business like mine... for a taxi driver job?'

'So Upton didn't fill in any forms?'

'Nah. Told him to come in and see me and bring his driving licence.'

Logan raised an eyebrow and scribbled a note in his notebook.

'How did the interview go?'

'It wasn't so much an interview as a little chat.'

'And you then employed him?'

'I did,' Andy confirmed, lighting up another cigarette.

'What made you take him on?'

Andy blew smoke up towards the ceiling. 'Said he'd been a driver in the army and had driven taxis before for about eighteen years. Seemed a decent and capable chap.'

'Did he say where he drove taxis before?'

'London.'

'Why did he move from London to Oxford?'

'Didn't ask him. I wasn't interested in his private life... just whether he could drive.'

'Did he say which unit of the army he served in?'

'Likewise... didn't seem relevant to ask him.'

'Did you get references?'

'Three, all good.'

'Have you still got them?'

Andy looked embarrassed. 'Nah. Got rid of them after a year. Didn't need them anymore.'

'Sounds like you didn't get much information about Upton's background.'

'As I said... I was only interested in whether he could drive.'

'What about after he started work. Did he ever talk about his past?'

Andy shook his head. 'Come to think of it, never. There's another driver who he was friendly with. He might know.'

'Can I have his name and contact details? I'd better have them for the other three drivers as well.'

Andy fished into one of his box files and gave Fleming a piece of paper.

Fleming handed it to Logan to make a note. 'One final question. Did you get an enhanced Disclosure and Barring Service check done on him?'

'Oh, yeah. Forgot about that. He filled in a form. I sent it off and he brought the certificate in to say everything was okay.'

Fleming thanked Andy for his time and he and Logan left.

'Want me and Naomi to see if there's any record of army service for Upton?' Logan asked as they got in the car. 'And check out what must be loads of taxi firms in London?'

'Afraid so, Harry. Better check with the DBS as well. See if they still have a record of his application.'

'I'll get Naomi started on that one.'

Fleming turned on the ignition and the squad car sparked into life. 'Seems our Mr Upton's background is a bit of a mystery.'

16

OXFORD

Anderson looked at the list Logan had given her. 'Overtime forms will be piling up again by the time we get through this lot, Sarge.'

'Might start with the quickest. Check with DBS to see if they still have a record of Upton's application when he applied for the driver's job at Andy Cabs.'

'Okay, I'll get on to that when I get back from St Aldates.'

'Going to check what the Lone Ranger's got?'

'What?'

'The Lone Ranger. It's what the boss calls DI Rainger. Some western fanatic at St Aldates gave him the nickname.'

Anderson smiled. 'Think I'd better stick to "sir".'

'It might be wise. Boss gets on with him, but he is renowned for being a bit of a dour character. Sense of humour escaped him some time ago.'

'Job getting to him?'

'Boss reckons all Rainger is looking forward to is his retirement.'

'Doesn't bode well for enthusiastic help and support then?'

'He may be dour and looking for the golden handshake, but they reckon he's a good detective.'

'Not reached DCI though.'

'Some people reach their level. Lack of further promotion doesn't mean they're not good at their job.'

'Yeah, good point, Sarge.'

'Think I'll make a start on London taxi companies.'

'Rather than the army connection?'

'Taxi driving was more recent.'

'There's always a logic to how you go about things, Sarge.'

Logan grinned. 'You being sarcastic?'

'Not at all. Would I ever be?'

'Most of the time. Now be off with you. And bring some fish and chips back for lunch if you feel like it, seeing as we missed out on them the other day.'

Anderson had left Logan starting the painstaking process of checking London taxi companies. They wanted to see if there were any with four- or five-year-old records of Upton being a driver there.

She was now walking through the open-plan office area, heading for DI Rainger's office. She'd been to St Aldates police station many a time and knew one or two of the DCs.

Yorkie called out from his desk. 'If it isn't DC Anderson. What brings you here?'

'Hi, Yorkie. Popping in to see your boss for an update.'

'Ah, the Lone Ranger!'

Anderson put a finger to her lips. 'He might hear you.'

'Nah.' He pointed to Rainger's office. 'Door's closed.'

'Was it you who gave him the nickname?'

'Guilty as charged. By the way, your boss hasn't half dumped a load of work on us.'

Anderson smiled sweetly. 'It's called co-operation. Police work is what you do... at least when you're not watching westerns.'

'Buy you a drink sometime,' Yorkie called out as Anderson reached Rainger's office door.

'That'll be the day,' someone shouted out above the din of chatter and phones ringing.

Anderson knocked on the glass door.

Rainger looked up from his desk and waved Anderson in. 'Take a seat. I'll be with you in a second.'

Anderson watched as Rainger scribbled a note in a file before looking up at her. He straightened against the back of his chair. 'Right. You want to know what we've got so far for your boss?'

'Please. Anything come out of questioning Upton's neighbours, sir?'

'Nothing. The man's a complete mystery. No one seems to know anything about him other than he drives a taxi for Andy Cabs.'

'He never speaks to the neighbours?'

'Only to say hello, nice day, goodbye.'

'Not met many taxi drivers who didn't want to talk.'

'He's one it seems.'

'Anything on CCTV on the roads round the golf course?'

'Loads. It was busy. Told your boss it would take till Christmas to trace and question all the drivers.'

'Literally?'

Rainger gave one of his rare attempts at a weak smile. 'No, but I'm afraid it'll take some time. I'll give Alex a buzz if we find anything. Nothing of interest so far.'

'Okay. What about Upton's mobile? DCI Fleming said you'd

found nothing on social media, but you were checking out all his contacts and calls.'

Rainger shook his head. 'We've questioned all his contacts, including the ones in his address book. There weren't many. Nothing worth following up on there, I'm afraid. Interesting though... no one seems to know much about him.'

'Calls?' Anderson asked without much hope of a positive reply.

'Not many. Couple to Andy Cabs. A few to his partner. Some to a company he'd ordered something from. Nothing of interest.'

'Incoming?' Anderson asked.

'Andy Cabs, and Upton's partner, Jamila Kazan. That's about it. Not surprising.'

'Oh?'

'He was obviously a man who kept himself to himself. Not many people knew him enough to ring him.'

'Very odd,' Anderson remarked. 'I mean for someone to have so few contacts and for no one to know much about him.'

'You're not far wrong. Maybe he has something to hide.'

'I daren't ask if you found out anything about him from the golf club members.'

'Still questioning them, but of those we've seen so far, you'll not be surprised there's very little known about the man.'

'Maybe he's a retired spook who wants to keep his head down.'

Rainger raised an eyebrow. 'Many a true word...'

17

LONDON

Logan was behind the wheel of the squad car speeding down the M40 on the way to London. Fleming had decided to go to speak to Jamila Kazan again who was staying with her sister, Zaina Mwangi. He wanted to question her about the row she'd had with her husband a couple of weeks earlier.

Fleming was deep in thought when Logan broke the silence. 'Five days since Upton's murder and little or nothing to go on so far. Just an aggrieved husband and a disgruntled golfer. We've had Upton's laptop checked. No clues there. Emails were all the junk he hadn't bothered to delete. Nothing on Word or Excel. No other contacts that weren't in the address book and DI Rainger's checked them all out. A few internet searches for golf stuff and orders off Amazon. Nothing to point to a potential killer. What do you reckon, boss?'

'I've read through all the statements DI Rainer's officers took from people who were on the golf course or in the clubhouse on the morning of the murder. No clues there, I'm afraid.'

'What about Atticus Kazan and Ian Hunter?'

'Atticus Kazan has a motive. Not sure about the means. As for opportunity; he has an alibi.'

'We've still got to check it out.'

'Next on my list of things to do,' Fleming said.

'Where would he get a rifle from though?'

'Good question. Handguns are more common when killers use firearms. He may know how to use a rifle and preferred to shoot from a distance while in hiding rather than get up close.'

'Still doesn't answer how he would've got hold of one.'

'You told me ballistics reckoned the killer used a Remington Model 700 bolt-action sniper rifle. Remington claim it's one of the most popular sporting rifles. You can buy them if you have a licence. Or he could have got it on the black market if he had the right contacts.'

'How'd you know that?'

'Looked it up after you told me what was in the ballistics report.'

'Okay, so he could have had motive and means. Be interesting if his alibi doesn't stack up.'

'It's about all we have to go on so far.'

'What about the disgruntled golfer, Ian Hunter? Would he kill a man over a stolen club?'

'Super had the same thought. I'm keeping an open mind at this stage. Maybe more to it than meets the eye.'

'I take it he's also on your list of things to do?'

'He is. A couple of other things to check out first.'

'Oh?'

'I want to check Kazan's alibi and his claim it was a few months ago when he last played golf where Upton was shot. Also see if he went more recently, maybe to get the lie of the land.'

'And the other thing?'

'Andy Cabs gave me contact details for the four remaining drivers on their books. One of them was quite friendly with

Upton. I want to see if any of them can throw any light on Upton's background.'

~

Zaina Mwangi's house was a mid-terrace property in a street not far from the edge of Clapham Common. Logan found a parking space near the house and pulled in.

Jamila answered the door. 'Zaina and her husband are both at work,' she explained. She showed Fleming and Logan down a short hallway and into a sitting room furnished in light colours. A large bookcase occupied the wall on one side of an electric fire which was set into an ornate fireplace. There were two armchairs and a two-seater settee. The aroma of fresh coffee filled the room. A bay window looked out over the front of the house.

'Can I get you both a drink?' Jamila asked. 'I've just had a coffee.'

Fleming shook his head. 'No, thanks. We won't take up much of your time. We wanted to ask you a few more questions if we may.'

'Of course.'

'We've brought the laptop back. It didn't give any clues into who might have killed Oliver,' Logan said, handing it over.

Jamila took it and put it down by the side of her armchair.

'Had your husband ever met Oliver?'

'Not to my knowledge. He saw us in town a few times. Pretended not to see us.'

'Your husband said you went back to the house a couple of weeks ago to pick some things up.'

'That's right, I did.'

'Quite a long time after you'd left him. Didn't you take all your things then?'

'I did take *most* of my stuff. I left all the furniture. Didn't need any of it. I took all my clothes. There were a few things I thought of afterwards. Personal things like letters, some of my research work and some books.'

'He said you had a row.'

'We did, yes.'

'He told me you were gloating about how happy you were now. Was that what caused the row?'

'He was getting agitated. Started shouting I'd used him, betrayed him, and had no morality. He upset me and I lashed out. I told him how happy I was with Oliver.'

'So he was angry?'

'Yes. He frightened me.'

'Was he a volatile person?'

'I wouldn't go that far, but he had his moments when he lost his temper.'

'Violent?'

Jamila shook her head.

'Do you still see him at work?'

'Not much. He tries to avoid me.'

'Did your husband play golf at the course where Oliver was shot?'

'A few times. I wouldn't say very often though.'

'Does your husband have a rifle?'

'No.'

'Did he ever say he'd like to kill Oliver?'

'Oh my God! You think it was him, don't you?'

'Did he... I mean ever say he'd like to kill Oliver?'

'No.' Jamila paused for a second. 'Doesn't mean he wouldn't have thought it, I suppose.'

'Jealous men can do stupid things,' Fleming said. 'He had a motive to kill Oliver, but at present, we're only trying to gather information. Other than the fact he's an aggrieved husband, we have no evidence to link him to the shooting. We're following other lines of enquiry.'

Fleming and Logan rose to leave, thanked Jamila for her time and promised to be in touch if they had any further news.

'He was angry and frightened her,' Logan said, getting into the car. 'I'd put my bet on him rather than Ian Hunter.'

18

EDINBURGH

The constant loud ringing of phones hit DI Aitken's ears when he opened his office door on the first floor of Gayfield Square police station. He looked across the open-plan area where officers sat at banks of desks and waved for DS Quigley to come and join him.

Quigley stuck a thumb up in the air to acknowledge the summons, ended a call and walked over. 'Something come up?'

Aitken closed the door behind Quigley to drown out the noise from the office. 'I'm going down to St Leonard's shortly to see DS McCabe. Before I go, I thought you might be interested in a casual conversation I had with the assistant chief constable.'

Quigley raised an eyebrow. 'You asked Ramsay Irvin about the black-tie dinner?'

'Bumped into him coming out of a meeting. He exchanged pleasantries for a minute, so I took the opportunity to ask about the dinner.'

'What'd he say?'

'He looked a bit wary and asked how I knew.'

'You told him about our visit to see Big Col Calhoun?'

Aitken nodded. 'I told him how Calhoun had gloated he'd been to the same event.'

'What was his reaction?'

'Brushed it off. Said he didn't know Calhoun would be there.'

'Must have been embarrassing for him, on account of us having our suspicions Calhoun has a finger in the pie somewhere in the drugs and gun smuggling racket.'

'He did say it was an embarrassment, but once he was there, he said he could hardly leave.'

'Did he say who had organised the dinner?'

'A prominent councillor. Someone who they say is friendly with the council chief executive. That's why Irvin reckoned he couldn't leave.'

'But he knew we were looking into Calhoun's possible involvement in a major investigation?'

'He had to know. Anyway, I asked him if Doug Jenner was there as well.'

'Was he?'

'He was. I asked Irvin if he noticed Jenner and Calhoun talking together at any stage in the evening.'

'And?'

'He reckoned he wasn't paying any attention to them and didn't notice whether they had.'

'Strange,' Quigley said. 'I mean, he knew we're looking into Calhoun. He must have known about the alleged link with Jenner Transport. Wouldn't you think Irvin would have kept an eye on them, being as he was there?'

'That's what I thought, so I decided to throw him a curved ball.'

'Meaning?'

'I told him Calhoun always seemed to know when the police

were going to turn up at his club. Suspected he might have a bent cop in his pocket.'

'Wow. You're sailing close to the wind, boss.'

'Got a reaction though. He wagged a finger at me and said I'd better have proof if I was going to make wild claims.'

Quigley's eyes opened wide. 'Christ! You... you don't think the hostile reaction was because he's the bent cop?'

'Keeping an open mind, Jock. That's all.'

It was only a ten-minute drive from Gayfield Square to St Leonard's under normal circumstances, but due to roadworks, it had taken Aitken twenty. 'Could almost have bloody walked it as quick,' Aitken muttered to himself.

Aitken knew the uniformed sergeant on the front desk. 'Hi there. I'm here to see DS McCabe. Where can I find him?'

'First floor, open-plan area. You met him before?'

'No.'

'Tall, well-built man with short brown hair, beard and moustache. Mid-thirties.'

'They'll make a policeman out of you yet,' Aitken joked.

Aitken found his way upstairs into the open plan office and spoke to the officer on the first desk. 'Which one's DS McCabe?'

'That'll be me,' said a man with a soft Scottish drawl.

Aitken turned to see a man walking towards him, matching the description the desk sergeant had given.

'DS McCabe. I've booked a small room over there.' He pointed to the end of the open-plan area. 'Afraid I can't offer tea or coffee. Hospitality isn't extended to internal meetings. Vending machine only if you want to take a chance.'

Aitken feigned affront. 'I'm external if you don't regard Gayfield Square as being part of St Leonard's.'

'Splitting hairs there, sir. We're all part of Police Scotland.'

'I'll pass on the vending machine. But I take it I can expect a lot of co-operation since we're all part of the same outfit?'

McCabe smiled and indicated for them to take a seat at a small circular table in the middle of the room. 'Of course. What is it you think I can help you with, sir?'

'I'm starting an investigation into drugs and gun smuggling. I'm betting Big Col Calhoun knows something about it.'

'Ah! Might have guessed.'

Aitken tilted his head to one side. 'Oh?'

'Goes without saying. Everyone thinks he has a hand in everything in the Edinburgh crime scene. Apart from that, any reason to suspect he's involved?'

'Just gut feeling at this stage. I hear one of the last things DI Taylor was working on before he retired was a possible link between Calhoun and Jenner Transport.'

'That's right. He had previously tried to link Calhoun to an attempted jewellery shop robbery five years ago. Couldn't prove anything. He reckoned Doug Jenner and Calhoun were thick as thieves. Didn't get anywhere with that either and he closed the files.'

'Did you agree with his decision?' Aitken asked.

'I thought if we'd dug a bit deeper, we might have found something, but he was the boss. I think he just wanted to close the books and retire.'

'Calhoun and Jenner were at a black-tie dinner organised by one of the councillors for City of Edinburgh Council. Maybe a connection there.'

McCabe stretched his legs under the table. 'How'd you know they were there?'

'Calhoun told us. Went to pay him a visit at his club. Just to let him know we're watching him.'

'And he told you he was there with Jenner?'

'No, the assistant chief constable, Ramsay Irvin, did.'

McCabe shook his head. 'How'd he know?'

'He was there.'

'Bloody hell! What was he doing mixing with them?'

'Said he didn't know they would be there.'

'I take it you're thinking Jenner Transport might be involved in the smuggling operation?'

'Keeping an open mind. I have no evidence, so I have no grounds to pull him in for questioning yet.'

'Right. I haven't been much use to you, have I?'

Aitken smiled. 'Worth a try. You'll let me know if you hear anything to do with Jenner or Calhoun?'

'Sure, anything to help you put Calhoun behind bars.'

19

OXFORD

The trip to London to see Jamila Kazan hadn't advanced the Upton murder enquiry much. In fact, Fleming reflected, it had revealed next to nothing. All he'd found out was confirmation that Jamila and her husband had a row when she went to pick some of her things up. Logan had offered the view they ought to be treating Atticus Kazan as the number one suspect. All things considered, they had little else to go on. *He was angry and frightened her*, Logan had said.

Fleming knew Oxford University was a large institution and had set Anderson the task of trying to find someone who would be able to verify Atticus Kazan's timetable. After getting passed from pillar to post, she finally found a senior lecturer in the computer science department. Parking would be a challenge, so Fleming decided to get a taxi into town.

The taxi, which was not one of Andy Cabs's tiny fleet of cars, turned up in good time. 'Where to, guv?' the driver asked, winding down his window.

'Oxford University, computer science department, corner of Parks Road and Keble Road.'

'I know it,' the driver said.

Ten minutes later, the taxi dropped Fleming off. He made his way past a large number of bicycles parked outside and found a young lady manning reception inside the front door.

'Can I help you?' she asked.

Fleming showed his warrant card. 'DCI Fleming. I'm here to see Yusef Zabow. He's expecting me.'

'If you bear with me, I'll give him a call and get him to come down.'

A few minutes later, a tall thin bespectacled man with short silver hair appeared. 'Sorry to keep you waiting. I had a student with me.'

'No problem. Thank you for seeing me. I won't take up much of your time.'

Zabow pointed to a small room opposite reception. 'We can talk in there.'

'May I ask,' Fleming said as they sat at a small coffee table, 'what your connection is with Atticus Kazan?'

'I take it this is to do with the shooting of Oliver Upton on the golf course?'

'It is, yes.'

'I see. In answer to your question, I'm a senior lecturer and I have management responsibility for Atticus.'

'Are you aware Mr Kazan's wife left him about six months ago to go and live with Mr Upton?'

'I did know, yes. That's why I assumed your visit was to do with the shooting.'

'Do you know Mr Kazan on a personal basis?'

'If you're asking whether we socialise, the answer would be yes and no. I mean, we don't socialise as friends do. It's more work-related dinners, parties, and social events if colleagues have a birthday, or if someone's getting engaged or married.'

'So you know him quite well?'

'From a work perspective, very well. Not so much about his private life.'

'But you did know about the split with his wife?'

'As I said, yes I did.'

'Did he volunteer the information?'

'In a way. I was having a conversation with him about work one day and he seemed a bit... distracted. Not his usual self. I asked him if everything was okay.'

'And he told you his wife had left him.'

'After trying to insist there was nothing wrong, he finally admitted it.'

'Did he say whether he knew his wife was having an affair or just walked out on the day?'

'He said he'd suspected it, but he didn't know it was Mr Upton.'

'Until his wife moved out?'

'I got that impression, yes.'

'Is Mr Kazan a good lecturer?'

'Yes. He's intelligent, capable, and *very* meticulous.'

'Did his performance suffer after his wife left him?'

Zabow pondered for a second. 'I suppose it did, but not to the point he became inefficient.'

'Maybe to do with his mental state?'

'He became a bit distant, serious. Though to be fair, he was always a serious character.'

'Had he become even more distant in recent weeks?'

'Can't say I noticed, no.'

'Did he ever mention Mr Upton after his wife left him?'

Zabow rubbed his chin. 'He got angry one day, must be about two weeks ago. Told me his wife had come back to the house to get some of her things and had goaded him about how much happier she was with Upton.'

'He was angry.'

'Most men would be, would they not?'

'One final question. Mr Kazan told me he was lecturing on the morning of the shooting. Can you confirm that?'

Zabow hesitated for a second. 'I'm sure he must have made a mistake. He would have been free of lectures that day. He always has Fridays clear for preparing lectures, research and marking.'

'Would he do that at home, or here?'

'Here in the library most of the time, but sometimes at home.'

Fleming rose to go. 'Thank you for your time, Mr Zabow. You've been very helpful.'

Zabow frowned. 'I do hope I haven't said anything that will get Atticus into trouble. He must have got his days mixed up. He couldn't possibly have had anything to do with the shooting.'

'You may be right, but we do need to check these things out. It's routine procedure.'

On his way back to the flat to pick up his car to drive to HQ, Fleming recalled something else Logan had said: *Be interesting if his alibi doesn't stack up.*

20

OXFORD

The golf course car park was full by the time Fleming got there. He'd left Logan and Anderson in the office. Logan was going through the painstaking process of checking all London taxi companies. He was looking for any information on Upton who had claimed he drove taxis there before moving to Oxford. Anderson was checking with the DBS to see if they still had a record of Upton's application for the job with Andy Cabs.

Fleming parked his car and walked over to the golf shop at the end of the clubhouse. It was a bright sunny day. Perfect for golf, hence the full car park. Fleming could see a group of four men about to tee off for the first hole. One of them was limbering up with a few practice swings.

Sam Galland was in the shop as Fleming entered. 'Oh, hello. Thought you'd finished your enquiries here.'

'There are a few more things I wanted to check.' He pointed outside to the men about to start their round. 'Looks like they're going to have a nice day. Car park's quite full. Seems business is doing all right despite the drama of a murder.'

'Yeah. Surprising how busy it is. I thought the shooting would put people off coming here.'

'Curiosity of people,' Fleming suggested. 'You'd be surprised how many people come to visit a murder scene. I can imagine golfers gossiping, telling friends they played on the course where a man was recently murdered.'

'Nowt as queer as folk, eh?'

Fleming smiled. 'I guess you're right.'

'What is it you wanted to ask?'

'You told me Mr Upton had been a member for about two years. Did he have a handicap when he joined?'

Galland frowned and tapped into a computer. 'Yes, he did. Eighteen.'

'Did he say where he played before?'

'I don't think he ever did.'

'When he turned up on the day he was shot, did he appear nervous or anxious?'

Galland shrugged. 'Didn't notice. I just booked him in and off he went.'

'He didn't say anything?'

'Said he was here for a bit of practise. He was never one for long conversations.'

'You any good at identifying dialects?'

Galland smiled. 'Are you about to test me?'

'Where would you say Mr Upton hailed from?'

'That one's easy. Scotland. No idea what part though. It all sounds the same to me.'

'Thanks, Sam. That's the first bit of background information I've got about the man. Don't know why I didn't think to ask anyone else before now, or why no one else mentioned it.'

'Glad to be of some help.'

'You said there was a big commotion in the clubhouse a few weeks ago involving Mr Upton and another member, Ian Hunter. Was it just an argument or was there a bit of a scuffle?'

'I didn't witness it. Someone came into the shop and

said hell had broken loose in the clubhouse. It was all to do with Mr Hunter accusing Mr Upton of stealing a golf club.'

'Were you aware of any previous or further hostilities between the two of them?'

'Can't say I was, no.'

'Mr Hunter was here on the morning of the shooting. Did you know that?'

'Sure. He'd booked a round for ten thirty, but said he was going to have some breakfast and a read of the paper in the clubhouse first.'

Fleming made a mental note to ask Hunter if anyone could confirm he was in the clubhouse café all the time before the four golfers found Upton.

'Is a man called Atticus Kazan a member here?'

'Don't recognise the name. I'll have a quick look.' His fingers danced across his keyboard until he found what he was looking for. 'Thought so. He's not a member.'

'How long do you keep records of tee times booked?'

Galland smiled. 'There's no need to keep them beyond the day in question. I tend to delete them when I've got nothing better to do.'

'When did you last delete them?'

'A few days ago. Why?'

'Would you have any way of knowing whether Atticus Kazan played here in the last few weeks or so?'

'I'm afraid not, no.'

'Okay, thanks for your time, Sam. Just one last thing, is there a road which runs near where the fifth hole would be?'

Galland thought for a moment. 'Yes, there is. If you turn right out of the golf course entrance, then first right again, there's a narrow country lane that takes you up the side of the course. About a mile up the road, you should be able to see the flag for the fifth hole through the trees. Maybe a couple of hundred yards in.'

'Thanks.'

Fleming left and made his way across the car park to his car. He turned on the ignition and wondered if it was worth a look. He was hardly likely to find anything. The SOCOs had checked the woods up near where they thought the shots may have come from but found nothing. He put the car into gear and eased out of the car park.

At the entrance, Fleming tapped the driving wheel and then indicated right. *No harm in having a look now I'm here.*

It was a narrow country lane as Galland had said, and there were no other cars on the road. Fleming took his time, driving slowly whilst keeping an eye out to the right for any sign of a flag. After about three-quarters of a mile, he spotted a white flag fluttering in the slight breeze through a gap in the trees. He slowed the car to a crawl and noticed a bit of a clearing on the side of the road up ahead. Pulling the car over, he parked, switched off the ignition, and wound his window down.

Fleming got out of the car to stretch his legs and walked over to the side of the road forming the boundary to the golf course. There was a small hedge, but where he was standing, there was a narrow gap. Fleming picked his way through the gap and made off through the trees towards the direction of the flag.

Reaching the edge of the treeline, Fleming looked down the fairway towards where golfers would tee off for the fifth hole; the place where they found Upton's body. About 200 yards from here, Fleming reckoned. *The estimated distance from the target is 200 yards,* Logan had read from the ballistics report.

Down by the tee, Fleming could see four golfers about to tee off. He decided this was probably where the gunman had fired the shots from, but the SOCOs had already searched there.

There was no point in searching further. He melted into the trees and made his way back to his car.

On his way to Long Hanborough, Fleming concluded that the killer either knew the course well or about this road. Or he had time to carry out detailed reconnaissance.

21

———————

LONDON

I t didn't take long for Toby to drive from the school to his mother's house, even though traffic was heavy. He parked on the road as near to the house as he could get and sat for a moment. He'd stopped off at a convenience store on the way to buy himself a bottle of wine. He was sure he was going to need a drink by the time he got home.

Toby's hands trembled when he took them off the steering wheel. The visits to his mother were becoming more stressful each time he came to see her. He loved his mother, but had tired of her domineering and manipulative interference in his life. Toby knew she didn't see it like that, of course. She'd often remark that Toby was clever and wanted to help people. That's why he'd become a teacher, she'd say. Just needed someone like her to make sure he made the right decisions in life, she'd say.

The business about the teaching job up in Scotland had caused a major upset. Toby agonised between loyalty toward his mother and the need to break free and do something for himself for once. Something that would be good for his self-esteem, peace of mind, and physical well-being. The chance to apply for the job up in Scotland had been too good an opportunity to miss.

A neighbour was walking past the car and recognised Toby sitting there, lost in his thoughts. She tapped on the window and waved. Toby smiled and wound the window down. 'You look like you're a million miles away,' she said. 'Everything all right?'

'Yeah, fine. Just had a busy day. Thinking about a problem at work,' was all Toby could think of saying. He didn't want to tell her what was really going through his mind.

'Well, I'm sure a visit to see your mother will help. Take care.'

Toby watched her walk on up the street. He wasn't at all sure his visit would stop what was worrying him. Taking a deep breath, Toby opened the car door and swung his long legs out.

He let himself into the house. It was unusually quiet. There was no sound coming from the sitting room. 'It's me,' Toby called out, closing the front door. Still no sound.

Frowning, Toby opened the sitting room door to find his mother's chair empty. He walked through to the kitchen, but there was no sign of his mother. A bread knife lying on a breadboard covered in crumbs suggested she had recently made herself a sandwich. Toby put a hand on the kettle. It was still warm.

He walked over to the door leading out to the back garden.

It was a long narrow garden with tall wooden fences on either side. A mixture of established shrubs and perennials lined the edges in shallow borders. At the far end, there was a stunning magnolia tree in full bloom. Deep pink flowers danced in the light breeze. By the back of the house, there was a small patio area of pink and buff paving slabs. Doreen Enderby was sitting in a chair drinking tea. On a small table by her side was a plate containing the hard crust remains of the sandwich she had made herself.

'Oh, there you are. Glad to see you're getting out for a bit of fresh air,' Toby said, his voice drowned out by the roar of engines from a passing plane.

'What'd you say?' Doreen asked. 'Too many planes flying overhead these days.'

'I said good to see you getting out into the garden.'

'Just having an afternoon sandwich and a cup of tea. Did you remember my cigarettes this time?'

'Left them on the kitchen worktop.'

'Be a dear and get them for me, will you?'

Toby fetched the cigarettes and watched his mother light up. She threw the matches and cigarette packet onto the table, took a deep drag, and blew a cloud of smoke up into the air. 'Had a good day?' she asked.

'Busy, as usual. I've got something to tell you.'

Doreen took another deep draw on her cigarette and smoke trickled out of her nostrils as she spoke. 'Kettle might still be hot enough if you want some tea.'

'It's okay. I'm fine. I came to–'

Doreen interrupted. 'Did I switch the TV off?'

She knows why I've come and she's trying to delay me telling her. 'Yes. Listen, I've something important to tell you.'

Doreen examined the glowing tip of her cigarette. 'I hope it's not about the stupid job you told me about.'

Toby couldn't put it off any longer. 'Yes... it is. I've been invited up for an interview.'

Doreen fell silent.

Toby shifted from one foot to the other. 'I'm excited about it.'

'Well I'm not,' Doreen said. 'I told you not to apply. It'll all come to nothing.' She sniffed and stubbed out her cigarette with more force than was necessary.

'I know you don't want me to get the job. I understand that. But can't you at least accept that I've managed to get an interview and show some enthusiasm?'

'Don't have much choice, do I? You might have an interview, but remember what I said.'

'What?'

'They won't want an outsider. You'll go all the way up there and they'll already have made up their minds.'

'I don't think so. They can't do that these days. It has to be a fair and open competition. They'll offer the job to the best person they think fits.'

'I doubt it.'

'You're getting very cynical, Mother. There's no way they would invite me to go up for an interview if they had no intention of offering me the job. I stand as good a chance as anyone else they speak to.'

'And if you do get the job, what about me? Who's going to look after me?'

'We've been through all this. You're not an invalid. Anyway, Quentin and Margo will still be here, and you have good neighbours.'

'I've told you... Quentin is too busy.'

Toby was getting tired of her stubbornness. It was one of the reasons he felt it was time to leave London. 'Rubbish! He's not so busy he or Margo couldn't do the odd bit of shopping for you.'

Doreen sniffed. 'You're getting angry with me.'

'No, I'm not.'

'What about the garden. Who's going to do it?'

'No reason you can't do some light work. You could get a gardener to do any heavy stuff. You can afford it.'

'But you like doing the garden, Toby.'

'I can still do some when I come down in the school holidays.'

'I don't want you to go. You'll only be disappointed if you don't get it. It'll all come to nothing.'

'I'll take my chances.'

'Don't say I didn't warn you. They'll ask why you want to leave your current job. If you tell them what you told me, they'll think you're not up to it.'

Toby shook his head. 'I'll remember what you said. If it's meant to be, I'll get it. If not, I won't.'

Toby made his mother another cup of tea before he left. On his way home he prayed she wouldn't get the chance to gloat if he didn't get the job.

22

OXFORD

A ndy Cabs driver Phil Odde's wife had told Fleming how to get to her husband's allotment. 'When you get there, follow the grass pathway up the middle of the allotments and you'll find him near the top end on the left-hand side,' she'd said. 'He's of medium height, has a bit of a paunch on him, and has a full head of grey hair. He's wearing a pink shirt and blue jeans. You can't miss him.'

The sun was shining and only a few white puffs of cloud drifted across the blue sky. There were a few keen gardeners out tending to their patches. Fleming left his jacket in the car and made his way up the grass pathway, tie undone and shirt sleeves rolled up to the elbow. He admired the creativity of some gardeners who had made an art form of building rustic sheds out of all manner of materials.

As Fleming neared the top end, he spotted a man who met the description Odde's wife had given him. Fleming waved and walked across to him. 'DCI Fleming, your wife told me where to find you.'

Odde smiled and pushed the spade he'd been digging with into the ground. He leaned on the handle. 'I have most Sundays off driving. Weather permitting, I'll always be up here this time of year.'

'What're you busy with today?'

'Bit of weeding and getting runner bean, beetroot, and lettuce seeds into the ground. Time permitting, I may get some sweetcorn in as well.'

Fleming swatted a fly away from his face. 'I'll try not to hold you up then.'

'My wife texted me to say you were coming round. Said you wanted to have a word about poor old Oliver Upton.'

'Yes. Your boss said you might be able to help me with a bit of background information on him. He said you were friendly with Mr Upton.'

'I guess you could say so, insofar as we got on okay. Went for the odd pint together, but I wouldn't go so far as to say we were lifelong friends.'

'How long had you known him?'

'Four, maybe five years, since he came to work for Andy Cabs. We got talking when he joined us and I offered to take him for a pint. Sort of welcome to the job, I suppose.'

'Did that become a regular thing... going for a drink?'

'Not really. We went for a pint together a few times. As I said, we weren't bosom buddies.'

'What sort of things did you talk about when you went out?'

Odde rubbed his chin. 'Driving taxis, sport, state of the world. I asked him once how he came to get a job with Andy Cabs.'

'What did he say?'

'Only that driving was what he did. There was a vacancy, so he applied.'

'Did he tell you he used to drive a taxi in London?'

'Yeah, he did.'

'Did he say why he moved up to Oxford?'

'I asked him. Said London was a nightmare to work in. He wanted a change.'

'Why Oxford?'

Odde shook his head. 'No idea.'

'He told your boss he'd driven taxis for about eighteen years. Did he happen to say how long he was in London?'

'Don't think he did, no.'

'I gather he had a Scottish accent. Did you ever ask him where he originated from?'

'I did, yes. It was interesting. He'd had a bit too much to drink.'

'What did he say?'

'He always seemed to be evasive about his background. Almost as though he was being careful not to let something slip. But that night he did. Said he used to drive taxis in Edinburgh.'

'Did he say any more about Edinburgh?'

'No. I remember it well because I thought it odd.'

'Oh?'

Odde's spade was starting to lean over so he pushed it further into the ground with his foot. 'He tried to change his story. I asked him to tell me about Edinburgh. He looked shocked and claimed he hadn't mentioned it. I said he had and he laughed it off saying he'd had too much to drink. Said he couldn't think why he would have mentioned Edinburgh. He mumbled something about not knowing what he was saying. Said it must have been a friend of his who worked there.'

'Did you ask why he moved south to work in London?'

'Reckoned he wanted a change.'

'Did you ever meet his wife?'

Odde frowned. 'No, I didn't, now you come to mention it.'

'You knew he was divorced though?'

'Yeah, I remember him getting married. Very quiet affair.

They went to a registry office. No guests, no reception, nothing as I recall.'

'Mr Upton seems as though he was a very private person, and wanted to remain so,' Fleming mused. 'I wonder why?'

'Beats me.'

'Do you know why he got divorced?'

'No, but I guess it must have been something to do with Jamila Kazan who moved in with him.'

'Did he talk about the divorce?'

'No, never.'

'Ever mention Jamila or her husband, Atticus Kazan?'

Odde shook his head.

'Did you ever play golf with him?'

'Nah. Never played the game.'

'Did he mention a row he had with another golfer called Ian Hunter a few weeks ago?'

'He did, yes. Said there was this prat, a real golfing snob, one of those people who get agitated if you don't stick rigidly to the rules.'

'Ian Hunter?'

'Yeah. Reckoned Oliver pinched one of his clubs.'

'I guess Oliver told you it wasn't him.'

'He got a bit agitated and said the man had a cheek. More than likely left it behind on the course. Oliver didn't nick it. Said he wouldn't even want to touch a club that had been in Hunter's hands other than to wrap it round his neck.'

'So there was bad blood between them?'

'I'll say. Oliver couldn't stand the man.'

23

OXFORD

Logan and Anderson were in the office at HQ going through the list of actions while Fleming went to speak to Upton's taxi driver colleague. It was late afternoon and Logan had gone to fetch some coffee. He put a mug in front of Anderson. 'Don't say I never do anything for you.'

'You're all heart, Sarge.'

'You were starting to look a bit tired. Thought a caffeine hit might keep you awake.'

'Very thoughtful. Bet you only got the coffees because *you'd* hit a slump.'

Logan grinned. 'Must admit, ploughing through all this stuff is enough to send you to sleep.'

'Bit painstaking, isn't it?'

'Yeah, but meticulous attention to detail can often come up with results.'

Anderson took a deep breath and exhaled. 'I suppose so.'

Logan took a sip of his coffee and eyed Anderson who was staring ahead. 'You okay?'

Anderson nodded. 'Just thinking.'

'Don't overdo it.'

Anderson scrunched up a piece of paper and threw it across the desk at Logan.

Logan ducked to avoid the missile. 'Go on, tell me.'

'What?'

'What you were thinking about.'

'Upton. He seems a complete enigma. DI Rainger's lot haven't been able to find out anything about him.'

'We know he worked for Andy Cabs and that Jamila Kazan lived with him.'

'That's about it though. Don't you find it strange?'

'I guess so. Did Rainger find anything from the check of CCTV footage on the roads around the golf course?'

'He said it was busy first thing in the morning. They picked up loads of vehicles and local bobbies have questioned a lot of drivers. They've still got a lot to go through, but no leads have come up so far.'

'Anything from golf club members?'

'No luck there either. It seems no one knows much about our mysterious Mr Upton.'

'We're not getting very far, are we?' Logan moaned.

'Maybe something will turn up eventually.'

Logan laughed. 'Sounds like you're hoping for a spot of luck.' He considered this for a moment, then added, 'But sometimes you *do* get a bit of luck in an investigation.'

'One can but hope.'

'What about the DBS? Get anything back from them on Upton's application for a job with Andy Cabs?'

'Yeah. It was all clear. No problems.'

'No information on his application at all?'

'Just his name, address, that he had no previous convictions, cautions, or warnings. Local police held nothing on him and he's not on any lists of barred people from any role or profession.'

'Not very helpful in terms of finding out anything about his background.'

'What about your check of London taxi companies?'

Logan sipped the last of his coffee. 'Not much luck there either, I'm afraid. Haven't been able to find anyone with any knowledge of Upton so far.'

'Like I said, we could do with a lucky break.'

'Talking about breaks, why don't we call it a day, pack in and go home?'

'Good idea.' Anderson paused for a second. 'Know what I reckon?'

'What?'

'Upton could have been a retired spook. Maybe someone thought he had information they wanted kept secret, tracked him down and made sure he stayed silent.'

'You've been reading too many spy stories.'

'Maybe, but it's a possibility, don't you think?'

24

OXFORD

I t was early morning and the streets in Oxford were already busy. The good weather had brought shoppers out in force, and workers were making their way to offices, shops and banks. Ian Hunter was sitting at his desk. Since going freelance as an accountant, he'd rented a room on the first floor above an estate agent's office near the town centre.

Fleming entered the outer hallway of the estate agent's office. Their office was through a door to his left. An arrow pointed up a wooden staircase. Fleming took the steps up to a small landing. A sign printed on a frosted glass window set into the top half of the door informed clients this was the office of I Hunter FCA. Fleming knocked and entered. 'DCI Fleming. You're expecting me.'

Hunter was sitting behind an antique desk with an inlaid leather top. A stack of wire baskets occupied one end of the surface. A computer screen sat on the other side, angled towards Hunter's chair.

Hunter stood and came round his desk, glancing at his watch. 'On time, I see. I've always been one for punctuality,' he said, offering a hand. Hunter was a tall, stocky man. What little remained of his hair was short and grey. Beneath a stubble beard, Fleming noticed a ruddy complexion. He put Hunter in his late fifties.

'I suppose it pays in business,' Fleming replied. 'How long have you been self-employed?'

Hunter went back to sit behind his desk and waved for Fleming to pull up a chair. 'A little over twenty years. I worked for an accountancy firm in Oxford for sixteen years before that.'

Fleming noted there was no smile on Hunter's face. He fixed Fleming with a steady gaze. His brown eyes were like pools of dark stagnant water.

'How's business?' Fleming asked.

'I am a busy man, Inspector. I've tax returns to complete for several clients who like to get them in early. I don't expect you came here to ask about my business.'

'No, you're right. I came to ask you about Oliver Upton. And it's detective chief inspector, by the way.' Fleming smiled. 'I've always been one for correctness.'

Hunter's right cheek twitched as though a sharp object had jabbed him. He frowned. 'Police have already questioned me about him. I gave them a statement.'

'Yes, I know. I've read it. Just wanted to ask a few more questions.'

'I'm not sure I can be of any more help.'

'You're a member of the club where Mr Upton met his demise.'

'If that's a question, the answer is yes.'

'How long for?'

'I can't see what that's got to do with anything.'

'Always useful to get as much background information as we can.' Fleming couldn't resist another dig. 'I'm a stickler for detail.'

Another twitch of Hunter's cheek. 'About twenty years.'

'Mr Upton became a member about two years ago. Did you know him?'

'Not at all.'

'You ever play together in competitions or small groups?'

'Yes, but not very often. Depends who's there on the day and which names they draw out of the bag. We may have played in the same team two or three times. Doesn't mean I knew him well.'

'You didn't learn anything of his private life?'

'I go to play golf, not get the life history of other golfers.'

'You accused Mr Upton of stealing one of your golf clubs a few weeks ago. Why did you think it was him?'

'I didn't like the man. He didn't stick to the rules and golf etiquette.'

'Doesn't make him a thief. You must have had another reason to suspect him.'

'We did play together a few weeks ago. He asked me about a driver I was using. It was a very expensive club. Paid about five hundred quid for it.'

'And you think he stole it because he asked you about it?'

'I saw him eyeing it up. Strange it went missing out of my golf bag the same day.'

'So you confronted him in the clubhouse?'

'Damn right I did.'

'Then what happened?'

'He got abusive. Claimed it wasn't him and I was free to check his car. Called me a golfing snob. Pushed me back into my chair and said he'd wrap the club round my neck if he had it.'

'Did you check his car?'

'I was too frightened to go out into the car park with him.'

'Why didn't you report it to the police?'

'No point these days. Your lot aren't interesting in petty crime. I claimed off my insurance and that was the end of it.'

'Had you had any fallouts with Upton before that?'

'No.'

'Any afterward?'

'No. I tried to steer clear of him.'

'So there was nothing more to your mutual dislike of each other than the fallout over your golf club?'

'Let's just say we didn't hit it off.'

'In your statement, you said you turned up to have a round of golf the day Upton was shot. You said you went into the clubhouse to have some breakfast before starting your round.'

Hunter glared at Fleming. 'Correct.'

'Is there anyone who can verify you were there all the time before they found Upton's body?'

'Are you serious? You think I'm a suspect because of a fallout over a golf club? You must be mad.'

'We have to follow up every single lead, including all recent contacts with a victim. You happen to be someone who had contact with Upton on less than friendly terms. Treat my questions as being more to do with eliminating people from my enquiries.'

Hunter seemed to relax. For the first time, he smiled. 'Yes, of course, I understand. The girl serving behind the counter can verify I was there all the time with several other members. I can give you their names if you need them.'

'Yes please.'

Hunter scribbled a few names on a sheet of paper and passed it to Fleming. 'Are we done?'

'We are. Thank you for your time, Mr Hunter. I won't keep you any longer from your tax returns.'

Fleming let himself out and wondered whether he could drop Hunter from his enquiries. But then he recalled what he'd said to Temple when she queried whether someone would kill a man over a golf club: *I've known people to kill for less.*

Is it possible Hunter could have paid someone to shoot Upton for him?

25

BALCORIE

Toby had decided to drive up to Scotland to keep costs down. It was an epic journey of 658 miles from London to Lochinver, taking almost twelve hours. He'd set off at seven in the morning and had three twenty-minute stops so it was nearing eight when he arrived at the bed and breakfast accommodation he'd booked.

Traffic had been heavy on the motorways in England. But once over the border, it dwindled the further up into the Highlands he drove. His interview with Highland Council was at nine thirty in the morning. Ailsa Brodie, who he'd spoken to on the phone, had sent the letter of invitation with instructions.

The next morning Toby's heart was pounding. Despite his nerves, he forced himself to have a full breakfast. The landlady had served up bacon, egg, sausage, baked beans, fried tomatoes and mushrooms. She had also asked if he would like some black pudding, tattie scones, and haggis. Toby had declined the extras. He'd eaten less in a three-course dinner, but had managed to eat most of it. *Won't need to eat for a week*, he'd thought.

To work off the calories consumed, he made his way on foot to the Highland Council office. The exercise would also help control his nerves. He found the office without any trouble. It was small, but a convenient place to hold the interviews.

Toby arrived there early at nine fifteen. He entered the building to find a young woman sitting behind a solitary desk in a small reception area. 'Hello, I'm Toby Enderby,' he said. 'I have an interview at nine thirty.'

The woman smiled. 'I'll get Ailsa to come down for you. Take a seat.'

As Toby settled into a chair, the pounding in his heart returned. He wished he hadn't eaten so much for breakfast. Trying to distract himself, he rehearsed answers to anticipated questions:

Why should we offer the position to you, Mr Enderby?

I've been a primary school teacher for ten years. I'm experienced, conscientious, and loyal.

So why do you want to leave your current job?

I–

A slim attractive woman, who looked to be a little younger than Toby, interrupted his thoughts. Wavy brown hair cascaded over her shoulders onto a white shirt tucked into a black skirt. 'Hello, I'm Ailsa Brodie. We've spoken on the phone,' she said in a soft Scottish accent and offered a hand. 'I hope you had a pleasant journey up here.'

Toby stood and shook hands. 'Thanks. It was a long drive though.'

'Gosh, yes, you have come a long way. I take it you're staying over?'

'Yes. I'm booked into a bed and breakfast place for two nights. Came up yesterday and going home tomorrow.'

'In which case, I can recommend a nice restaurant for you to eat in tonight.'

Toby attempted a smile. 'After the breakfast I've had this morning, I don't think I'll need to eat again for a week.'

'Bet that's Mrs McIntyre's place,' Ailsa said. 'She's renowned for piling it on.'

'Yes, I am staying there, and I can vouch for the size of breakfast helpings.'

Ailsa laughed. 'You're a few minutes early, but I'll take you up. You can wait in my office.'

Toby sat opposite Ailsa who was sitting behind her desk writing something into a file. He crossed and uncrossed his arms and legs and felt a trickle of sweat run down his back.

'After your interview, I'll get someone to take you up to Balcorie so you can have a look at the school,' Ailsa said. 'It's only six miles from here. It won't be open though. It's the May holiday. You'll be able to look round the outside and you can peep through the windows.'

'Thank you,' Toby managed to say, clearing a throat about to dry up.

After a few minutes, a door to the side opened and a red-haired man looked out. 'Ah, you must be Mr Enderby.' He held the door open. 'If you'd like to come in.'

The interview had gone well, Toby thought. They'd explained the current teacher was retiring. The plan was to get someone in place to start after the summer school holidays in mid-August. They would let him know whether he'd been successful in the next week.

Kenny, one of Ailsa's colleagues, had offered to drive Toby up to Balcorie to see the school and drop Ailsa off. The car wound its way north through the hills and soon the sea appeared beyond the clifftops to the left. Over to the east, mountains were visible in the distance.

It was a bright sunny day with large white clouds drifting

across a blue sky. There was a stiff breeze coming in from the west, and whitecaps topped the waves of the azure sea. A small fishing boat bobbed up and down on the swell, a quarter of a mile out. They rounded a corner and Toby saw the road winding down the hill towards Balcorie, past a white sandy bay, then rising into the hills again on the other side.

'Wow,' Toby exclaimed from the back seat. 'What a view!'

Ailsa turned from the passenger seat and smiled. 'Bit different to London, eh?'

'I'll say!'

Kenny drove on down into the tiny village and parked the car outside the small primary school.

Toby had a good look round. He was impressed. It felt like he was meant to be here.

'Okay to have a quick drive through the village so Toby can see the place while we're here?' Ailsa asked Kenny. 'You can drop me off at the post office.'

'Sure, no problem.'

Kenny drove through Balcorie, down to the small bay and Ailsa pointed out the church and the tiny village hall on the way. Waves were gently lapping up against the white sand and seagulls screeched overhead as they soared up on thermals.

'Beautiful,' Toby whispered. 'It's so peaceful here. Amazing. I'd always wanted to come and see Scotland.'

'Never been to Scotland before?' Ailsa asked.

'No.'

'You're far from the maddening crowds here, for sure.'

'No air pollution either,' Kenny added.

'How many people live here?' Toby asked.

'About 160,' Ailsa said.

'And only ten pupils at the primary school?'

'It's an ageing population. A lot of the youngsters leave to go to university or down to Edinburgh or Glasgow to find work. Oh dear, I hope that doesn't put you off.'

'No, not at all. I'm sure I'd love it here. But what's the long-term future of the school?'

'Oh, it's safe for a long time yet. There are a few toddlers who'll be coming up to school age to keep it going.'

Perfect, Toby thought.

Kenny had turned the car round and had parked outside the post office which also served as a small shop where you could buy essential food items.

'Have you always lived here?' Toby asked Ailsa.

Toby noticed a slight hesitation before she answered.

'No.'

'Where'd you come from?'

'Further south.'

Toby was curious Ailsa wasn't more specific.

She got out of the car. 'Thanks, Kenny. I'd best let you get Toby back to Lochinver.'

26

OXFORD

Fleming and Logan were on their way in a marked car to see Atticus Kazan. He'd lied about where he was on the morning of Upton's murder. Either that or he'd mixed his days up.

Logan was driving. 'No way he got confused over the days,' he said, looking across at Fleming then back to the road. 'The man was lying.'

'We need to be able to prove it if he was.'

'It'll be interesting to hear what he says,' Logan said, indicating to turn into Kazan's cul-de-sac.

'Looks like we've arrived just in time,' Fleming said, seeing Kazan come out of his house and walk over to his car.

Logan parked in front of the gravelled parking area, blocking off Kazan's exit.

Fleming climbed out. 'We need a quick word, Mr Kazan.'

'Afraid it'll have to wait. I'm on my way to meet a friend.'

'This won't take long.'

'I'm late as it is. If you don't mind,' Kazan said with an ingratiating smile, 'I'd be grateful if you could move your car so I can get out.'

'Call your friend if you like and tell them you're running late. Could be five minutes if you answer my questions here, maybe an hour or more if I have to take you in.'

Atticus frowned and looked at Fleming. 'Look, I've already answered your questions. What can be so urgent?'

'There appears to be a problem over your explanation of where you were on the day Oliver Upton was shot.'

'Oh? I told you where I was.'

'You said you were lecturing at the university. I checked, and it seems you didn't have any lectures that day.'

'Who says?'

'Yusef Zabow. He reckons you don't have any on Fridays.'

Kazan smiled. 'Ah, of course, I must have got the days mixed up. I do apologise.'

'So where were you?'

'I must have been in the college library doing research or preparing lectures.'

'Not at home?'

'No, I rarely work from home. I would have been in the library.'

'Can anyone verify that?'

Kazan frowned as though deep in thought. He snapped his fingers. 'Yes, a chap called Chris Owen was there.'

'Did you speak to him?'

'Yes... yes, I did. I remember it now. Sorry, I got confused about the days.'

'What time would that be?'

'I have no recollection of the time. Recording the timing of all the conversations I have is not something I make a habit of,' Kazan mocked.

Fleming ignored Kazan's irritating smile. 'I do make a habit of recording and checking everything people tell me if it's to do with their whereabouts at the time of a crime,' he retorted.

'Good for you, Inspector.' There was no mistaking the sarcasm in his voice.

'Be a bit unfortunate for you if Mr Owen can confirm what time he spoke to you and the timing would have allowed you to be at the scene of Upton's murder.'

'I'm sure you'll find it won't. But even if it did, doesn't mean I killed him.'

'True, but in the meantime don't plan on going anywhere.'

'*Anywhere?* Am I to take it you see me as the prime suspect?'

'It doesn't help when people give a wrong account of where they were at the time of a serious crime. For your sake, I hope it doesn't happen twice. You can go meet your friend now.'

'Excuse the French, boss, but he's a slimy bastard,' Logan said as they climbed back in the car. 'Full of himself if you ask me. No wonder his wife left him.'

Fleming smiled. 'Must admit I don't take to the man, but we can't let that prejudice the enquiry.'

Logan grunted. 'What if his second attempt at providing an alibi proves to be false?'

'Then he's in serious trouble.'

27

EDINBURGH

The period of dry sunny weather in Edinburgh had come to a sudden end. A summer storm had hit the city and the wipers on the squad car were going full pelt as rain pounded in gusts against the windscreen. DI Aitken and DS Quigley were speeding east towards Doug Jenner's house in Portobello with tyres hissing on the waterlogged roads.

'This is it,' Quigley said, turning into a cul-de-sac. Two police cars had answered the 999 call and had parked outside the house with blue lights still flashing.

Faces peered out the windows of neighbouring houses, but no one had ventured out onto the street in the pouring rain. A uniformed officer wearing a yellow hi-vis jacket stood guard by the front door of the house. He looked miserable, rain dripping off the brim of his black baseball cap.

Aitken showed the man his warrant card. 'DI Aitken and DS Quigley.'

'Okay, sir, you can go in.'

There were three uniformed police inside, one female officer was sitting with Jenner's wife, trying to comfort her. Another was on his radio while the third was standing by him.

'What's happened?' Aitken asked the third officer.

'Husband tried to kill her, she reckons.'

'Here?' Aitken asked.

'No. Over at his depot. He's the owner of Jenner Transport, a small one-man operation not too far from here.'

'I know. Jenner happens to be someone we're already interested in.'

'Oh?'

'Possible connection with Big Col Calhoun.'

'Add attempted murder to the list then, sir,' the officer said.

The officer who'd been on the radio joined the conversation. 'I sent cars round to the depot, but there's no sign of Jenner. We've launched a manhunt.'

'Good. Let me know when you find him.'

'Sure. I think we're all done here, sir. We'll leave you to speak to Mrs Jenner. An ambulance is on its way.'

The three officers left and Aitken sat next to Jenner's wife. She had a black eye and bruising round her neck. She was an attractive woman with short auburn hair. Maybe mid-forties, Aitken guessed. There were dirty marks on the white shirt she was wearing, and a tear in her jeans exposed a bloody knee.

'Feel like answering a few questions while we're waiting for the ambulance?' Aitken asked.

'Yes, okay.'

'What's your first name?'

'Sheena.'

'Tell me what happened, Sheena.'

Tears welled up in Sheena's eyes and she dabbed at them with a handkerchief she pulled out of her jeans pocket. 'I... I'm sorry. It was awful.'

Aitken put a hand on her arm. 'Take your time.'

Sheena sniffed. 'I went out to do some shopping this morning and called in at Doug's depot on the way home. He'd told me he would be there most of the day doing paperwork as he had no trips planned. I bought him some sandwiches for lunch.'

'How long ago was that?'

Sheena looked confused. 'An hour and a half... maybe two hours ago.'

'What happened when you arrived there?'

'I drove into the yard. Doug's car was there with another one. I didn't recognise it.'

'What kind of car was it?'

'I don't know. Didn't pay much attention to it.'

'Colour?'

'Dark. Black maybe.'

'What happened next?'

'Doug keeps his lorry in the big warehouse garage at the depot. He'd shut the big sliding doors on the front so I went round to the side door. Doug's office is next to the door and his window was open. I heard Doug's voice. There was another man with him.'

'Did you see him?'

'No. It's a high window. You can't see into the office from it.'

'Go on.'

'Something about the way they were talking made me curious.'

'Arguing, furtive?'

'Not arguing, no. More like animated I suppose. I listened to what they were saying.'

'And?'

Sheena a deep breath. Her hands shook. 'I was shocked. I had no idea...'

'About what?' Aitken pressed.

'The other man was saying there was another consignment to pick up from the Netherlands.'

'Did he say what it was?'

'Doug asked. The man said more drugs and guns. He said the guns were coming from Syria, smuggled over the border to Turkey, then up through Eastern Europe to the Netherlands.'

'And the drugs?'

'Would be waiting there with the guns.'

'You had no idea your husband was involved in this?'

'No, didn't have a clue.'

'So what did you do?'

'I was shaking. Couldn't believe what I was hearing. The man said he'd get details to Doug in the next few days.'

'He left then?'

'Yes.'

'Did you see him?'

'No, I was frightened he would see me so I kept hidden round the corner.'

'Then what did you do?'

'After I heard the car drive off, I went into the office and asked Doug what he thought he was doing. He looked surprised to see me and asked what I was talking about. I told him I heard everything and was going to go to the police before he got mixed up in something stupid.'

'What did he say?'

'He went mad. Said he'd done several trips before and I couldn't go to the police.'

'What did you do?'

'I said I was going to the police anyway, broke away from him and ran out of the office. He... he came after me and I slipped and fell. Doug had a violent temper. I was frightened. He punched me in the face and had his hands round my neck. I thought he was going to kill me. I... I poked him in the eyes with my fingers and managed to push him off, got up and ran to my car. He came after me and was thumping on the window as I drove off. I came back here, locked myself in the bathroom and rang for the police.'

'You've been very brave, Sheena,' Aitken said. 'We'll wait for the ambulance to get here and then arrange somewhere safe for you to stay until we find your husband.'

Back in the car, Quigley asked, 'We going to pull Calhoun in for questioning?'

'Not yet. Let's wait till we find Jenner and question him first.'

Back at Gayfield square with Quigley, Aitken picked up the phone and called DS McCabe. 'Thought you'd like to know, there's been a major development.'

'Oh?'

'Jenner just tried to kill his wife. She overheard a conversation between him and another man discussing a shipment of guns and drugs.'

'You've arrested him?'

'Not yet. He's gone on the run.'

'What about the other man?'

'We don't know who he is. Jenner's wife didn't see him.'

'Pity. I'll get my guys here to keep their ears to the ground. I'll let you know if there's any word of Jenner.'

28

SPAIN

Logan had offered to drive Fleming to Luton Airport to get an early flight to Malaga, suggesting it would be a good chance to catch up.

'What time's your flight back?' Logan asked.

'Not due in till after midnight. No need to pick me up. I'll get a taxi home.'

'I'm surprised the super didn't tell you to question Upton's ex-wife over the phone instead of going out to Spain to see her.'

'I wanted to speak to her new partner as well. Local police out there did check on Mrs Upton for me but they were less than enthusiastic. Told the super I wanted to speak to her partner in person and ask Mrs Upton about him first.'

'I know, face to face is best. Still a drain on the budget though.'

'Got cheap flights.'

'Right. By the way, I'm still checking London taxi companies. So far, I haven't been able to find anyone who'd heard of a driver called Oliver Upton.'

'One of Upton's taxi driver mates reckoned Upton let slip one night that he used to drive taxis in Edinburgh. When his mate asked him about it, he made out he was talking about a friend.'

'You want me to check with Edinburgh as well?'

Fleming laughed. 'No, carry on checking the London angle. I can always get my old friend DI Aitken up in Edinburgh to ask around if needs be.'

'Okay. Naomi's spoken with DI Rainger. So far, his team hasn't found anything to go on from the CCTV footage on the roads round the golf course. But there isn't coverage on every road, especially the country lanes next to the course.'

'Anything from golf club members?'

'Likewise... nothing. No one seems to know anything about Upton's private life or background.'

Fleming sighed. 'So far, everything to do with Upton is drawing a blank. It's as though he didn't have a past life.'

'Know what Naomi's latest theory is?'

'What?'

'She reckons Upton could have been a retired spook.'

Fleming smiled as they approached the airport. 'Anything's possible until it's proven not to be.'

The EasyJet flight landed with a slight bump and the engine noise increased as the pilot engaged reverse thrust. Five minutes later, the plane pulled into its bay next to the terminal building. After a short delay, the doors opened and Fleming made his way to passport control. He hadn't any baggage to pick up so made his way straight to the Avis car hire desk.

He'd hired a Seat Leon with air conditioning and was soon heading north from the airport on the motorway up to the junction with the A-357. Turning left, he headed west for about ten miles before taking a left-hand turn down a minor road for about a further four miles. The villa where Vivian Upton lived was set off the road up a small dusty track. Panoramic mountain views surrounded the villa, and orange, lemon, and palm trees filled the garden.

Fleming parked the car next to a red Suzuki Jimny and opened the door of his Seat to a blast of hot air. He walked up a path leading round to a large patio area next to a swimming pool at the rear of the villa. A shaded porch supported by four pillars ran the full length of the building. Terracotta plant pots holding pink and red geraniums lined the front of the porch.

A slim woman of medium height appeared through an open door. She had shoulder-length platinum blonde hair and wore a blue short-sleeved shirt, cream shorts, and leather sandals. Late forties, maybe fifty, Fleming guessed. Dark sunglasses with pink frames sat on top of her head. Fleming noticed a tattoo of an artist's palette on her right arm as she approached him.

'I heard your car,' she said, holding out a hand. 'I'm Vivian Upton. I guess you must be Chief Inspector Fleming?'

Fleming shook the offered hand and smiled. 'Good guess. Nice place you have here.'

'Oh, it's not mine. It's Will's.'

'Your partner?'

'Yes, Will Palmer. I moved over to live with him last year.' Vivian pointed to two chairs on the porch. 'Let's sit here. Can I get you a cold drink? A beer maybe?'

'Water would be fine.'

Vivian disappeared back into the villa and returned with two glasses of water. 'I take it you want to ask me about Oliver?' she said, taking a seat next to Fleming.

'Yes. How did you hear about the shooting?'

'A friend rang me to tell me. Are you anywhere near to finding out who killed him?'

'We're following a couple of leads, but it's still early.'

'I'm not surprised someone wanted to kill him. He was a bastard.'

'When did you get married?'

'Four years ago. I met him when he moved to Oxford. It was a quick romance. We married the year after. Big mistake. We were divorced last year.'

'What went wrong?'

'He was, untrustworthy, violent... secretive even.'

'In what way was he secretive?'

'He would never talk about his past or background. It was as though he had something to hide. I was curious and kept asking him why he was reluctant to tell me things. He would get angry and abusive.'

'Did he harm you?'

'Yes. He would lash out and hit me, usually when he'd had too much to drink. Then, two years ago, I found out he was having an affair with a woman called Jamila Kazan. We'd only been married two years. I left him and she moved in with him. We divorced last year.'

'When did you meet Will?'

'Soon after I left Oliver. A couple of years ago. He's an actor and we share an interest in art. I met him at a London art exhibition. He has a flat in London and bought this place as a second home.'

'Do you live here all the time?'

'Most of the time. Will still uses the London flat when he's working in England. I sometimes stay there as well, but prefer to be here.'

'Is Will here with you now?'

'No, he went back to England last month. He's filming there. It's a new crime drama. They're filming most of it in Oxford and some in London. You may have heard of it.'

Fleming took a sip of his water and nodded. 'Yes. I read about it. Does he play a lead role?'

'No. He worked in theatre in London for eight years then started to get support roles in TV and film. Pays well though. It's why he could afford this place.'

'I take it your divorce was acrimonious?'

'Yes. I could have killed him. Oops, sorry, I shouldn't have said that should I.'

'Have you any idea who would want to kill him?'

Vivian blew air through clenched lips. 'Almost anyone who got to know him.'

'That's the strange thing. No one *does* seem to know anything about him.'

'As I said, he never did talk about life before we were married. He seemed charming at first, then changed.'

'Did you see, or had you been in touch with him since the divorce?'

'You're joking! Why would I want to have anything more to do with the scumbag?'

'Did Will know how Oliver treated you?'

'Yeah. I started seeing Will after I left Oliver so he knew what had gone on.'

'Did he know about the domestic abuse?'

'I told him, yes. He was furious. Wanted to go and have it out with Oliver on several occasions but I told him not to get involved.'

'So he didn't?'

'No. Look... I know what you must be thinking, but there's no way Will would harm anyone. He's played the part of tough villains but it's all an act. Might slip into broody moods from time to time. Problems at work, I guess, but wouldn't harm a fly. He's normally a cheery chap.'

'Has he kept in regular touch while he's been filming in England?'

'Yeah, bless him. He rings every night.'

'And he seems his normal self?'

Vivian frowned. 'What do you mean?'

'Cheery, not sounding gloomy, depressed, or distant?'

Vivian avoided Fleming's gaze. 'Cheery.'

'Okay, you've been very helpful. Thanks for your time. Just one more thing, I'll need contact details for Will. Routine, but I'll need to speak to him.'

'Why?'

'Because he knew how your husband had treated you. We need to question everyone who had any connection with Oliver.'

29

LONDON

Toby rushed home from school to check for any post. Highland Council had said they would let him know the result of his interview in the next week. The next week had arrived. He unlocked the front door and pushed it open. There was some post. Toby rifled through it and threw it all unopened on the small telephone table in the hallway. It was all junk mail.

Disappointed, Toby wandered through to the kitchen to put the kettle on. He'd promised his mother he would call in to see her later and pick up some shopping on the way, but he had time for a cup of tea first. Before the kettle could boil, the telephone rang. He dashed through to the hallway and picked it up. 'Hello?'

'Oh, hi, is that Toby Enderby?'

Toby's pulse raced. He recognised the Scottish accent. 'Yes.'

'It's Ailsa Brodie. Have you had a letter yet?'

'No. I wondered—'

'Sorry,' Ailsa cut in, 'there's been a bit of a hiccup in the office and the letter was only posted this morning.'

'Oh, I see.'

'Under the circumstances, I thought it only fair to ring you to let you know... in case you had any other applications on the go.'

'No... no. There are no others.'

There was a slight pause before Ailsa spoke again. 'Right. Well... I'm sorry to call you with bad news. I'm afraid you didn't get the job.'

Toby felt a tightness in his chest and took a deep breath.

'Toby? You still there?'

'Yes, I'm still on the line. Thank you for letting me know.'

'I'm sorry. You should know it was close. They've put you on a reserve list until they conclude final checks on the successful candidate.'

'I see. May I ask where I am on the list?'

'There isn't a list as such. You're the only other candidate under consideration.'

'When will I know... whether the other candidate has accepted the job or not?'

'In the next day or two. I'm sorry once again but felt I had to ring to let you know as there was a delay in getting your letter out.'

Toby felt a crushing disappointment. He wanted to cry. 'It's fine. Thank you for letting me know.'

'I'll call. Okay?'

'Okay.'

'Bye.'

'Bye,' Toby whispered in reply.

Toby didn't feel at all like going to see his mother, but he had promised and she would panic if he didn't turn up. He pulled the shopping bag from the passenger seat, locked the car, and let himself into the house. As soon as he opened the front door, he could hear the TV on full blast.

'Mother, I'm here.'

There was no reply.

Toby opened the sitting room door and saw his mother slumped in the easy chair in front of the TV. Her arm was hanging over the armrest and an empty mug was lying on the floor. 'Mother!' Toby shouted as he rushed across the room.

'What!' came his mother's strangulated voice.

Toby switched the TV off. 'I... I thought something had happened to you. Your arm was hanging over the edge of the chair and you've dropped your mug on the floor.'

'Oh dear. Must have fallen asleep.'

'Not sure how you could with the TV volume up so loud.'

'My hearing isn't so good these days. I need to have the sound up a bit.'

'I've brought your shopping,' Toby said, picking up the mug.

Doreen grunted. 'I'll sort it out later. Have you heard anything about the job up in Scotland yet?'

Toby sat next to his mother. 'I had a phone call before I came out.'

Doreen's eyes flashed concern. 'From them?'

'Yes.'

'Spit it out, Toby. What'd they say?'

'I didn't get it.'

Toby couldn't help but notice the slight twitch of his mother's lips as a faint smile crossed her face.

'Didn't I tell you? There's no way they were ever going to give you the job. Should have listened to me in the first place instead of putting me through all that worry. You should never have applied for it.'

Toby took in a deep breath. 'Well, I did, and I didn't get it.'

'I hope that's the end of your ridiculous idea of moving out of London.'

'They've put me on a reserve list though.'

The smile had left Doreen's face. 'A what?'

'It was Ailsa Brodie who rang me. She said it was close, but they still have to complete checks on the man who came first, and he still has to accept the job.'

'I don't believe it! Can't you see, Toby? She's stringing you along. All they're doing is prolonging the agony for you... and for me, may I say. Anyway... how many people have they got on this... this list?'

'It isn't a list as such. I'm the only reserve.'

Doreen said nothing. The stern unsmiling look on his mother's face told Toby it was time to leave.

30

OXFORD

The rifle club wasn't far from Oxford. Atticus Kazan's university colleague, Chris Owen, had told Fleming he would be there all morning. He'd said he would be able to speak to him at the club if Fleming didn't mind the drive out there. The alternative was to catch him at home or between lectures at the university. Fleming was happy to go to the club, his curiosity aroused by the fact that Kazan's colleague was a member as well.

He found Owen sitting in the café where he said he'd be at ten in the morning. The man wearing a bright pink shirt matched the description Owen had given Fleming. He'd omitted to add that he was bald, and wore rimless spectacles perched on a large hooked nose.

'Mr Owen?' Fleming asked as he approached Owen's table.

Owen stood to greet Fleming and offered a hand with long, thin fingers. The handshake was weak. Fleming felt like he was shaking Owen's fingers rather than his hand. 'DCI Fleming, how lovely to meet you.' The voice was soft and melodious. 'Do have a seat. Can I get you some tea, or coffee?'

'No, thanks. I won't take up much of your time. You're a member here I take it?'

'Yes, my partner and I are both members. There is an Oxford University rifle club, but it's mainly for students who also run it.'

'She's not with you today?'

'Who?'

'Your partner.'

'Oh, sorry, my partner is a man, Francis. We both have a passion for music.'

Fleming smiled. 'So you both joined a rifle club.'

Owen giggled. 'Yes, I suppose it does seem a bit out of character.'

'What do you do at the university?'

'I'm an associate professor, lecturing in music.'

'Is that where you met Francis?'

'No, he plays the violin in an Oxford orchestra. Met him at a concert two years ago.'

Fleming shook his head. 'Shooting does seem an unusual pastime for an associate professor in music and a musician.'

'Ah, you'd be surprised how many members there are here from all walks of life. You don't have to be a macho guy to want to learn how to shoot and take part in competitions.'

Fleming held up his hands as though in surrender. 'You're right. I once knew a detective in the Met who was in the specialist firearms command. He used to sing in a church choir.'

'There you are then.'

'So whose idea was it to join the rifle club?'

'Francis was already a member when I met him. He persuaded me to join.'

'You enjoy it?'

'Yes. It's something completely different from what I do. I can't explain why, but it's very satisfying... exhilarating.' Owen glanced at his watch. 'My practise is in half an hour. You said you wanted to check something with me to do with a colleague.'

'Yes. You know a lecturer called Atticus Kazan?'

'I know of him, yes. We're not friends, just colleagues who pass the time of day if we happen to bump into each other.'

'And would the university library be a place where you might meet?'

'More likely than not. I've met him here at the club a couple of times.'

Fleming froze. 'He's a member?'

'Yes, he joined about six months ago. I sponsored him.'

'Were you aware that Mr Kazan's wife, Jamila Kazan, left him?'

'Yes, he did mention it to me a while back. I knew he was married and asked how his wife was. I had no particular interest. It was one of those things you ask out of politeness without caring much how she was.'

'Did he offer any information about why she left him?'

'No need to, my dear chap. The man's intelligent but dull and far too serious. He has no interest in anything other than mathematics.'

'Did you know she left him to go and live with Oliver Upton, the man who was shot on a local golf course recently?'

'Oh my God! That's what this is about. You're not thinking Atticus killed him, are you?'

'Just following up on every angle. It was about six months ago when Jamila left him. Did he say why he'd joined the rifle club?'

'No, not at all. I never asked him and he never volunteered the information. Do you really think it was him?'

'You may be able to help me out there.'

Owen frowned. 'How come?'

'So I can cross him off my list of possible suspects.'

'I'm not with you.'

'Mr Kazan told me he was in the college library on the morning Mr Upton was shot.'

'I don't see how...'

'He said he was talking to you. Can you confirm that?'

'Oh, I see. I did speak to him one day in the library. Let me think now. I'm trying to remember what day it was.'

Fleming waited as Owen concentrated.

'Ah! Got it!' Owen said. 'It *was* that day. I was in the library in the morning and did speak to Atticus. Someone told me later the same day that a man had been shot on the golf course.'

'Can you remember what time in the morning you spoke to Mr Kazan?'

'Not exactly, no, but it would've been late morning. I had a lecture first thing. It would be nearer lunchtime I guess.'

Fleming rose to leave. 'Thank you for your time, Mr Owen. Enjoy your practise.'

On the way back to HQ, Fleming was working out the maths.

Upton's tee time was first thing at eight.

About an hour and a half later, some golfers found his body.

The killer must have shot Upton around eight fifty, the time it would take for Upton to get round the course to where they found him.

Kazan could have made it back to the university library by late morning.

Fleming frowned. Kazan's alibi still wasn't watertight.

And he joined a rifle club around the time his wife left him.

31

OXFORD

Fleming was in the office talking to Logan and Anderson after an update meeting with Temple. He hadn't had much to tell her apart from the fact Kazan's alibi wasn't conclusive and he'd joined a rifle club. There was still Ian Hunter's alibi to check out, and he was yet to question Will Palmer, Upton's ex-wife's new partner.

'How'd your meeting with the super go?' Logan asked.

'She's got the chief constable on her back. Murder with a firearm tends to make people nervous. She's looking for progress.'

Logan shrugged. 'Might be slow, but we *are* making some progress. She should know as well as anyone that investigative work can take time.'

'Talking of which, have you finished checking out all London taxi firms for any old records of Upton?'

'Yep. No one's heard of him.'

Fleming sighed. 'At least we've established Upton's a man who lied about his background for whatever reason.'

'Do you want me to start checking with Edinburgh now?'

'No. I'll speak to my old mate DI Aitken up there. See if he can help out.'

Anderson had been flipping through her notebook. 'I've been checking for any record of army service.'

'Any luck?' Fleming asked.

'No.'

'Might have guessed,' Logan muttered.

Fleming rubbed his chin. 'Upton's bit of a mystery, no doubt about that. Why would he lie about being in the army and driving taxis in London?'

'He has a dodgy past he wants to keep secret,' Logan offered.

'Or,' Anderson reminded him, 'he could be a retired spook who can't let on what he did.'

Logan laughed. 'I'm beginning to think you may have a point there, Naomi. Maybe we should check with MI5 and the cousins across the river.'

'MI6,' Anderson mouthed, looking at Logan who nodded.

Fleming continued. 'But maybe we ought to exhaust all other possibilities first. Not that I don't think there's any merit in what you say, Naomi,' he added hastily. 'I've still got one more taxi driver from Andy Cabs to question. He might be able to throw some light on Upton.'

'Think you're being a bit optimistic there, boss. No one else seems to know anything about him,' Logan said.

'You never know. It's worth speaking to him. Sometimes you get information from where you least expect it.'

'Maybe you'll get the lucky break Naomi was looking for,' Logan said.

Fleming's mobile indicated an incoming call: *Rainger*. 'Better get this,' he said, tapping on the answer icon. 'Fleming.'

'Hi, it's DI Rainger. You'll never believe this, but a guy called Earl Yates has just walked into the station and claimed he killed Upton.'

'What!'

'Don't get too excited. This guy is weird. Sounds to me like he's... well... not all there, if you know what I mean. He's creepy.'

'Weird people have been known to be killers,' Fleming said. 'I'll come over to question him. Got an interview room spare?'

'Sure. We'll wait for you.'

~

An hour later, Fleming and Rainger were facing an ashen Earl Yates across a table in interview room two at St Aldates police station. He was mid-thirties, slim, with tousled brown hair. His grey eyes stared straight ahead. The blue jeans and white open-neck shirt he wore looked as though they hadn't seen a washing machine for some time.

Rainger had switched on the digital interview recorder and Fleming had gone through all the usual formalities.

Bearing in mind Rainer's assessment of Yates, Fleming had decided to play safe. He was treating Yates as a vulnerable adult and had found a social worker to sit in on the interview. He'd established no family could be present. Yates was single and his parents were both deceased. He had no siblings.

A bead of sweat had formed on Yates's forehead and his heels tapped nervously on the floor as he listened to Fleming's caution. He sniffed and waited for the first question.

'You came to St Aldates police station of your own volition and confessed to killing Oliver Upton. Is that correct?'

Yates stared at Fleming. 'I did, yes,' he murmured in a soft adenoidal voice.

'What made you decide to hand yourself in?'

Yates's legs stopped twitching. He stayed silent for a few seconds before answering. 'A voice in my head.'

'Do you often get voices in your head?'

'Sometimes.'

'Why did you kill Mr Upton?'

'Someone told me to.'

'Who?'

Yates looked confused. 'I can't remember.'

'Was it one of those voices... in your head?'

Yates rubbed his chin and looked at the ceiling. 'No, not in my head. Thing is... I can't mention names... know what I mean?'

'I'm not sure I do.'

'Security services...'

Fleming glanced sideways at Logan who remained impassive.

'Can you remember why this person told you to kill Upton?'

Yates placed both hands against the edge of the table and took a deep breath. 'He was a threat to national security. Had to be eliminated.'

'How did you kill him?'

'Shot him.'

'With a handgun?'

'No, a rifle.'

'Where?'

Yates stared ahead. 'On a golf course.'

'What time of day was it?'

'Can't remember.'

'Know what I think, Earl? The how, where, and when were all published in the papers. You're making all this up from the information you've read, aren't you?'

'Why would I do that?'

'I don't know, but I don't believe you did kill Mr Upton. I'm going to stop this interview and we'll arrange for a healthcare professional to see you.'

～

Later, back in Rainger's office, Fleming was waiting for the assessment of the on-call psychiatrist who was with Yates in the custody suite.

'Why did you tell Yates it was a healthcare professional we were calling in and not a psychiatrist?' Rainger asked.

'I don't know. Maybe it sounded less like I was suggesting he wasn't quite with it. A bit less intimidating.'

'You're sure he isn't the killer?'

'I'm certain he isn't. My guess is DID.'

'DID?'

'Dissociative identity disorder.'

Rainger was about to reply when the psychiatrist knocked on his door and popped her head in. 'Okay to come in?'

'Sure. What's the verdict?' Rainger said.

'There's no doubt he has mental health issues. He's delusional. Probably confessed hoping to get some attention. I suggest you request access to his health records on the basis it's required in relation to a murder enquiry.'

'I aim to release him without charge. Is it safe to do so in your judgement?' Fleming asked.

'Yes. I don't think he's a danger to anyone. He's more of a Walter Mitty character. But do get his medical records.'

'Okay, thanks.'

Fleming turned to Rainger. 'Release him but give him a conditional caution.'

'Conditional on what?'

'He doesn't waste police time again. I'll leave it to you to request his medical records. Let me know what they say.'

32

LONDON

School had ended for the day and Toby was walking across to his car when his mobile rang. He tapped the answer icon. 'Hello.'

'Is that Toby Enderby?'

Toby drew a quick breath. He recognised the voice.

'Speaking.'

'Hi. It's Ailsa Brodie.'

Toby's pulse quickened. 'Hello.'

'Thought I'd give you a call to say there's a letter in the post for you. All the checks were okay on the successful candidate, but he's turned the job down.'

'Really? May I ask why?'

'He said he wanted the job but his wife changed her mind. Had second thoughts about moving up here. Reckoned they would be too isolated.'

'Why did she let him apply for the job if she didn't want to move?'

'From what I gather, he was keen to move up here, but she wasn't. Rather than burst his bubble, she let him apply hoping he might not get the job.'

'Bit disingenuous. Is that what he told you?'

'More or less. It's what he guessed. He was sorry he'd wasted our time. It seems she likes city life too much.'

'Where were they going to move from?'

Ailsa hesitated as if deliberating whether she should say. 'Bristol.'

'I see. There's no chance he'll persuade her to change her mind and call to say he'll take the job after all?'

'The letter on its way to you is offering you the job. He can't change his mind unless you decline the offer.'

Toby felt a surge of elation. 'I don't know what to say. I'm delighted. There's no doubt in my mind. I want the job.'

'I'm so pleased. Just write back to confirm you're accepting as soon as you get the letter.'

'References and checks... are they all done?'

'All done. We've also completed the character and previous employer references. The Disclosure and Barring Service check was okay as well, so the job is yours.'

'Great. When can I start?'

'The school breaks up for the summer at the beginning of July. That's when Pherson Dalglish retires. The new term starts mid-August so then would be the perfect time for you to start.'

'That fits in with our term times, more or less. I could hand my notice in, finish next month and come up during the summer break. Get my bearings and settle in before starting.'

'Perfect. I'll arrange for you to meet Pherson. I know there's a cottage available to rent and could make enquiries for you if you like. Give you a chance to get to know the area before you get anything long-term sorted out.'

'That's very kind of you. I'd be most grateful. One less thing for me to worry about.'

'Fantastic. I'll look forward to your letter and get things

moving. Be in touch soon. Bye.' Ailsa rang off and Toby punched a hand in the air.

'You okay there?' one of Toby's teaching colleagues asked, coming up behind him. 'Found out you've won the pools?'

'Could say that. I've hit the jackpot.'

'Do tell.'

'I'm moving out of London.'

'Wow! Where are you going?'

'Scottish Highlands.'

'Far cry from London. Any particular reason?'

'I've been offered a teaching job in a tiny primary school up there. A place called Balcorie.'

'I can understand why you might want to move out of London, but the Highlands... that's some change.'

'Doctor reckons London isn't good for my asthma. Air up there will be much better for me, and the job will be less stressful.'

'Lucky you. I wish you all the best with it. When are you going?'

Toby laughed. 'As soon as I hand my notice in and get my bags packed.'

After a quick bite to eat at home, Toby set off for his mother's house. His stomach was churning, knowing how she would take the news. He parked outside the house and took a deep breath. Picking up the flowers he'd bought on the way, he let himself in.

Doreen was in the kitchen preparing a salad to go with some cold chicken for dinner. 'Oh hello, Toby. I didn't hear you come in.'

Toby handed over the flowers. 'I brought you these.'

'How... lovely.'

Toby sensed the hesitation in the response and wondered whether buying flowers had been a good idea. 'I thought it might brighten the place up a bit.'

'I'll put them in the sitting room,' Doreen said, reaching for a vase on the worktop. 'Is this a peace offering after you upset me on your last visit?'

'I didn't mean to upset you but I had to tell you what the position was with the job.'

'I don't want to hear any more of this nonsense. You didn't get it. I told you they were stringing you along with all this talk of a reserve list. Very thoughtless of them, I have to say. They should never have tried to keep your hopes up.'

'The thing is–'

'I don't want to hear it!'

Toby was losing patience. 'Okay, I can leave without telling you if that's what you'd prefer. I'll see you next week.' He turned to go.

'Toby!'

He turned back. 'What!'

'Sorry, I was maybe a bit hasty. Has the other man accepted the job? Is that why you're so tetchy?'

'No, I'm getting irritated because of your attitude. Ailsa rang to *offer* me the job. The other man turned it down.'

Doreen's face hardened. 'Why?'

'His wife changed her mind and decided she didn't want to move up there.'

'She has more sense than you then. Unless you've changed your mind as well. Have you?'

'No. I've told Ailsa I'll accept the job.'

'What about me? You can't leave me here on my own.'

'We've been through this before, Mother. You can manage fine and I'll have lots of school holidays when I can come and stay with you.'

Doreen sobbed. 'You're being very selfish. Think of all I've done for you and this is how you repay me.'

'Sorry, it's time for me to move on... find a new life.'

'Without me! How could you?'

'I'm sorry. This is something I have to do. I'll let Quentin know. He can come round to put your mind at rest.'

'He'll be too busy.'

Toby kissed his mother on the forehead. 'I'll call you tomorrow.'

He left wondering why he'd been so loyal for so long. *How many times do I have to hear Quentin's too busy!*

33

OXFORD

Fleming was on his way to the rifle club to see the secretary, Gavin Noble. He wanted to ask him about Atticus Kazan's membership. Kazan was about all Fleming had to go on. Earl Yates had claimed he'd killed Upton, but it was clear he had mental health issues. The psychiatrist had reckoned he was seeking attention or notoriety for some reason. Fleming wasn't treating him as a serious suspect.

Ian Hunter was another suspect he'd ruled out. Logan had checked out his alibi. The girl serving behind the counter in the golf clubhouse café had confirmed Hunter was there up until the time Upton was found. Fleming had yet to speak to Will Palmer.

Clouds were gathering in a pale blue sky and a slight breeze was coming in from the west as Fleming parked his car. He made his way to the reception office. A young man looked up from a computer screen as Fleming entered. 'Hi there. Can I help you?'

Fleming showed his warrant card. 'DCI Fleming. I'm here to see Gavin Noble.'

'Ah, okay. Give me a sec and I'll let him know you're here.'

A few minutes later, Noble appeared, looking every bit the ex-military type. He was tall and stocky, but with a solid frame. His back was ramrod straight, and he had short grey hair. The blue eyes were bright and alert. A motif showing two crossed rifles was prominent on the left breast of his white T-shirt. 'Hi, care to come up to my office?'

Fleming followed him through a door and up some wooden stairs to a small landing. A door to the right had a glass window with a sign which announced this was the office of the club secretary. It was a small affair, furnished with a desk, a couple of chairs, and two metal filing cabinets. There was a computer screen on one corner of the desk. On the wall behind Noble, there was a photograph of him receiving a silver cup.

'Take a seat,' Noble said, sitting behind the desk. 'You said on the phone you wanted to make enquiries about our membership. Would this be in connection with the recent shooting on the golf course?'

'Yes.' Fleming pointed at the photo. 'What'd you win?'

'A league competition. Two years ago. We're doing well again so far this year. We have some pretty good marksmen.'

'How many members have you got?'

'At the moment we have over a hundred. It's a sport with growing interest.'

'What's the process for accepting new members?'

'Some clubs have junior members, but up until now we only accept people over eighteen. Anyone can apply, providing they pass all the police checks. At least one full club member has to sponsor them.'

'I'm interested in a man called Atticus Kazan. Do you know who sponsored *him*?'

'Tell you in a minute.' Noble pulled a keyboard closer to the edge of the desk and tapped away on it. A quick manoeuvre with the mouse to scroll down the list appearing on his screen and he found what he was looking for. 'It was one of his university colleagues, a chap called Chris Owen.'

'And the police checks were satisfactory?'

'Yes. All good.'

'Mr Owen said he thought Kazan joined about six months ago. Is that right?'

Noble tapped on the keyboard again and peered at the screen. 'Yep. Bang on. Six months ago.'

'Do you see all new members before they join?'

'Most of the time, yes. I try to meet everyone if I can.'

'Did you see Mr Kazan?'

'I did. I remember him well.'

'Anything else required before you can accept people as members?'

'Before anyone can become a full member, they have to have a probationary period of at least three months.'

'What does that entail?'

'They have to attend and shoot regularly. There's also a course they have to take on the safe handling and use of firearms on a one-to-one basis.'

'Who with?'

'Someone who's either a full member or is a qualified coach. In his case, it happened to be me. That's how I remember him well.'

'What did you make of him?'

'Strange man, I thought. Struck me as being an intense sort of guy, very serious, dull. He was methodical and meticulous though. I'll give him that. Didn't come as a surprise to me when he said he lectured maths and computing science at Oxford University. Had a bit of an ingratiating way about him. Didn't take to him much, but there was no reason to deny him membership.'

'Did he say why he wanted to join the club?'

'I asked him. Said he wanted to take up something new... completely different. Reckoned Chris Owen had talked about it, and he got interested.'

'You said members on probation had to attend often. Did Mr Kazan make frequent visits?'

'I can tell you exactly how often. We keep a register of attendance.' Noble had another quick check on his computer screen. 'He came once a week during his probationary period. In fact, he's continued to attend regularly since.'

'When did he last come?'

Noble traced a finger across the screen. 'Two weeks ago.'

'Thank you, you've been most helpful.' Fleming rose to leave. 'I'll see myself out.'

Noble frowned. 'All this interest in one member. You're not thinking he shot Mr Upton, are you?'

'Did you know Kazan's wife had left him?'

'No.'

'She went to go and live with Upton.'

Noble's mouth dropped open. 'Oh my God! You *do* think he did it.'

'I'd rather you didn't tell anyone about this conversation. It could prejudice the enquiry if information about the investigation became public knowledge. Mr Kazan is just someone we need to investigate due to his connection to Upton, nothing more.'

'I see.'

'I take it I can rely on your complete discretion?'

'Of course.'

Fleming left a worried Noble at his desk and made his way out to the car park. He got into his car and sat for a minute before turning on the ignition. His mind was racing.

Kazan's last visit to the rifle club had been two days before Upton was shot.

147

34

OXFORD

It was 6pm and Fleming and Logan were sitting in the Bear Inn waiting for Will Palmer. They'd settled behind a table where they could see who was coming in. Much to Logan's delight, Fleming had decided they should consider themselves to be off duty. He'd suggested they treat the meeting with Will Palmer in the pub as being down to pure chance. 'In which case,' Logan had said, 'I'll have a pint of London Pride.' Fleming had ordered the same.

Logan looked at his watch. 'Should be here by now.'

'To be fair, he did say he would be working on the set and couldn't be sure exactly what time he would be here.'

'What are they filming?' Logan asked after taking a sip of his beer and wiping the froth from his mouth.

'Would you believe it, a crime drama? Filming some of it here, some in London.'

'He doesn't play a sniper by any chance?'

'Support role, according to Vivian Upton.'

'How do we know who Palmer is when he does arrive?'

'Vivian Upton showed me a photograph. Look out for a

hippy. Tall, slim guy with long black hair, complete with beard and moustache. He could play the part of one of the three musketeers... without much make-up.'

'How old?'

'Forty-eight. Bit of an extrovert by all accounts.'

Logan peered over the rim of his glass. 'Think he may have arrived.'

Fleming turned to the door and saw a tanned Palmer enter. He was wearing a light pink coat with black lapels over a white T-shirt. Large round glasses with orange-tinted lenses completed the picture of a flamboyant dresser.

Palmer looked round the pub and his eyes fastened on Fleming and Logan. He sauntered over. 'I guess you must be DCI Fleming and DS Logan.' The Irish lilt in the voice was unmistakable.

'You guessed right,' Fleming said. 'What'll you have?'

'Pint of whatever you two are drinking, please.'

Logan got up from the table. 'My round.' He looked at Fleming's near-empty glass. 'Ready for another?'

Fleming downed the rest of his beer and handed the glass to Logan. 'Thanks.'

Palmer pulled up a chair. 'Vivian said on the phone you wanted to speak to me so your call didn't come as a surprise.' He laughed. 'What does surprise me is you do your police work in a pub.'

'We do sometimes retire to a pub after work and, as you were filming in Oxford, it seemed too good an opportunity to miss.'

'I like your thinking. Must say I'm ready for a drink after a hard day on the set.'

'What are you filming? Mrs Upton said it was a crime drama.'

'Ah, to be sure, it is. *The Marksman's Target.*'

Fleming raised an eyebrow. 'Bit unfortunate... given current circumstances.'

'Yeah, I suppose so.'

'What part do you play in it.'

'A drug dealer. A small part but it pays the bills.'

'Did I hear something about a drug dealer?' Logan said, returning with three pints.

'That's me,' Palmer said.

Logan took his place back at the table. 'Didn't take you long to get that out of him, boss,' Logan quipped.

Fleming smiled. 'It's in the film they're shooting.'

'Where in Oxford are you filming?' Logan asked.

'Various locations. One of them is Exeter College where they filmed at least one of the Inspector Morse episodes.'

'I believe this pub might have featured in one of the Morse films as well,' Fleming said.

'Really?' Palmer queried before taking a swig of his beer. 'I didn't know that.' He held his glass up to examine the contents. 'Nice, by the way.'

Being midweek, and early, the pub wasn't busy. But it didn't stop raucous laughter coming from a table in the far corner.

Palmer took another long swig of his beer. 'So how can I help you guys?'

'You met Vivian Upton at a London art exhibition, and she moved into your villa in Spain last year. Is that right?' Fleming asked.

'Yes.'

'And you still have a flat in London?'

'Yes, they do a lot of the filming in London, so it's handy to keep it.'

'Do you travel up to Oxford each day while you're filming here?'

'Nah. Too much hassle. I stay in a caravan on one of the sets. Much easier.'

'Did Vivian ever talk about her husband?'

'Yeah. Said she made a big mistake marrying him. She reckoned he was charming and generous, but after they married, she learned he had a dark side.'

'Did she elaborate?'

'Reckoned he was a bit strange about his past.'

'In what way?'

'Vivian told me he would never talk about his background. Got upset if she pressed him. Even became violent.'

'She told me he sometimes hit her,' Fleming said. 'Did she ever tell you about what went on?'

'Yeah, she told me. I was livid. Wanted to go and sort him out but she begged me not to get involved. He was a real bastard by all accounts.'

'So you didn't go to have it out with him?'

'No. Vivian finally divorced him when she found out he was having an affair.'

'What do you do up here when you're not filming?'

'Read, go to art galleries, ring Vivian, eat out.'

'Do you play golf?'

'Sometimes. Prefer to play in Spain. Better weather.'

'Have you played around Oxford while you're here?'

Palmer's mood changed and his eyes darkened. 'I can see where this line of questioning is going.' He thumped his beer glass on the table. 'I'm done here. If you want to speak to me again, I'll have a solicitor with me.'

'We can arrange an interview at the local police station if you'd prefer. But you could save yourself the trouble if you cared to tell me where you were on the morning Upton was shot.'

Palmer stood and glared down at Fleming. 'On the set,' he snarled then left.

Logan looked at his empty glass. 'That went well then. He got a bit tetchy there, don't you think? Either he's a suspect, or there's some nutter who knows about the film and wanted to play it out in real life. Another pint?'

35

EDINBURGH

'They've found him!' DS Quigley shouted across the room as DI Aitken entered shaking a wet umbrella.

'Jenner? Where?'

'Port Edgar Marina. Two coppers on the beat spotted him coming out of the café.'

'Where did he go?'

'He walked along the pontoon and got into a boat.'

'Coppers keeping an eye on it?'

'Sure. They've been warned to keep out of sight and not to approach the boat in case Jenner's armed.'

'Let's get over there... and get the armed response unit on the phone. We need backup. Can't take any chances.'

Quigley made some calls, grabbed his coat and made his way down to the Gayfield Square car compound. Aitken was already there climbing into a squad car. Another car with four uniformed officers was sitting behind. Quigley dashed to the first car and jumped into the passenger seat next to the driver.

'Armed response unit on the way?' Aitken asked.

'Yeah. We should get there before them.'

Aitken tapped the driver on the shoulder. 'Okay. Let's go! Port Edgar Marina.'

The two cars sped west through the streets of Edinburgh, and out to Port Edgar, tyres hissing on the wet roads. Fifteen minutes later, they pulled into the marina car park. A couple of armed response unit vehicles had caught up with the squad cars. They screeched to a halt beside them and eight officers, in full black protective gear poured out of the vehicles carrying Heckler and Koch carbines and Glock 17 pistols.

The uniformed officers who had spotted Jenner walked over to Aitken's car and one of them pointed out the boat that Jenner had boarded. It was about fifty yards along the pontoon on the left-hand side.

'Area cleared of people?' Aitken asked.

'Yes, sir,' the officer who had pointed out the boat replied.

'Good.' Aitken pulled out a megaphone from the boot of the car. He walked over to the side of a building next to the entrance to the pontoon. The armed officers fanned out across the car park and followed him. Making sure everyone was ready, Aitken lifted the megaphone to his mouth.

'Mr Jenner. We know you are on board. We have armed officers here. Please come out with your hands held high.'

There was no sign of movement.

'I repeat. Please come out with your hands up.'

Aitken waited for a few more seconds and was about to speak again when the cabin door creaked open. No one appeared.

Aitken spoke into the megaphone again. 'Be assured it's safe to come out.'

'I hear you!' Jenner shouted through the open door. 'There's no way I'm coming out. I'm armed and have a hostage. If anyone comes closer, I'll shoot him.'

'Fuck!' Aitken muttered. He lifted the megaphone to his

mouth once more. 'There's nowhere for you to go, Jenner. Be sensible and give yourself up.'

'I want to see the armed officers get back in their vehicles and drive off.'

'You know that isn't going to happen.'

'I'll tell you what *is* going to happen: I'm going to sail out of here. No police patrol boats or helicopters anywhere in sight... you hear me?'

Aitken paused. 'I heard you. Where do you think you're going? There's no escape.'

'We'll see about that.'

'You're going to make things worse for yourself. Why not do us all a favour and give up.'

'No way!'

'If you give yourself up without anyone getting hurt, a judge is more likely to be lenient.'

'Pull the other one.'

'If you harm the hostage, you'll get life for attempted murder, kidnapping... take your pick.'

'I've nothing to lose now.'

'Except your life, if you're stupid.'

'Go to hell!'

'Your wife–'

The sound of a sudden scuffle and a shot going off cut Aitken short. 'Fuck!' He waved the armed officers forward. They dashed down the pontoon to the boat. One officer jumped aboard and stood to one side of the cabin door, carbine at the ready. Another followed him and took the other side. The remaining officers positioned themselves along the pontoon. They'd trained their carbines on the door and windows.

The two officers by the door looked at each other and nodded. They burst into the cabin and saw Jenner on the floor with blood streaming from a gash on his head. A handgun was lying beside him. One of the officers kicked the gun out of reach and slapped handcuffs on Jenner's wrists.

A man wearing shorts and a flowery shirt stood behind Jenner holding a large glass ashtray. He dropped it on the floor. 'He untied me to get the boat going. Had his back to me for a second while he was shouting out the door. I grabbed the ashtray and hit him on the head with it. He turned and fired a shot but missed me. Couldn't see straight, I guess. I hit him again and he fell. He could have killed me!'

'Take it easy,' one of the officers said. 'You okay?'

The man nodded, looking wide-eyed as the other officer hauled Jenner to his feet. 'All clear!' the officer shouted to the armed men outside. 'Coming out.'

The two officers manhandled Jenner onto the pontoon where Aitken stood. He showed a scowling Jenner his warrant card. 'Mr Jenner, I'm DI Aitken. I'm arresting you for the attempted murder of your wife, kidnapping, and suspected involvement in drugs and gun smuggling. You do not have to say anything, but it may harm your defence if you do not mention when questioned something which you later rely on in court. Anything you do say may be given in evidence.'

Jenner snorted blood from a nose someone had broken long before the ashtray hit him. 'Go to hell!'

36

OXFORD

Fleming and Logan were back in interview room two at St Aldates police station facing Atticus Kazan across a table. It was a hot day outside and the room, having no windows, was stuffy. Fleming nodded at Logan who switched on the digital interview recorder.

'This interview is with...' Fleming began. He looked at Kazan. 'State your full name, date of birth and address please.'

Kazan smiled and obliged.

'I'm DCI Fleming. Also present is DS Logan. Mr Kazan has declined the opportunity to have legal representation. There are no other persons present.' He looked across the table at Kazan. 'Can you confirm I gave you the opportunity to have a solicitor with you and you declined?'

Kazan sighed. 'Yes, you did offer me the chance to have legal representation. And I decided I had no reason to require such services.'

'Thank you.' Fleming went on to state the date and time. 'We are in interview room two at St Aldates police station in Oxford. You do not have to say anything, but it may harm your defence if you do not mention when questioned something which you later rely on in court. Anything you do say may be given in evidence. Do you understand the caution, Mr Kazan?'

Another sigh. 'Yes, I do.'

'You are not under arrest and you're not obliged to remain at the station, so you can leave at any time.'

'After all that, I could get up and go?'

'You could unless we decide to arrest you,' Logan said.

'In which case, I presume I would have no choice?'

'Correct.'

'Then I'm happy to stay.'

'When first questioned, you claimed to be lecturing at the university on the morning Oliver Upton was shot. That was a lie, wasn't it?' Fleming said.

'No, it was not. I made a mistake. I told you.'

'You later said you were in the university library the morning of the shooting.'

'I did, and I was. I apologised for the mistake over my whereabouts.'

'You said you spoke to Chris Owen. Is he a friend of yours?'

'Not as such. More like work colleagues.'

Fleming looked at his notes. 'You said you couldn't recollect what time it was.'

'I told you. I don't make a habit of checking what time I speak to people.'

'I checked with Chris Owen and he confirmed you did speak to him.'

'So there you are. You've established where I was at the time of the murder.'

'Not quite. You see, Chris Owen had a lecture first thing. He reckoned he wouldn't have been in the library until late morning.'

Kazan placed his hands on the table and examined his

manicured fingernails. 'Maybe a bit difficult for a policeman to grasp, but he could have been mistaken about the time.'

Fleming ignored the attempt to rile him and fixed Kazan with a steely glare. 'Maybe difficult for *you* to grasp, but some policemen can spot a liar when they see one.'

Kazan leaned back in his chair and ran both hands through his long grey hair. 'I'm not lying. I did speak to him. He's confirmed what I told you, has he not?'

'For a mathematician, you don't seem to be able to work out the maths.'

'What do you mean?'

'No one's disputing you were in the library and that you spoke to Chris Owen. The timing doesn't do you any favours though.'

Kazan thought for a second and his lips curled into one of those sardonic smiles. 'What exactly are you suggesting, Mr Fleming?'

'Detective Chief Inspector,' Fleming reminded him. 'Memory as good as your maths, eh?'

Kazan glowered across the table at Fleming. 'Are you usually this disrespectful?'

'Respect is something earned. It doesn't come with your position. The point I'm making is that I checked up on the lecture Chris Owen was giving and it didn't end until 11am.'

'Meaning?'

'Oliver Upton teed off at 8am and about an hour and a half later, some golfers found his body where he was about to tee off for the fifth hole. It would take him about fifty minutes to get there, suggesting the approximate time of death would be around 8.50am.'

'Very precise, I have to say. What's that got to do with me speaking to Chris Owen?'

'Even allowing for heavy traffic, it would take no longer than thirty minutes to drive from the golf course to the university. Fifty minutes absolute tops if you had to get back to your car and change clothing.'

A flicker of concern flashed in Kazan's brown eyes. 'Are you suggesting what I think you're suggesting?'

'Ah, you're beginning to grasp the point at last. You could have shot Upton and have been back in the library long before you saw Chris Owen.'

Even his beard couldn't hide the fact that the blood had drained from Kazan's face.

'I... I–'

'Your alibi isn't quite conclusive, is it, Mr Kazan?' Fleming cut in.

Kazan shook his head.

'Did you shoot Oliver Upton?'

'No... no, I did not!'

'You did play golf at the same club, didn't you?'

'Yes... I–'

'Did you know the area well enough to know there was a narrow lane which takes you up the side of the course, pretty near to where they found Oliver Upton's body?'

'No, I told you, it was ages ago when I last played there. I didn't go very often.'

'You had a row with your wife when she came home to collect some things, did you not?'

'Yes, what's that got to do with it?'

'She told me you were angry and you frightened her.'

'She's exaggerating.'

'When I spoke to your manager, Yusef Zabow, he said you got angry one day when you were telling him about your wife coming home. Would you say you're a volatile man?'

An obsequious smile crossed Kazan's face. 'Of course I was

angry. Have you never been angry, *Detective Chief Inspector*?' There was no attempt to hide the sarcasm in his voice.

Fleming continued pressing. 'You joined a rifle club soon after your wife left you. Why?'

'I wanted to find something different to do... a new pastime once I was on my own. It was Chris Owen who got me interested in it.'

'You attended almost every week. Is that correct?'

'Yes.' The smile was there again. 'It was a requirement of the probationary period.'

'Do you have a firearm?'

'No.'

'You last attended the range two weeks ago, is that correct?'

'About then, yes.'

'It was, in fact, two days before Oliver Upton was shot.'

Kazan shrugged. 'Pure coincidence.'

'Okay. That's all for now, Mr Kazan. You're free to go.'

'You decided not to charge him then?' Logan asked after Kazan had left.

'Not enough evidence to secure a conviction, Harry.'

'Guilty as hell, if you ask me.'

'All we have on him is he had a motive, made a mistake about his alibi, his revised alibi doesn't quite stack up, and he joined a rifle club. No fingerprints, CCTV, murder weapon or DNA.'

'See what you mean.'

Fleming tapped his folder of notes. 'We need more evidence.'

37

LONDON

The Oriental Wok Chinese restaurant wasn't far from Toby's flat, so he'd decided to walk. It wasn't a big place, having only one long rectangular dining area. Tables for four with orange tablecloths were set out in lines down each side. Wall lanterns illuminated decorative patterned wallpaper a shade paler than the tablecloths. It was early evening and there weren't many people in. A glance round revealed Quentin had not yet arrived.

A waiter approached Toby with a large smile on his face. 'Table for one?'

'No, for two. I'm meeting my brother but he hasn't arrived yet.'

'That's okay. It's not busy, so you can sit anywhere.'

'Thanks. Could I have a beer while I'm waiting, please?'

The waiter nodded. 'Of course.'

Toby found a table that wasn't near to any other people. He'd have preferred to have had the conversation with Quentin in private at his flat, but Quentin had insisted he treat Toby to a meal. He was looking through the menu when Quentin's entrance coincided with the arrival of Toby's beer.

Quentin sat opposite Toby and flashed a smile at the waiter. 'Could I have one of those as well, please? Have you decided what you want?' he asked Toby.

'Not yet. There's so much to choose from.'

'Been here long? Got a bit delayed.'

'No, just arrived. Are we having a starter as well as a main?'

'Go for it. Have what you want.'

The waiter was hovering, notepad and pen at the ready.

Toby looked up. 'I'll have the chicken and sweetcorn soup for a starter. Then lamb with ginger and spring onions and special fried rice, please.'

'I'll have the spare ribs with honey sauce, followed by king prawns and mixed vegetable fried rice,' Quentin added.

'Wine?' the waiter enquired.

Quentin looked at Toby. 'Red or white?'

'House white all right?'

Quentin nodded and the waiter disappeared off to the kitchen.

'You said over the phone you were going to accept the job,' Quentin said. 'Have you?'

Toby sipped on his beer. 'I got the acceptance letter yesterday and wrote straight back to accept.'

'Have you handed your notice in?'

'Did that yesterday as well.'

'You're going for it then?'

'No going back now.'

'What about this other candidate who turned the job down?'

'His wife changed her mind. Decided she couldn't move up there.'

'Any chance you'll change *your* mind?'

'Bit late now. I've given the school written notice that I'm leaving.'

'Did they try to persuade you not to?'

'They did, but I'm determined to make a go of this. Have you been to see Mother?'

Quentin groaned. 'Yes. As you can imagine, she's distraught.'

'I said you'd put her mind at rest.'

'Tried. But you know Mother. Kept saying how she relied on you and how I would be too busy to run around after her.'

'Did you try to tell her it wouldn't be a problem?'

The arrival of the starters gave Quentin time to consider his response. 'It *will* be a problem though. There's no way I can afford the same time you had on your hands.'

Toby stirred a spoon in his soup. 'If you haven't got the time, she could get a cleaner and a gardener. And online shopping is easy.'

'Have you seen Mother trying to operate a computer?'

'I could show her before I leave, and you're a whizz on computers. You could help her.'

Quentin pursed his lips.

'I'm sure you could pop in to see her from time to time on your way home from work,' Toby added. 'And I can come down during the school holidays.'

'You make it sound easy.'

'It is.'

Quentin frowned and picked at his spare ribs. 'When do you start?'

'Middle of August, but I'm going up as soon as I've worked my notice. Good chance during the summer holiday to get my bearings and settle in.'

'You're making a big mistake, Toby. You could withdraw your notice. As you said, they tried to persuade you to stay. They'd happily tear up your resignation.'

'Not going to happen, Quentin.'

'What about your flat?'

'I'll sell it.'

Quentin shook his head. 'Toby, I think you need to take a step back from this. You're not thinking straight. What if you sell the flat and buy something up there and it doesn't work out?'

'They've found me a cottage to rent. I'll wait and see before I buy anywhere.'

'You do realise, once you sell your flat and go up to Scotland, you'll never be able to afford to move back to London?'

'There's no way I'd want to, so not a problem.'

Quentin drew a deep breath. 'This will devastate Mother.'

'She'll get over it. Anyway, I have a life of my own to lead and this feels right.'

The main courses arrived with the wine but Toby didn't enjoy it. There was nothing wrong with the food. He felt unsettled by the attempts by his brother and mother to persuade him he was making a bad decision and get him to stay.

38

OXFORD

The movie vehicles had parked on a campsite set in six acres of land a few miles west of Oxford. Fleming was on his way there to speak to Marco Valerio who was the director for *The Marksman's Target* film. It was Sunday and Valerio had said over the phone they wouldn't be filming.

Will Palmer's reaction when Fleming had questioned him about playing golf locally had intrigued Fleming. He'd decided to check with DI Rainger to see whether anyone on his team had questioned Palmer. There was always the off-chance he might have been one of the drivers whose vehicle had shown up on CCTV on roads near the golf course. Rainger had told him he would check and get back to him.

Fleming pushed the thought from his mind as he drove into the campsite. There was a house at the end of a long driveway with a few parking spaces. A sign above a porch indicated this was the way into reception. Fleming got out of his car and walked over. Before he reached the door a woman dressed in shorts and a sleeveless shirt came out. 'Hi, can I help you?'

'DCI Fleming. I'm here to see Marco Valerio, the film director.'

The woman gave Fleming a wary look. 'Is there a problem?'

'No. He's expecting me.'

'Oh, right. All the trailers are up past the lodges. You can't miss them.'

'Thanks.' Fleming climbed back into his car and drove up the driveway past rows of wooden lodges. The film-set trailers were unmistakable. There were about twenty of them of various sizes. Fleming parked beside the largest one thinking it looked like it belonged to someone higher up the pecking order.

A short stocky man with receding curly black hair and a cigar tucked into the side of his mouth appeared from round the side of the trailer. 'Heard your car coming up the drive,' the man said with an Italian accent.

'I'm looking for Marco Valerio,' Fleming said. 'He's expecting me.' Fleming pulled out his warrant card and held it up for the man to see. 'DCI Fleming.'

'You've found him. That's me. What can I do for you?'

'Just a few questions if I may. Quite a gathering of trailers you have here.'

'Yeah.' Valerio took a deep drag on his cigar and blew smoke up into the air. He took it out of his mouth and pointed up the driveway. 'Twenty-eight in all. Mine, the producer's, film crew, technicians, lighting experts, make-up people, and actors. We keep all the filming equipment in some of them.'

'I can see why you couldn't find space in the middle of Oxford.'

Valerio took another drag on the cigar. 'The owner very kindly said we were welcome to park here... for a fee of course.'

'Most of your filming is done in Oxford I believe.'

'Yeah. But we do some in London.'

'It's crime drama, isn't it?'

'It is. We're calling it *The Marksman's Target.*'

'So I gather. Does filming involve the use of firearms?'

'It does. We strive for authenticity and use real guns, but they're props which use blanks to create realistic gun sounds.'

'How many, and what type?'

Valerio removed the cigar from his mouth and tapped ash from the end. 'As you might expect for a film called *The Marksman's Target*, we have a rifle. Just the one.'

'Is that all?'

'Couple of handguns as well.'

'Presumably there are still health and safety protocols and procedures?'

'Of course. We make sure we keep all weapons under strict control and they're accounted for.'

'And I take it there's never any live ammunition about?'

'Never, but everyone is still trained in gun safety.'

'And how to use firearms?'

'Yes.'

'How *do* you control the handling of weapons?'

'We're subject to health and safety regulations which require us to carry out a risk assessment. We have to have appropriate control measures in place.'

'Which are?'

'We have a set weapons manager who keeps all weapons under lock and key in gun cabinets.'

'In one of the trailers?'

'Yes. There are only two keys to the trailer. I have one and the weapons manager has the other.'

'And the keys to the gun cabinet?'

'Likewise, only two. I have one and the weapons manager has the other.'

'They're never handed to anyone else?'

'Never.'

'What about when they're needed for a scene?'

'The weapons manager books them out and has to ensure their security at all times... for delivery to the set and on it.'

'You've never had anyone break into the trailer and gun cabinet?'

Valerio took a deep drag on his cigar and blew a cloud of smoke into the air. 'No.'

'Is it possible for someone to get hold of one of the keys without you or the weapons manager knowing?'

'No chance. They're secured to our belts during the day and locked away at night in our trailers. And, before you ask, the gun cabinet also has an alarm on it.'

Fleming scratched his chin and changed tack. 'Did you know Will Palmer has a villa in Spain?'

'Yes.'

'You knew the ex-wife of Oliver Upton, the man shot dead on a local golf course recently, moved in with him?'

Valerio dropped his cigar on the ground and stubbed it out with his shoe. 'I didn't know about Upton's ex-wife.'

'The thing is, it turns out Upton abused his wife, knocked her about, and Will knew about it.'

'Whoa there! Are you saying Will's a suspect because Upton knocked his partner about?'

'It's just a case of eliminating everyone from our enquiries who had any connection with Upton.'

'I see.'

'I spoke to Will. He said he was on the set on the morning Upton was shot. Can you confirm that?'

'Remind me what day it was.'

'Friday, fourteenth of May.'

Valerio frowned. 'There was a Thursday night, Will knocked on my trailer door. Said he had a stomach bug and wouldn't be able to film the next day.'

'Was it the thirteenth when he came to see you?'

'I'd need to go and check my schedules. Hang on.' Valerio disappeared into his trailer.

A couple of minutes later, he returned having lit up another cigar. He had a worried look on his face. 'Yep, it was Friday fourteenth he called off.'

'Did anyone check on him the day he cried off filming?'

'I did,' Marco said. 'He was in his trailer.'

'What time?'

'About ten.'

'Okay, thanks for your time, Mr Valerio.'

Valerio took a deep drag on his cigar and tapped the ash off the end. He blew out a cloud of smoke. 'Should I worry about Will?'

Fleming wasn't quite sure how to answer. 'You can always ask him. I'll need to speak to him again to ask why he said he was filming when he wasn't. Is he here?'

'No, went back to London for some reason this morning. Returning late tonight.'

'Okay, tell him I'll need to speak to him at St Aldates police station. I'll call him to arrange.'

Back in his car on the way to Long Hanborough, Fleming pondered over the fact Palmer didn't appear to have the means to shoot Upton. Unless, of course, he had access to a rifle from somewhere else. He was in his trailer that morning, but could have been back there by ten if he did kill Upton. The case against him seemed weaker all of a sudden.

39

OXFORD

Logan tapped a newspaper on his desk as Fleming arrived in the office. 'Have you seen this, boss?'

'What is it?'

Logan turned the paper round and slid it across the desk.

Fleming saw the headline: *The Marksman's Target*. The first sentence of the report said Thames Valley Police had visited the film director. The reporter had gone on to point out the uncanny relevance of the title after the recent shooting.

'How did the reporter get hold of this?' Logan asked. 'You only went there yesterday.'

'Either Marco Valerio told him, or it could have been the woman I met outside reception. I told her who I was and that I was there to see Valerio.'

Before Logan could say any more, Temple appeared with a face like thunder. 'A word, Alex. My office.' She turned and strode off.

Fleming looked at Logan and grimaced.

'Sounds like she's seen the article as well,' Logan said.

Fleming turned to follow Temple. Her door was open and she was sitting behind her desk. Fleming knocked anyway and went in. He saw a copy of the paper Logan had been reading in Temple's hands.

'Have you seen this, Alex?'

'Only just. Logan showed it to me.'

'The chief constable's been on the phone. She's livid she didn't know about this and it's leaked out. Care to tell me what it's all about?'

'I didn't think it necessary to let you or the chief constable know every time I planned to question someone.'

'Only this article seems to be suggesting there's some sort of link between Upton's murder and the film. It would have been nice to have known about it before you went haring off questioning people.'

'I'm sure there isn't a connection. Just an unfortunate title and bad timing.'

'So why did you go to question the director?'

'An actor by the name of Will Palmer plays a support role in the film–'

'So?' Temple cut in.

'You know I told you Oliver Upton's ex-wife lives in Spain with a new partner?'

'Yes.'

'Turns out the partner is Will Palmer.'

'And?'

'I spoke to Palmer and he knew Upton had treated his wife badly.'

'Meaning he was violent towards her?'

'Yes. Palmer was angry and wanted to have it out with Upton, but Mrs Upton persuaded him not to get involved.'

'So you think that might have been a motive for shooting Upton?'

'I asked Palmer where he was on the day of the murder and he told me he was filming on set.'

'So you went to see the director to check his story?'

'Yes.'

'And was he filming?'

'No. I'm going to pull him in for questioning under caution.'

'You're not going to arrest him?'

'Not enough evidence, ma'am. I'm going to ask him to come in of his own volition at this stage. And we still have Atticus Kazan as a possible suspect. Too early for any arrests.'

'I'll let the chief constable know, but she'll be expecting results sooner rather than later.'

'Want me to get in touch with this reporter? Get him to issue a statement to say the visit to see the film director was just routine. I could say we have no reason to believe there's any link between the filming and Upton's murder.'

'No. Best to stay clear of the press. They'll only want to know why you went to see the director.'

'DI Rainger's in your office,' Logan said when Fleming returned from seeing Temple. 'Says he has some news for you.'

'Okay.'

The door to his office was open and Rainger was sitting in a chair by the window looking out over the open-plan area. 'Hi, Alex. You see this morning's paper?'

'You're the third person to ask me that.'

'Anything in the story?'

'Not as much as the article implies. I was just following up on a lead. Routine. Logan said you had some news for me.'

'Not a lot, but thought I'd drop by.'

'Did you get anything on Earl Yates?'

'Yeah. Medical records show he has a history of anxiety and depression, and suffers from delusions. He served in

Afghanistan and came back with post-traumatic stress disorder. Yates's doctor thought there was no need to section him. He's treating him for his condition.'

'Anything else?'

'You asked me about Will Palmer. My lot have finished trawling through CCTV footage of the roads near the golf course. They've questioned the drivers of all vehicles picked up.'

'And?'

'He was one of them. But the uniform questioning him wasn't aware that Palmer was the partner of Upton's ex-wife. He decided there was no need for any further action.'

After Rainger had gone, Fleming sat behind his desk thinking over what he'd just been told.

40

LONDON AND BALCORIE

Toby was back at his flat for a final check before he set off for Scotland. He'd been to say goodbye to his mother and, as expected, it had been a traumatic experience. Toby had prepared for his mother's anger, tears, emotional blackmail, and exaggeration about being ill.

What he faced was not what he expected. His mother had refused to speak to him. She sat in her chair with a face like thunder, staring straight ahead to avoid eye contact with Toby. He'd left saying he didn't want to leave her like this, but it made no difference. On his way out, he'd turned hoping she would say something, but her eyes remained fixed on the wall.

Toby felt remorseful. Of course, that's exactly what his mother had wanted him to feel. She hadn't managed to get Toby to change his mind about leaving, so she was going to make him suffer. He finished checking the flat, picked up his suitcase, and slammed the door behind him. Remorse had given way to anger. This was why he had to leave. There also his doctor's observation about London air not being good for his asthma.

Things had worked out well in the end. The headmaster had surprised him. He'd bullied Toby in the past, but he'd been flexible. He'd agreed Toby could work his notice up to the end of term and through the summer break when he wasn't working, so he'd be able to start his new job when the autumn term started. The school had broken up the day before. Toby had already worked three weeks of his notice.

Toby took the lift down to the communal car park and threw his case in the boot. He'd booked into a Travelodge at Penrith, calculating it was about halfway to Balcorie. The journey planner estimated it would take over five hours. Toby reckoned it would be more like seven, taking into account traffic and rest breaks. He looked at his watch. It was past eleven so he should be in Penrith by six. Toby knew there were lots of roadworks and speed restrictions on the M1 so had decided to go via the M25, M40, and M6. He made good time, arriving at the Travelodge by quarter to six.

After settling in and having a rest, Toby found somewhere to eat a short walk from the hotel. It was then back for an early night. He had another long drive ahead of him the next day.

Toby didn't sleep well. He worried about his mother and how he'd upset her. The silence when he'd gone to say goodbye, and the vision of her sitting staring at the wall preyed on his mind. The enormity of the decision he'd made had caught up with him and a twinge of self-doubt had crept in. He was also nervous about the new job and the move. It was a major milestone in his life. Tension had built up in his neck and shoulders and a headache followed. He'd taken painkillers with a swig of water and decided he would call his mother the next day to make sure she was okay.

After an early breakfast, Toby made three calls. The first was to his mother. There was no answer. The second was to his brother. No answer there either. Toby left a message asking him to check on their mother as she wasn't answering her phone, and to call him later.

The third call was to Ailsa. She picked up after three rings.

'Hi, Ailsa. It's Toby. Just to let you know, I'm on my way. I stopped over at Penrith to break the journey and I'll be setting off for Balcorie in a few minutes.'

'Oh, hello. When do you think you'll get here?'

'It's about six and three-quarter hours from here. I'll have one or two stops on the way, so I reckon I could be in Balcorie by six.'

'Okay. I'll be over at Pherson's place. When you get to Balcorie, park by the post office and pip your horn. We'll come and get you. I've got the keys for your cottage so we can take you there and let you in. I've put some food in the fridge so you can get something to eat.'

'That's very kind. Thank you. See you both later.' Toby ended the call and checked out of the hotel.

Five minutes later, Toby was on his way up the M6 heading for Carlisle. From there it was up the M74 to Glasgow, then Stirling, Perth, Inverness, Ullapool, Lochinver, and finally up to Balcorie.

Ailsa had warned Toby temperatures rarely exceeded sixteen degrees Celsius in Balcorie in summer. She'd also told him that rainfall was high and, sure enough, the first drops of rain splattered on his windscreen as he left Lochinver. The rain didn't stop Toby from enjoying the last leg of his journey. The road wound its way through rocky hills. At times it hugged the shoreline where waves pounded against the rocks. Then it went up into the hills. Clifftops soon became visible over to the left with the sea beyond. Driving round a corner, Toby saw the narrow road winding down the hill to Balcorie. This would be his final destination where a new life awaited him.

Despite poor visibility with the rain, the white sandy bay stood out. Toby took in the view. There was a small cluster of buildings set back from the bay. Toby could see small cottages dotted here and there on the foothills rising behind the village. He drove on down into the village, parked outside the post office, and pipped his horn.

A couple of minutes later, Ailsa and Pherson appeared. Toby got out of the car to greet them. 'Hi. Made it!'

'Toby, great to see you,' Ailsa said. 'Trip okay?'

'Fine, thanks.'

'It's just a short walk from here to your cottage so you can leave your car here for now.'

Later, once settled in after a chat with Ailsa and Pherson, Toby made a quick dinner of ham and eggs he found in the fridge. He'd washed up and was starting to unpack his things when his mobile rang: *Quentin.*

Toby listened for a short while, saying little other than to make the odd one-word response. He ended the call looking pensive.

His mother had phoned Quentin to say she was feeling ill.

41

OXFORD

I t was the day after an irate Temple had tackled Fleming about the newspaper article hinting at a connection between the film making in Oxford and Upton's murder. Fleming had made an early start and had called Logan and Anderson into his office.

'The super and chief constable are getting a bit twitchy over the Upton murder. They're not happy we haven't made an arrest yet.'

Logan drew in a deep breath. 'Unbelievable! What the hell do they expect? We can't make an arrest unless we have enough conclusive evidence that would stand up in court.'

'Bit unfair,' Anderson added. 'We're doing our best.'

Fleming held up his hands. 'I know. They seem to think we're not doing enough to get the evidence we need. Results are what they want, and quickly.'

'Unbelievable!' Logan repeated.

'Steady, Sarge. You'll give yourself a heart attack,' Anderson said.

'It's a bit rich, isn't it? Easy for them to sit behind their desks and expect an arrest just because they demand it.'

'I understand your frustration, Harry, but let's not get ourselves wound up,' Fleming said. 'They're under pressure, same as we are. We just need to keep clear heads and take stock of where we're at.'

'Cool headed as always, eh, boss?' Logan said. 'How about we start with Ian Hunter? Are we definitely ruling him out as a suspect?'

'I have,' Fleming said, 'unless, of course, everyone at the golf club is covering up for him.'

'Atticus Kazan?' Logan queried.

'His alibi timing doesn't stack up. He joined the rifle club around the time his wife left him, and attended as required under the probationary rules. His last visit was two days before Upton was shot. Otherwise, we have nothing conclusive, apart from the fact he had a motive.'

'So what do we do about him?'

'Wait and see if anything else turns up. Keep an eye on him to make sure he's not planning on going anywhere.'

Logan ticked another name off his list. 'That leaves Will Palmer.'

'Interesting,' Fleming said. 'They use real guns on the film he's in, and he was a bit tetchy when I asked about the golf club.'

'Yeah,' Logan agreed. He looked at Anderson. 'Wanted to get a solicitor involved.'

'Sounds like a man who's getting worried,' Anderson said.

'He said he was working on the set the day Upton was shot, but he wasn't,' Fleming said. 'The director told me he'd cried off filming that day with a stomach bug.'

Logan grunted. 'Not looking good for him right now. Going to pull him in?'

'Tomorrow,' Fleming said. 'I don't think there's enough evidence to arrest him, but he's volunteered to come in for questioning.'

'Be interesting to hear what he's got to say for himself. Guess he's having a solicitor present, is he?'

'He is.'

'Worried man,' Anderson repeated.

Fleming nodded. 'He should be. He was one of the owners of vehicles caught on CCTV near the golf course on the day of Upton's murder. One of DI Rainger's guys questioned him. He didn't know Palmer was Upton's ex-wife's partner so didn't see any reason to treat him as a potential suspect.'

'He's guilty,' Logan said.

'That's what you said about Kazan,' Fleming reminded him.

'So I did. Well... maybe it was Palmer all along.'

'Okay, other things,' Fleming said. 'I've still got one more taxi driver who works for Andy Cabs to go and see. I'll call my old friend DI Aitken up in Edinburgh. See if he can check if any taxi companies have any record of Upton being a driver up there.'

'We could have checked there earlier,' Logan said.

'I know but I was hoping you might find a London company that knew him before I got DI Aitken involved. Now you've exhausted that angle we'll try Edinburgh.'

'I could do that.'

'Let's try DI Aitken first. Anything else?'

'No,' Logan and Anderson said together.

'Okay, I'll give Aitken a call.'

Fleming picked up his phone and dialled the number he had for Gordon Aitken. He answered after a long delay.

'DI Aitken speaking.'

'Hi, Gordon, it's Alex Fleming. You busy?'

'As always. Been a while since we last spoke. What can I do for you?'

'A very big favour if you can. I'm working on a murder case and I'm struggling to find any information about the victim's past from four to five years back. He turned up in Oxford then and started work with a taxi firm. One of the other drivers reckoned he let slip he used to drive taxis up in Edinburgh. Any chance you could get someone to dig around to see if any taxi companies have any record or recollection of him?'

'What's his name?'

'Upton... Oliver Upton.'

'As it happens,' Aitken said, 'I've got a new rookie DC. I'll get him on it. May take some time though.'

'Just grateful you can help, Gordon. Many thanks.'

42

OXFORD

Fleming and Logan were outside interview room two at St Aldates police station, about to go in to question Will Palmer.

'Think we've kept him and his solicitor waiting long enough?' Logan asked.

'Yes. Let's go in and see what he has to say for himself.'

Palmer was whispering to his solicitor, Sita Sadak, when Fleming and Logan came into the room. He stopped talking when they entered.

'Sorry to keep you waiting,' Fleming said. 'Something urgent came up.'

Sadak frowned. 'My client volunteered to attend,' she reminded Fleming. 'You're lucky we're still here.'

'Yes, thank you. We won't keep you too long.'

Palmer had decided to tone down his showy dress sense for this occasion. The pink coat, white T-shirt, and orange-tinted glasses had given way to a white sleeveless shirt and glasses with round blue-tinted lenses. Sadak, wearing a smart black jacket and white shirt, sat beside him.

Fleming and Logan drew up chairs on the opposite side of

the interview room table. Logan switched on the digital recorder and Fleming went through all the usual preliminaries. He cautioned Palmer and reminded him he was free to leave at any time.

'I know we covered some of this when we met in the pub, but for the benefit of the recording, I need to go over some things again.'

'Whatever keeps you happy,' Palmer drawled in his strong Irish accent.

'You're currently filming in Oxford and are staying in a film set trailer. Is that correct?'

'Yes.'

'How long have you been there for?'

'A few weeks.'

'So you would have been staying there at the time Oliver Upton was shot?'

'I have to object,' Sadak cut in before Palmer could answer. 'You've only just started questioning my client, and you're trying to get him to implicate himself.'

'I only wanted to verify Mr Palmer was in Oxfordshire, and not at his flat in London.'

'I was in Oxford,' Palmer volunteered, 'as were you and thousands of others. Doesn't implicate me in the least.'

'Thank you. Oliver Upton's ex-wife moved into your villa in Spain last year. Didn't she?'

'She did, yes.'

'And she told you about how her husband was sometimes violent towards her. Is that correct?'

'Yes.'

'How did that make you feel?'

'I was angry.'

'She had to restrain you from going to have it out with him, didn't she?'

'DCI Fleming,' Sadak said, 'you are trying to get my client to admit to things which could incriminate him.'

'I'm only going over things which he has already told me in an informal chat. This is for the record.'

'I don't mind answering the questions,' Palmer said with a smile. 'I have nothing to hide.'

'You were a little less helpful when DS Logan and I spoke to you last. You got angry and walked out when I asked you if you played golf around Oxford.'

'Because I knew someone shot Oliver Upton on a local course and thought you were about to try to link me to the murder.'

'It's a simple question. Have you ever been on the same golf course?'

'No.'

'You told me you were filming on the set on the morning Upton was shot. Do you stand by what you said?'

'Of course I do. It's what I was doing. Why would I say anything else?'

'I checked with the director. He told me you went to see him the night before and said you wouldn't be able to work the next day because you had a stomach bug.'

'He must have got the days mixed up.'

'He has the day you called off on his printed schedules.'

'Doesn't prove anything. He could have put in the wrong date.'

'Is he prone to making mistakes?'

Palmer shrugged. 'He's human. We all make mistakes.'

'So are you still claiming you were filming even though the director is adamant you called off sick that day?'

'Okay, maybe I got it wrong.'

'If we agree you were not on the film set, where were you?'

'I'd have been in bed in my trailer.'

'You didn't go out?'

'No.'

Fleming looked inside a folder in front of him, then stared straight at Palmer. 'If that's the case, how do you explain why a CCTV camera picked up your car on a road near the golf course early on the morning of the shooting?'

Palmer glanced at Sadak as though for help.

'A no comment answer might not be helpful,' she suggested.

'It is you, isn't it,' Fleming pressed. 'Why were you there?'

'I... I–'

'You use real guns on the set, don't you?' Fleming cut in.

'Yes, bu–'

Fleming interrupted again before Palmer could say any more. His questioning was relentless. 'You took a rifle, had some bullets, went to the golf course and shot Upton, didn't you?'

'No... no. I know it looks bad. That's why I lied about where I was. It seemed easier than trying to explain why I was there.'

'So why were you there if you didn't shoot Upton?'

Palmer's eyes darted between Logan and Fleming. 'Okay. I was going to have it out with him and drove to his house early in the morning. He was packing his golf things into his car. I followed him to the golf course and changed my mind. Thought it was a stupid idea. There would have been too many people about. I came back to my trailer in case Marco sent someone to check up on me.'

Fleming looked at Logan. 'Anything else?'

'No.'

Fleming looked across at the DIR. 'Interview terminated at 11am.'

'Can I ask a question, boss?' Logan asked outside the room.

'Sure, go ahead.'

'How come you thought Palmer shot Upton, but didn't charge him?'

'Not enough evidence to secure a conviction. All we have on him is he despised Upton. He could have had access to a rifle, and lied about his alibi.'

'A CCTV camera *did* pick him up near the golf course,' Logan reminded Fleming.

'True.'

'Isn't that enough?'

'I don't think so. Hating someone isn't evidence of killing them. We'd need to prove he took a rifle from the set and had bullets for it, and he's explained why he lied about his whereabouts. At the moment, we can't disprove his explanation.'

'So why accuse him and then stop the interview?'

'I was trying to provoke him into either confessing, or explaining why his car was near the golf course on the morning of the murder. He gave us a reason which we can check out. And... I wanted to keep him sweating.'

43

BALCORIE

The fisherman's cottage Ailsa had arranged for Toby to rent was on the edge of Balcorie. It was near to the bay, about fifty yards from the sea, up a slight rocky rise. A blue door with flaking paint sat in the middle of the single-storey stone building. It had a slate roof and there were two windows, one on each side of the door.

Worn stone steps led up to the door from a gravel driveway. Inside, there was a combined kitchen and living room, a bathroom, a utility room, and one bedroom. Although sparsely furnished, it was homely and had a log-burning stove.

It was Saturday, the day after Toby had arrived in Balcorie. The rain of the day before had given way to a brighter, breezy morning. He walked over to the window and looked out over the sea. Whitecaps were riding on the waves and spume flew off in the wind. White clouds drifted across an otherwise-blue sky. Toby opened the window and took in a deep breath. He felt elated and better than he had for years. This was the new beginning.

Ailsa was coming up the driveway, saw Toby at the window, and waved. She had promised to come down to the cottage and take Toby up for coffee with Pherson. Toby waved back and opened the door.

'Settle in all right last night?' Ailsa asked.

'Yes. Slept like a log.'

'Have you had breakfast? I left some bacon and eggs in the fridge for you.'

Toby smiled. 'Yes, had ham and eggs last night and a fried breakfast this morning. It was very thoughtful of you. I'll pay you back.'

Ailsa shook her head. 'No, it's fine. It's the least I could do when you had to drive all the way up here. I was sure you wouldn't have had time to get any food in.'

'Where's the nearest supermarket? I should go and do a bit of shopping later.'

'You can get some basics from the post office shop, but otherwise, it's Lochinver. In the meantime, are you ready to come up to Pherson's?'

'Sure, I'll grab a coat.'

Ailsa walked Toby up through the village, past the old church and village hall. Pherson Dalglish's house was a few hundred yards on from the school on the outskirts of Balcorie. It was of a similar structure to Toby's fisherman's cottage; stone with a slate roof, but with two storeys.

Pherson answered the door. 'Ah! Just in time Got the kettle on.'

Pherson was a short well-kept man in his late sixties. He had a rotund red face, though his wrinkled neck was showing signs of age. He was wearing brown tweed trousers, a checked shirt, and a woollen pullover. 'Come in... come in and make yourself at home.'

Pherson showed Toby and Ailsa into a sitting room furnished with vintage furniture. There was an old grandfather clock in one corner, and an antique table and chairs were set against a back wall. Tartan throws covered a settee and two easy chairs. 'Have a seat,' Pherson said. 'Mrs Dalglish has gone off to the shops in Lochinver. I'll just pop into the kitchen and get the coffee.'

A few minutes later, Pherson returned holding a tray with a coffee pot, three cups and a plate of biscuits. 'Help yourselves to biscuits,' he said, pouring the coffee.

'Just had breakfast so I'll give the biscuits a miss,' Toby said with a smile. 'But thank you.'

'Likewise,' Ailsa echoed.

'So,' Pherson said, looking at Toby, 'how are you settling in?'

'Fine, thank you. I thought it would be good to get to know the area and get organised before starting work.'

'Good idea. I'm sure Ailsa will help you out. Mind if I ask why you applied for the teaching job here? It's a far cry from London.'

'London's stressful and the air quality doesn't do my asthma any good. I saw the advert and felt it was too good an opportunity to let pass me by. Decided to apply, and here I am.'

'Good for you. I'm sure you'll be happy here. You'll love the school and the kids. I taught there for thirty-eight years. Finally decided it was time to put my feet up and enjoy retirement... with a little bit of encouragement from Mrs Dalglish,' he added with a faint smile.

'What did you do before teaching?' Toby asked.

'Joined the civil service after university. I worked in London for eight years, so I know what you mean about the place.'

'Oh, really? What did you do?'

'Started in the Home Office, then went on to other things. Nothing very interesting. Tell me about the school you've left.'

'It was a primary school for children aged three to eleven. About sixty kids there. It was okay, but could be stressful at times.'

'Only ten pupils at Balcorie Primary,' Pherson said.

They went on for another hour talking about the school, teaching, and life in Balcorie.

As Toby and Ailsa were getting up to leave, Pherson said, 'Oh, by the way, Ailsa, just remembered something.'

'Yes?'

'Meant to tell you, I was in the post office the other day and an old friend of yours called in. He was speaking to the postmistress. Said he was doing the famous north coast five-hundred-mile trip and decided to do a slight detour on the off-chance he might catch you in. Said he hadn't seen you in years and heard you'd moved up here. Unfortunately, you were out at work. He asked where you were staying so he'd know where to find you should he ever find his way up here again.'

Ailsa had turned ashen. 'Did he give a name?'

'No, he didn't.'

'Did the postmistress tell him where I lived?' Pherson laughed. 'Sorry, no she didn't. She's always a wee bit suspicious of strangers asking questions.'

'You didn't either?'

'He wasn't talking to me, so I kept quiet.'

'Thanks for telling me, Pherson.'

'No problem.'

After coffee, Toby decided to go down into Lochinver to get some provisions. He'd left a worried-looking Ailsa behind. She'd seemed concerned about the man asking where she lived. And... she'd been less than forthcoming about where she'd moved from when he'd asked after the interview. He shook his head. *I wonder why.*

44

OXFORD

'The chief constable's been on my back again over the lack of progress on the Upton case,' Temple said. 'She wants to know if there's any news. Anything I should be letting her know about?'

Fleming sighed. 'We *are* making some headway, but we're finding it difficult to get anything on Upton's background. The man's a complete enigma. If we could find out more about him, we might get closer to identifying who might have wanted to kill him.'

'Then I suggest you make it a priority to find a way to overcome the difficulties.'

A thought flashed through Fleming's head. *I don't need you to tell me that. What the fuck do you think I'm doing?* 'It's top of my list,' was all he said instead.

'Good. So how are you hoping to find more about the man?'

'A taxi driver colleague of his said he once let slip he used to drive taxis up in Edinburgh, then tried to retract it. I have an old friend up there. He's a DI with Police Scotland. I've asked him if he can check if any taxi companies up there ever employed Upton.'

'That's all you have to go on?'

'I've got one more driver who works for Andy Cabs to speak to. He's been on holiday. Maybe he'll be able to provide more information.'

'Anything else I can tell the chief constable to keep her happy?'

'I've questioned Will Palmer under caution. He lied about his alibi. CCTV picked up his car near the golf course on the morning of the murder. Also, the film set he's working on uses real guns, albeit with blanks.'

'Sounds like a prime suspect to me. Why didn't you charge him?'

'Not enough hard evidence, ma'am. We'd need to prove there was a rifle on the set he was able to take without anyone knowing, and that he had live bullets.'

'Better have a word with the film director.'

'I did but he said that was impossible, strict controls, he said.'

'What about Palmer's alibi and his car appearing on CCTV?'

'He had an explanation for why he lied about his whereabouts, and about CCTV picking him up near the golf course. So far, I'm unable to disprove what he claims.'

'Which was what?'

'He said he lied about where he was because if he'd told us where he really was it would look bad.'

'The reason being?'

'He went to Upton's house to have a go at him.'

'Over what?'

'How he treated his wife... who's now Palmer's partner.'

'And?'

'He saw him packing his golf clubs into his car and followed him to the golf club. Got there and decided it wasn't a good idea to have it out with him with so many people about. He went back to his trailer on the film set.'

'Very convenient way to explain why CCTV picked up his car, don't you think?'

'As I said, I can't disprove his explanation.'

'Have you got a warrant to search his house?'

'The Met is checking his flat in London for me, and DI Rainger's arranging to have Palmer's car and trailer searched.'

'And this guy, Ian Hunter, the golfing chap, what about him?'

'Witnesses confirm he couldn't have been anywhere near the scene of the crime at the time of the shooting. He's in the clear unless a lot of people are covering up for him.'

Temple took a deep breath. 'Okay, let me know the outcome of the searches. Close the door on your way out.'

Fleming left Temple's office and found Logan and Anderson in the incident room. Anderson was scribbling on the whiteboard while Logan sipped on a mug of coffee.

Anderson turned as Fleming arrived.

'Finish what you're doing,' Fleming said. 'I need to get some strong coffee.'

Five minutes later, Fleming returned. He looked at the whiteboard. Upton's name was in the centre. Outward lines pointed to Will Palmer, Vivian Upton, Atticus Kazan, Jamila Kazan, Ian Hunter, and Earl Yates. Lines with arrowheads linked Palmer and Vivian Upton; and Kazan and Jamila.

Logan took the marker pen from Anderson. He put a cross with a question mark against Hunter's name and wrote alibi confirmed in brackets. Another cross went against Yates's name, with false confession and mental health issues added in brackets.

'Good mind map,' Fleming observed. 'About sums up where we are. Two realistic suspects: Palmer and Kazan, with Palmer now looking the more likely.' He took the marker pen from Logan and wrote 'motive, opportunity and means' by Palmer's name.

On reflection, he put a question mark next to 'means'.

Next to Kazan, he scribbled 'motive and means' with a question mark next to 'means'. He added, 'joined a rifle club, alibi timing not conclusive'.

'Did Rainger's people find Kazan's car on the CCTV check of vehicles near the golf course?' Logan asked.

Fleming shook his head. 'They didn't.'

'Maybe he knew which roads didn't have CCTV or ANPR cameras on them,' Anderson suggested.

'So still two suspects,' Fleming said, scratching his chin.

'Got word from Rainger and the Met while you were with the super,' Logan said. 'No incriminating evidence found in the searches of Palmer's flat, car or trailer.'

Fleming sighed. 'This isn't going well, is it?'

45

OXFORD

Kamil Waclauski's terraced house was up a side street off the Iffley Road in Oxford. Fleming had checked with Andy Wade from Andy Cabs when Waclauski would be back from his holiday. He was the last of Wade's drivers Fleming had to question.

Fleming had left the office the night before feeling the pressure. Temple and the chief constable were pressing for a result. But all he had to offer was they had two possible suspects with insufficient evidence to arrest either of them. Palmer and Kazan were the two prime suspects. Palmer was looking the more likely, but the news that the searches of his flat, trailer and car had revealed nothing was a blow. Without witnesses, DNA samples or any forensic evidence, an arrest seemed a long way off.

A long shot was whether DI Aitken would be able to find any old record of Upton as a taxi driver up in Edinburgh. It all seemed as though the investigation was on hold. Fleming needed a breakthrough. Maybe Kamil Waclauski would provide it.

Fleming managed to find a space on the roadside not too far

from the house. Parking was for permit holders only so he left his Thames Valley Police card on top of his Audi dashboard. He walked back to the house and rang the doorbell.

A chubby man dressed in jeans and a blue T-shirt opened the door. He had short silver hair and a stubble beard to match. 'You police?'

'DCI Fleming. Mind if I come in to ask a few questions about Oliver Upton?'

'Ah, yes. Mr Wade, he told me you'd be coming to speak to me. Come in.'

Waclauski showed Fleming through a narrow hallway into a small sitting room furnished with a settee and two easy chairs. A folded table sat behind the settee and a large TV filled a corner by the front window. 'Please, take a seat,' Waclauski said, waving a hand at the seating options while slumping onto the settee.

Fleming took one of the easy chairs. 'Thank you for seeing me. I gather you're just back off holiday.'

Waclauski managed a brief smile on an otherwise-sombre face. 'Not a holiday. Mr Wade gave me extra unpaid time off to visit my old parents in Gdańsk. Been there four weeks. Came back yesterday.'

Fleming nodded. 'Mr Wade has no doubt informed you of the unfortunate demise of Mr Upton.'

'He did, yes. Big shock, no?'

'How long have you worked for Andy Cabs?'

''bout eight years.'

'You came straight from Poland to work here?'

'Yes. Casual, labouring work to start with. I drove taxis in Gdańsk and soon got a job with Mr Wade. I like it here.'

'So you were with Andy Cabs when Mr Wade took on Oliver Upton.'

'Yes. One driver left, so there was a vacancy. Oliver applied and Mr Wade took him on.'

'How well did you get to know Oliver?'

Waclauski shrugged. 'Not very well. He kept much to himself.'

'Did he ever tell you why he came to work for Andy Cabs?'

'No. Drivers come and go, you know.'

'Did he tell you he used to drive taxis in London?'

'No.'

'Edinburgh?'

A shake of the head. 'No.'

'Did you ever hear him mention being in the army?'

Another shake of the head.

'He was quite friendly with Phil Odde. Did you speak much with him?'

'Not really. We all just drove our taxis. Sometimes we meet at Mr Wade's house. He uses it as his office.'

'Did you know Oliver was divorced?'

'I heard, yeah.'

'Did you know a woman called Jamila Kazan moved in with him?'

'Heard someone had, but didn't know the name.'

'Jamila's husband is a lecturer at Oxford University... Atticus Kazan. Do you know of him?'

'No.' Waclauski gave another weak smile. 'Why would I know a university lecturer?'

'Maybe he used your taxi at some time.'

'If he did, I wouldn't have known.'

'Do customers not give you names when they book a taxi?'

'If they book, yes. But I don't remember names. Sometimes they just wave you down and jump in. No names given.'

Fleming was fishing and getting nothing. He tried another tack. 'Andy Cabs is a small company. How does Mr Wade get on with the bigger companies?'

Waclauski shifted in his seat. 'It's difficult, for sure. Some try to put him out of business... stealing customers, you know?'

'Have you ever had any trouble with competing companies?'

'Me? No.' Waclauski hesitated. 'But...'

'Go on.'

'I don't know if I should say...'

'What?' Fleming pressed.

'There's a guy, nasty piece of work. He had a big row with Oliver one day. I was there. I was going to pick up a fare and saw them arguing next to their taxis. I stopped and asked what was going on. Oliver poked a finger at this man and accused him of trying to run his taxi off the road.'

'What happened?'

'The man punched Oliver in the face and shouted he knew where Oliver lived and he had better watch his back.'

'Who was this man?'

'He works for a rival small company... Syed Taxis.'

'Know his name?'

'Raj Syed.'

'Did Oliver report the assault to the police?'

'No. He said he would sort it his way.'

'Do you know what he meant by that?'

'Not at the time. But later I read in the papers that Syed's taxi had been set alight by vandals. I was sure it must have been Oliver, but I kept quiet. I didn't want Oliver to get into trouble and lose his job.'

'Not going to happen now,' Fleming said. 'Thank you for letting me know this. I'll need to speak to Syed.'

'He is a nasty man. Please don't tell him I told you. I fear for my safety.'

'Don't worry. I'll keep you out of it.'

Fleming thanked Waclauski for his time. He left thinking he might have the breakthrough he needed. *Was this a feud that got out of hand?*

46

OXFORD

Fleming was on his way to see Andy Wade of Andy Cabs.

Wade was at home and showed Fleming into the small room off the hallway. 'Must get this office of mine tidied up one day,' Wade said, clearing papers off a chair so Fleming could sit. Smoke drifted up towards the ceiling from a cigarette dangling on the edge of a full ashtray. An empty mug with Andy Cabs printed on it sat next to the ashtray. 'Just had a coffee. Want one?'

Fleming shook his head. 'No, thanks. I won't take up much of your time.'

'Thought I told you all I could about poor old Oliver,' Wade said, taking a seat in front of his computer desk.

'I saw Kamil Waclauski yesterday,' Fleming said. 'He told me about a run-in Oliver had with a man called Raj Syed.' Fleming watched for a reaction from Wade and saw him stiffen.

'Oh yeah?' Wade finally answered.

'He told me he found them arguing by their taxis one day and it ended up with Syed punching Oliver in the face. Told him he knew where he lived and he had better watch his back. Did you know about that?'

Wade took a final drag from his cigarette and stubbed it out in the ashtray. 'I did, yes.'

'And you no doubt heard Syed's taxi was burnt out. Know anything about that?'

'I heard, yeah.'

'Was it Oliver?'

'I don't know. It could have been I suppose, but I don't know for sure.'

'Why didn't you tell me about this when I last spoke to you?'

Wade shifted in his seat and beads of sweat had formed on his forehead. 'Look, I don't want any trouble with Syed. He's a real nasty piece of work. I've had my run-ins with him. He'd like to put me out of business. I didn't want you going round questioning him and him thinking I'd put the finger on him as a suspect for killing Oliver.'

'Not good judgement, Mr Wade. He could have done, and you withheld important information.'

'I didn't think he would have shot Oliver over an argument they had.'

'It was more than an argument though, wasn't it? Syed threatened and assaulted Oliver who may have set Syed's taxi on fire.'

'As I said, I don't know anything about that, and I didn't think for a minute Syed would have killed Oliver.'

'Oliver didn't report the assault to the police. Did you discuss whether he should with him?'

Wade lit another cigarette, took a deep drag, and blew a cloud of smoke up towards the ceiling. 'We did, yes. Same reason. We didn't want to get into a deeper feud with Syed. Best left alone we thought.'

'But it seems like Oliver had other thoughts. He told Waclauski he would sort Syed out.'

'He didn't say anything to me.'

Fleming frowned and decided to give Wade a warning in case he was hiding any other pieces of potential evidence. 'I'm not happy you withheld important information which could have a bearing on Oliver's murder. I could charge you with attempting to pervert the course of justice.'

'You're joking!'

Fleming doubted such a charge would stick under the circumstances, but felt sure Wade wouldn't know. 'Withholding information is not a good idea.'

Wade sighed. 'Look, I could have pointed the finger at Syed, but kept quiet out of fear and because he may be innocent. As I said, I don't need any trouble.'

'Okay, I get why you kept quiet, but it's for the police to decide who's innocent and who isn't. I'll need to speak to Syed.'

Wade took another deep drag on his cigarette. 'In which case, I might need police protection.'

'You're *that* worried about him?'

'Yes.'

'And yet you say you didn't believe Syed could have killed Oliver.'

'Okay, I've been an idiot, but I don't want any trouble with Syed.'

'If he causes trouble, you report it to the police.'

Wade put his head in his hands. 'And then I get into more trouble with him.'

Fleming felt some sympathy for Wade. He put a hand on his arm. 'You made a mistake, but don't beat yourself up about it.'

47

EDINBURGH

On his way to interview room one at Gayfield Square, DI Aitken went to see young DC Iver Schultze to see how he was getting on with Alex Fleming's request. 'Any luck yet finding old records of the taxi driver Oliver Upton?'

Schultze looked up from his computer screen. 'Not yet, boss.'

Aitken grimaced. 'Okay, keep at it.'

'Right. I also checked the electoral registers for four and five years ago.'

Aitken raised an eyebrow. 'And?'

'There were ten Oliver Upton's registered. Four are still on the current register. One appears in the register of births, marriages and deaths. So DCI Fleming's man could be one of the other five who no longer appear on the current register.'

'Most likely one of them is. Not sure how that'll help him. He knows Upton moved to Oxford. It's background information he needs on the man.'

'I could make enquiries.'

'Such as?'

'Find out which one moved to Oxford. Check if the new

owners of the property he left, or old neighbours, can provide any information about him.'

'Hmm. Stick to checking the taxi firms for now. Don't want to start hares running and get you tied up in a major enquiry. Wouldn't be great if the super found out I was using our resources to help out an old friend of mine in Thames Valley.'

'Okay, sir. I'll make sure no one knows what I'm doing.'

Aitken found DS Quigley waiting for him outside the interview room, sipping on a mug of tea. 'All ready to go?'

'Doug Jenner and his solicitor are in there waiting for us,' Quigley said.

'Right, let's see what Jenner has to say for himself.'

Jenner was whispering to his solicitor when the two detectives entered the room. The solicitor's face was as colourless as the grey suit, white shirt and tie he was wearing. Jenner, who was in his fifties, had short grey hair, and a stubbled beard and moustache. His blue jeans and red T-shirt were the only sign of colour between the two men.

Aitken waited for Quigley to turn on the digital interview recorder then went through the usual protocols. He cautioned Jenner before he started to question him. 'You're facing the prospect of some pretty serious charges,' Aitken reminded Jenner. 'It's in your interest to give straight answers to my questions.'

Jenner stared at Aitken with steely blue eyes and said nothing.

'You own the haulier company, Jenner Transport, don't you?'

'I do,' Jenner mumbled.

'And do you ever need to drive to Europe in the course of your business?'

Jenner shrugged. 'Yes.'

'In particular, the Netherlands?'

'I've been there, yes.'

'What sort of things do you deliver, or pick up from there?'

Jenner sneered. 'You want me to take up all your time while I list them?'

'Lots of different things?'

'Yes.'

'What about drugs and guns?'

Jenner shook his head and offered a sly smile. 'No. Didn't find any in my lorry or depot, did you?'

'We didn't, no.' Aitken sifted through the folder of papers he had in front of him. 'What I do have is a statement from your wife. She says she overheard a conversation you had with another man. Reckons the man told you a consignment of drugs and guns was ready to pick up from the Netherlands.'

'Crap. She's lying.'

'She also says you admitted to her you'd already done several trips.'

The sly smile returned. 'She's right. Been to the Netherlands several times. As I said, I could give you a long list of goods I transport.'

'She said it in the context you were talking about drugs and guns and you warned her not to go to the police.'

'You can't prove that, because it didn't happen.'

'She said she was going to go to the police anyway, and then you attacked her. You could face a charge of attempted murder, at best assault.'

'Didn't touch her. She tripped and fell. Her word against mine. You can't prove a thing.'

'Do you know Big Col Calhoun?'

'Know *of* him, yeah.'

'You were recently seen at the same black-tie dinner as Calhoun.'

'So... doesn't mean we're friends. There were loads of people there I didn't know.'

'A DI Taylor questioned you some time ago. He was interested in Calhoun and thought you had links to him.'

'I remember. Nothing came of it. He was just fishing. I had nothing to do with Calhoun.'

'The man you were talking to at your depot... it was Calhoun, wasn't it?'

Jenner shifted in his chair. 'No.'

'So who was it?'

'No comment.'

'When we question Calhoun, you think he's going to protect you?'

Jenner stared over Aitken's shoulder and said nothing.

'My guess is he'll say you invited him to the depot to discuss a business proposition, but left as soon as he knew what it was. He'll say he didn't want to get involved and didn't report it to the police because you'd threatened him.'

'Bollocks!'

'He'll claim you told him you had a consignment of drugs and guns to pick up and asked if he had any contacts who could help you sell them.'

Jenner shook his head. 'No way!'

Aitken sighed. 'You could make things much easier on yourself if you co-operate. As things stand, you're facing three charges. There's attempted murder for one. Taking and threatening a hostage for two. Then there's the drugs and gun smuggling. If you co-operate, I could change the attempted murder charge to assault. A judge may show some leniency over drugs and gun smuggling if you testify against Calhoun. Remember, he won't think twice about dropping you in it.'

Jenner looked at his solicitor who gave an imperceptible nod. 'You'll put a good word in for me?' Jenner asked Aitken.

'I'll do what I can.'

Jenner licked his bottom lip. 'Okay, I'll tell you all you want to know about Calhoun.'

48

OXFORD

The taxi was sitting in a queue outside Oxford station. Fleming slipped into the passenger seat behind Raj Syed as the air turned cooler and dark clouds raced in from the south. Lightning flashed across the sky followed by a sharp crack of thunder. Rain started to beat against the roof of the taxi like a shower of hail.

Fleming saw Syed's dark, brown eyes staring at him through the rear-view mirror. 'I'm in a queue here,' Syed said. 'You need to get a taxi from the front.'

'I'm not going anywhere.' Fleming leaned forward to show his warrant card to Syed. 'Just want a quick word.'

Syed turned with a look of alarm and pulled his black and white shemagh scarf tighter round his neck. Fleming guessed he was in his fifties, but Syed still had thick black hair and a short beard and moustache to match. 'Strange place to want to have a chat,' he said in a brusque, harsh voice.

'Could invite you to St Aldates police station if you prefer.'

Syed shrugged. 'What's this about?'

'Andy Cabs.'

'What about them?'

'Wondered how you get on with them.'

'I don't. Bastards want to put me out of business.'

'Is that why you argued with Oliver Upton a few weeks ago?'

'Who says I had an argument?'

'I have an eyewitness.'

'Okay, we disagreed. So what?'

'Bit more than an argument. Wasn't it?'

'How'd you mean?'

'I hear you punched him in the face.'

'Rubbish! It was just a friendly slap.'

'That's not the way I heard it. Whatever it was, why'd you do it?'

'He poked me in the chest, so I clipped his ear.'

'Did you threaten him?'

'No.'

'Did you say you knew where he lived and he'd better watch his back?'

'No.'

'So what was the argument about?'

'He cut in front of me to pinch a customer. Almost caused an accident. Bloody stupid if you ask me... careless driving.'

'So you got out of your cab and had it out with him?'

'Too bloody right. Not the first time I'd had run-ins with Andy Cabs.'

'You said they were trying to put you out of business. What were they doing?'

'Muscling in on my regular customers, spreading rumours and lies about me.'

'What rumours and lies?'

'Claiming I didn't have a licence or insurance. Told their customers to steer clear of me because I overcharged. All sorts of things.'

'Thing is, Andy Cabs are saying it's you who's trying to put *them* out of business.'

'They would, wouldn't they?'

'Okay. I get that there's rivalry, but maybe it's getting a bit out of hand.'

The rain was coming down harder and Syed flicked his wipers on to clear the windscreen as he eased the taxi forward one space. He glanced in the rear-view mirror. 'What happens when I get to the front of the queue?'

'You tell anyone looking for a taxi to get in the one behind.'

'So I lose business. That bastard Andy Wade put you up to this, didn't he?'

'No. I happened to know you'd either be here or driving a customer. I didn't want your business to suffer by calling you in for questioning at this stage. Decided it would be better to wait for you to turn up here so we could have a nice informal chat.'

Syed's dark eyes glared at Fleming through the rear-view mirror. 'If the rivalry's getting out of hand, it's down to Andy Cabs.'

'You think it was Oliver Upton who set your taxi on fire?'

Syed paused before answering. 'Either him or someone else from Andy Cabs. My guess is it was Upton.'

'After the row you had with him and your taxi was torched, Upton was shot. Where were you on the morning of the shooting?'

'Driving my taxi.'

'Can anyone vouch for that?'

'The customers who I drove.'

'Can you give me their names?'

'No. They were just people who jumped in and asked me to take them to different locations.'

'Were any of them to home addresses?'

'Yes.'

Fleming passed a card over Syed's shoulder. 'Make a list of the ones you can remember and let me have it. Sooner the better.'

Fleming got out of the taxi and dashed through the rain to his car. He sat for a moment reflecting on the conversation with Syed. There wasn't any doubt there was no love lost between Andy Cabs and him. He wondered whose side of the story of intimidation he should believe. Maybe one was as bad as the other.

Syed seemed sure it was Upton who had torched his taxi but Fleming had his doubts whether he had shot Upton. He switched on the ignition and wondered whether the shooting was more like the actions of a cold calculated killer than an angry man.

49

LONDON

Zaina Mwangi's house was only a few hundred yards from the edge of Clapham Common. It was where Jamila Kazan had gone to stay with her sister and her husband. They'd left her on her own for a couple of days while Zaina and her husband went to visit his ill mother. Jamila had assured them she would be okay and that she was more than happy to look after Winston, their golden cocker retriever.

'Winston's very energetic,' Zaina had warned. 'He'll need loads of exercise and play.'

'Not a problem,' Jamila had replied, stroking Winston's head.

Jamila had finished breakfast and tidied up in the kitchen. She was wondering about the phone call from one of Oliver's neighbours up in Oxford. She'd told her an insurance agent had called round asking if she knew where Jamila was staying.

'She's the beneficiary on Mr Upton's life insurance policy,' the man had said. Jamila had no idea Oliver had taken out a life insurance policy, let alone he had named her the beneficiary. The neighbour had phoned Jamila a couple of days ago, but no one had contacted her yet.

Putting the thought from her mind, Jamila looked out of the

window and saw it was a bright sunny day. 'I think we should go for a nice long walk on the common, Winston. What do you think?'

Winston had been standing next to Jamila, chewing on a bone. He dropped the bone and looked up at Jamila with his head cocked to one side as though trying to work out what she said.

'Walkies,' Jamila repeated, heading for the hallway to get her shoes.

Winston barked and trotted after Jamila. He waited, wagging his tail while Jamila fixed the leash round his collar. She slipped a bag of dog treats into her handbag, slung it over her shoulder and opened the front door. Even though it was quite early in the day, she could feel the warmth of the sun. 'Come on then,' she said to Winston, 'let's go.'

It wasn't far to walk along the street to the main road running alongside the common. Jamila crossed the road and headed off in the direction of the bandstand. She let Winston off the leash knowing that if he bothered anyone, a sharp whistle would bring him bounding back looking for the inevitable treat.

Jamila decided to go up past the bandstand and then hang a left along the tree line. The common opened up in front of the trees to a large grassed area where she knew Winston would enjoy a good run. It wasn't long before Winston found a playmate to chase around. Jamila stood and watched as a man walked over to her, dog leash in his hand. 'Great day for the dogs to play, eh? Lovely dog. What's he called?'

'Winston. He's not mine though,' Jamila said. 'He's my sister's. I'm staying with her for a while.'

'I come here almost every day. Thought I hadn't seen you before. Nick, by the way,' the man said, holding out a hand.

Jamila shook his hand. 'Jamila.' She smiled and watched the two dogs running around after each other. Winston was getting near the tree line when he stopped and looked over to the trees. He bounded off towards them and disappeared. Jamila could hear him barking. 'Not like him,' she told Nick. 'I'd better go and see what he's found.'

Jamila started to walk over and saw Winston barking at a man with what looked like a long stick just inside the line of trees. She gave a loud whistle and Winston came bounding back to her. Before Winston reached Jamila, two bullets thumped into her chest. She was dead before she hit the ground.

Nick heard the shots and turned to see Jamila falling. 'Oh my God! What the fuck!'

He ran towards Jamila. Winston was lying by her side whining and Jamila's lifeless eyes were staring up at Nick. He looked over to the trees, but saw nothing. Two other wide-eyed walkers had joined him.

'Police!' Nick gasped. 'Either of you got a mobile? Too late for an ambulance by the looks of it, but get one anyway.'

One of the bystanders already had his phone out and was tapping numbers into it.

The man in the trees stuffed the rifle into a golf bag and threw a towel over it so it looked like one of his clubs. He made his way out of the common, and crossed the road heading for the street where Jamila had been staying. Three minutes later, he was throwing the golf bag into the back of his car.

He headed west, then north across the river towards the M4. Traffic was slow, but he took his time and it wasn't long before he was on the M25 going north.

50

OXFORD AND LONDON

Fleming was having an update meeting with Logan and Anderson when Temple came rushing in. 'There's been a shooting in London,' she said. 'Better come up to my office, Alex.' Before Fleming could say anything, she'd turned.

'What's a murder in London got to do with us?' Logan asked.

'Good question,' Fleming said. 'Met will be dealing with it. Better go and see what it's all about.'

Temple was sitting on the edge of her desk. 'Just had a call from a DI Gamez in the Met. Someone shot Jamila Kazan this morning on Clapham Common. Thought she should let us know because they found she has an address in Oxford.'

Fleming shook his head. 'What the hell's going on. First Upton and now Jamila?'

'Seems she was walking her sister's dog. She'd been talking to another dog owner when someone shot her.'

'Did you tell Gamez about Upton?'

'No. I'd rather you went down to London to speak to her and explain our interest.'

'I'll get Logan to drop me off at the station and get the next train down.'

'Good. I'll call her back to let her know you're on your way. Before you go, anything you need to tell me?'

'Couple of things. I spoke to the film director and it seems there's no way Palmer could have got access to a rifle off the set. He also confirmed he'd checked on Palmer. He was in his trailer on the morning he'd called off sick.'

'So he's off your suspect list?'

'Not entirely. He could have got a rifle from somewhere else, and he would have had time to get back to his trailer by the time the director went to check up on him.'

'Great. The other thing?'

'I found out Upton had a bit of a disagreement with a rival taxi firm. Guy called Raj Syed assaulted him and vandals later torched Syed's taxi. Spoke to him yesterday and he thinks it was Upton who was behind it. I'm waiting for Syed to supply a list of home addresses of people he taxied home on the morning of Upton's murder to see if I can pin down where he was.'

'If Palmer, Kazan, and Syed can account for their whereabouts when Jamila was shot, we have a problem. It means we're looking for someone else... if the same person did shoot Jamila.'

'This whole thing's becoming a nightmare,' Fleming said. 'It's too much of a coincidence. Has to be the same person who shot Upton.'

'All the more reason why you need to go and speak to DI Gamez. Let me know how you get on.'

Two minutes later, Fleming was back with Logan and Anderson. Logan raised an eyebrow at Fleming. 'Who's been shot?'

'Jamila Kazan. Met are dealing with it. I'm off down to London to speak to them. Drop me off at the station?'

~

Fleming had been based at the old headquarters on Broadway when he worked for the Met. It was after he joined Thames Valley Police that the headquarters moved to the new building on Victoria Embankment.

DI Yara Gamez's office was on the second floor at the end of an open-plan area lined with tiers of desks. Uniformed and plain-clothes officers sat behind computers, staring at screens. The noise of fingers tapping on keyboards, ringing phones and animated chatter filled the air as an officer led Fleming up to Gamez's office.

Gamez, wearing black trousers and a white shirt, got up from behind her desk. She strode over to greet Fleming, hand outstretched. 'Yara Gamez. Your boss told me to expect you.'

Fleming shook hands. 'Alex Fleming. Good of you to see me.' He guessed Gamez was in her forties. She had shoulder-length brown hair, though there were signs of greying.

'Come in and take a seat,' Gamez said. 'I hear you used to work for the Met.'

'Yes, a few years ago. I transferred to Thames Valley when they promoted me to DCI. I'm with the Major Crime Unit.'

'So how can I help you?'

'I'm interested in the murder of Jamila Kazan.'

'May I ask what your interest is?'

'I'm investigating the murder of Jamila's partner, Oliver Upton. Someone shot him dead on a local golf course near Oxford a few weeks ago.'

Gamez raised an eyebrow. 'You think it's the same killer?'

'Seems likely.'

'So someone had it in for them big time. Was Jamila married?'

'Yes, to an Oxford University lecturer. They're getting divorced.'

'Aggrieved husband? You've questioned him?'

'About the Upton murder, yes. He has an alibi, but the timings of his whereabouts are open to question. I'll need to speak to him again.'

'Correction. I'll need to speak to him about Jamila. Someone murdered Oliver Upton on your patch... *your case*. Jamila Kazan was on my patch... *my case*. No offence, but my boss won't be happy if I didn't question Mr Kazan myself.'

'Fine, but I'd like to be present.'

'Okay. Be interesting if he can prove he was elsewhere this morning,' Gamez observed.

'Indeed. What's the story on Jamila?' Fleming asked.

'Call came in about ten. A couple of squad cars were in the vicinity and were on the scene in minutes.'

'Any witnesses?'

'Yeah. Another dog walker had been talking to Jamila when he heard a shot. He turned and saw her falling to the ground. He ran over to her and guessed she was dead. Two more walkers ran to help and one of them rang for the police.'

'Is that all the first man saw? Jamila falling to the ground? No sight of who might have shot her or from where?'

'No. Nick, the man who'd been talking to Jamila, said whoever shot her must have been hiding in the trees not far away.'

'Makes sense he wouldn't be out in the open.'

'Nick did say something else.'

'Go on.'

'Jamila's dog had been running around but stopped and bounded off towards the trees. Jamila had started to walk over to investigate and that's when the killer shot her.'

'Have you appealed for any other witnesses? The killer would have to have made a quick escape and, if it is the same person who shot Upton, he'd be carrying a rifle.'

'You know for sure whoever killed Upton used a rifle?'

'Remington Model 700 bolt-action sniper.'

'Not easy to hide, I agree. We've appealed for witnesses, but so far no one's come forward. SOCOs are still scouring the area for any shell casings or forensic evidence.'

'Any CCTV nearby?'

'No. I'm assuming the killer must have followed her from her sister's house. There's a CCTV camera at the end of the street, but guess what?'

'It's out of action?'

'Spot on.'

'How did you know she was staying at her sister's house?'

'She told Nick she was staying with her sister and the dog collar had her sister's address on it.'

'She decided to go and stay with her for a while after her partner was shot,' Fleming confirmed.

'Was she frightened of her husband?'

'They had a big row one day when Jamila went back to the house to collect some of her things. She reckoned he got quite angry and frightened her.'

'My bet is Kazan shot her. I'll come up to Oxford to question him. Can you fix it?'

'Sure,' Fleming said. 'But you might be looking for someone else if he can account for his whereabouts this morning. I'll let you know when you can come.'

'Thanks.'

On his way back to Oxford, Fleming was deep in thought.

How did the killer know where to find Jamila?

51

OXFORD

Either Atticus Kazan was innocent, or he was very confident. He'd declined the opportunity to have a solicitor present at the interview. Fleming had told him DI Gamez wanted to question him about the murder of his wife. Fleming had switched on the digital recorder before Gamez issued a caution to Kazan.

'You're not under arrest and are free to leave at any time. However, it would be helpful if you could answer my questions,' Gamez said.

Kazan smiled. 'I am aware of my rights.' He flashed a glance towards the DIR. 'And, for the record, you've not arrested me because you can't prove I killed my wife, because I didn't. If it will help find the killer, I'm happy to answer your questions.'

Gamez ignored this and looked inside the folder on the table in front of her. 'You and your wife were getting divorced. Is that because she had an affair with Oliver Upton and moved out of your house to live with him?'

'Yes.'

'There's no other reason?'

'What other reason could there be?'

'You tell me.'

'Isn't the fact she went to live with someone else enough reason?'

'You had a big row with her when she came back home to collect some things. She said you were angry.'

'I'm sure you would agree it would be normal to be angry if your wife left you to live with another man, would you not?'

Gamez ignored Kazan's question. 'Jamila said you frightened her. Were you violent towards her?'

'No.'

'You joined a rifle club soon after Jamila left you, didn't you?'

'I did, yes.' Kazan looked at Fleming. 'I've been through all this with–'

Gamez continued. 'Why? Why did you join the rifle club?'

Kazan looked back at Gamez. 'A colleague of mine is a member. He got me interested. Taking up a new hobby would help take my mind off things he reckoned.'

'You went to the club often. In fact, your last visit was two days before someone shot Oliver Upton. Is that correct?'

Kazan sighed. 'I'd already explained to DCI Fleming that I had to attend on a regular basis. It was one of the rules a new member had to follow.'

'Do you have a firearm licence?'

Kazan smiled again. 'I don't need one as I don't have a gun.'

'You lied about where you were on the morning someone shot Oliver Upton, did you not?'

'No. I made a mistake and mixed my days up.'

'You eventually recollected where you were and a witness has confirmed he spoke to you on the day you claimed. But the timing of that discussion doesn't rule out the fact you could have been elsewhere at the time of the murder.'

'A shame, I must admit, but DCI Fleming has no proof I was at the scene of the murder. Furthermore, he *will* never find such proof because I wasn't there and I didn't shoot Oliver Upton. Stalemate, wouldn't you say?' Kazan glared at Gamez. 'Anyway, why is going over old ground DCI Fleming covered when he questioned me about Upton relevant to your enquiry?'

'Just interested that you lied… sorry, made a mistake over your whereabouts and that it *is* possible you could have murdered Upton. You had the motive to kill him and your wife. Did you?'

Kazan shook his head. 'No.'

'Do you still attend the rifle club?'

'Yes, as a matter of fact I do. I rather enjoy it.'

'Where were you yesterday morning?'

'I didn't have any lectures planned so I took the day off.'

'Doesn't answer my question. Where were you if not at work?'

'At home.'

'Can anyone vouch for that?'

'No. I was on my own.'

Gamez looked at Fleming who shook his head.

'Okay, that's all for now, Mr Kazan. Interview terminated at two thirty.'

'What do you think?' Gamez asked Fleming later.

'I can get a warrant to search his house in relation to the Upton murder. Regarding Jamila, it would be easy to check whether he bought a train ticket to get to London. I can also arrange a check of CCTV cameras at the station and the roads out of Oxford and on the M40 if you like.'

'That would be helpful. Let me know how you get on.'

'Sure. I have a feeling you won't find anything which proves he was at the scene of Jamila's murder though.'

'What about your other leads? You said you had one or two.'

'I did for the murder of Oliver Upton, but I can't see they had any reason to want to kill Jamila as well. I'm beginning to think we could be looking for a hitman.'

52

BALCORIE

The early morning rain in Balcorie had given way to some sunshine. Large white clouds drifted across a blue sky and screaming seagulls swooped overhead. A couple of fishing boats were taking the opportunity of better weather to head out to sea. Waves hissed against the sandy shore as Ailsa made her way down to Toby's cottage.

She had reason to be uneasy about new male acquaintances, but now felt she could trust Toby. They had, after all, completed all the background checks on him. Character references had been exemplary as had the previous employer reference. The enhanced DBS check had shown no criminal record. There were no cautions, reprimands or warnings. Nor were there any spent or unspent convictions.

She'd also established Toby had never been to Scotland before so had no Scottish connections. Toby's background and difficult relationship with his mother all seemed genuine. Ailsa had grown fond of Toby as she found out more about him and got to know him better. She'd decided there was no need to worry.

~

Toby had been delighted Ailsa had suggested a walk. She'd checked on the weather the night before and it was looking fine. 'It's lovely along the beach out of Balcorie. When the tide's out you can go for about two miles under the cliffs,' she'd said. 'You'll need boots on though,' she'd warned. 'The sandy bay gives way to a shingle and rocky shoreline after a few hundred yards.'

Toby had grown to like Ailsa and had welcomed the opportunity to get some fresh air, explore the surroundings and enjoy her company. They chatted away as they strolled along the beach and it wasn't long before sand gave way to clumps of rock.

'This is one of my favourite places,' Ailsa said, starting to clamber up the rocks. Once on top, the surface was reasonably flat, making walking easy as long as you avoided the deep rock pools.

'I guess there are lots of different walks you can go on from Balcorie,' Toby said, panting behind Ailsa.

'Yeah. You can head off inland up into the hills. If you want a whole day out hiking, you can get to the foot of the mountains. Fantastic views!'

'I'll bet. I'd very much like to do that one day.'

'Be okay with your asthma?'

Toby smiled. 'Feeling better on that front already. The move from London has worked wonders.'

'Right... we'll get something arranged and get you up into the hills.'

'I'll look forward to it.'

'Look!' Ailsa pointed out to sea. 'Dolphins!'

Toby looked out to where Ailsa was pointing and saw four of them leaping through the waves. 'Wow! Never seen anything like that in real life.'

'If you get up into the mountains you might be lucky and catch sight of an eagle.'

'Can't wait.'

'How are things with your mother?' Ailsa asked.

Toby looked out to sea. 'Pretty much the same. She's trying her best to make me feel guilty for leaving. She'll get over it.'

'Sounds like she's being a bit selfish.'

'She is. Another reason why I had to break free. She can be very domineering.'

'Oh, meant to tell you, they've arranged a ceilidh in the village hall tomorrow night. Would you like to come with me? It'll be a good chance to meet some of the villagers and parents of the school kids. And… it's always a lot of fun.'

'Sounds great… love to co–'

The sudden sound of crashing rocks cut Toby short. He turned in alarm and saw rocks falling off the cliff.

'Don't worry,' Ailsa said. 'I made sure we kept well away from the bottom of the cliff. Rockfalls are quite frequent round here, especially after heavy rain.'

'Glad you told me.' Toby peered up to the top of the cliff. He thought he caught a glimpse of something, but then it was gone.

Ailsa saw him looking. 'What is it?'

'Nothing. Thought I saw something. Must be imagining things. By the way, I meant to ask you, did you enquire at the post office about the man who came in and said he was a friend? You seemed a bit concerned he might have been shown where you lived when Pherson told you about him.'

Ailsa seemed to think for a moment before answering. She frowned. 'I did ask. The postmistress gave me a description, but I didn't recognise it as anyone I knew.'

'Isn't it worrying? I mean someone you don't recognise turning up here asking where you live.'

Ailsa shuddered. 'Getting a bit colder. We should head back.'

'I guess so.' Toby thought for a moment. 'Pherson said the man claimed he hadn't seen you in years. Can you think who that might be?'

'No. There are only a few people who know I moved up here.'

Toby frowned and shot Ailsa a quizzical look. 'Any particular reason?'

Ailsa smiled. 'I'll tell you about it someday, but not today.'

The man on the top of the cliff cursed. His foot had caught a large stone and sent it tumbling down, taking some loose rocks with it. He dropped his binoculars onto his chest and stood back. He'd seen the man with Ailsa glance up, but felt sure he hadn't spotted him.

Making tracks back to his car, he felt the days reconnaissance had been worthwhile.

It's her for sure.

53

OXFORD

'H e didn't buy a train ticket to go to London on the morning of Jamila's murder,' Logan said, parking the car outside Atticus Kazan's house. 'CCTV cameras didn't spot his car on the roads out of Oxford or on the M40 either.'

'I have a feeling this could be a waste of time,' Fleming said, getting out of the car.

'Did the super ask you to get the warrant?'

'No, but she did query whether I had one to search Palmer's house. My guess is she would think it an oversight if I failed to get one to search Kazan's. I also told DI Gamez I would get a warrant.'

'Bit of a superficial search then?'

'You could be right. I didn't take to the man, but he's not stupid. I'd be surprised if he had any incriminating evidence in his house.'

Fleming rang the doorbell three times. Kazan, dressed in smart casual clothes and brown shoes, opened the door. 'Saw you coming. What do you want now? I've answered all your questions about Upton.'

Fleming showed Kazan the authorisation. 'We have a warrant to search your house,' he said.

Kazan took the document, examined it through narrow eyes, shook his head, and passed it back to Fleming. 'I can assure you there's no rifle here. You think I'd be stupid enough to keep it here if I had one?'

'No, but we'd like to search the premises anyway. There's a lot of circumstantial evidence pointing to you as a suspect for the murders of Oliver Upton and your wife. We want to search your house to see if there's any evidence you had the means to do so.'

'Your so-called evidence is somewhat flimsy, I have to say. My wife left me for another man. Not a particularly unique event.'

'You either lied about your whereabouts on the morning of Oliver Upton's murder, or you confused the days as you claimed.'

'It was a mistake. How many times do I have to tell you?'

'Your second explanation doesn't entirely rule you out as a suspect. There's also the fact no one can confirm you were at home when someone shot your wife. Under the circumstances, a search of your house is justifiable.'

'Then you must do what you have to do,' Kazan said, waving a hand to usher the two detectives into the house. 'I could save you the trouble though. You won't find anything.'

'I'll take downstairs and you take upstairs,' Fleming told Logan.

Logan made his way to the staircase with Kazan shouting after him. 'I expect to find my things as I left them.'

'Sure,' Logan muttered over his shoulder.

Fleming browsed round the living room. There were some photos on the window ledge. One looked like it might have been of Kazan with his parents in Greece. Another was of Kazan's graduation. There was one of Kazan at the rifle club, but none of

Jamila. Fleming couldn't help but notice they were all spaced the same distance apart. Kazan had divided the books in the bookcase into fiction and non-fiction, each genre filed in alphabetical order of author.

Having completed a cursory scan of the living room, Fleming wandered into the kitchen with Kazan following him. He had a glance inside all the kitchen units under the worktop, before opening the first wall unit.

'Think you're going to find a rifle in there, Fleming?' Kazan mocked.

'Doubt it. Maybe a pack of bullets hidden amongst the tins, eh?' Fleming teased.

Kazan was a meticulous and methodical man. Soup and vegetable tins were all lined up with labels facing outwards in one cabinet. He'd stored tins of fruit in a separate unit, all in neat lines, as were spices and herbs in another cabinet. All labels were facing outwards.

'Find any bullets then?' Kazan taunted.

Fleming closed the last wall unit door. 'Nope. Lucky you, eh?'

Kazan was about to say something when Logan reappeared. 'Nothing upstairs, boss.'

'Could have told you that,' Kazan sneered. 'Hope you've left all my things neat and tidy.'

'Of course,' Logan retorted.

'About all done then,' Fleming said. 'Just the cupboard under the stairs in the hallway and we're finished.'

Fleming opened the cupboard door. Coats hung on hooks on the back wall and a wooden rack contained a mix of casual and smart shoes. An ironing board leaned against the wall to the right of the door and next to it was a golf bag full of clubs. There was one section empty apart from a short black towel stuffed in the top.

'What do you keep in here?' Fleming asked Kazan, pointing at the empty section.

'Nothing. I don't have a full set of clubs.'

'Okay. That's all for now, Mr Kazan. We'll let ourselves out.'

'Total waste of time, as you predicted,' Logan said back in the car. 'Notice how neat everywhere is? Touch of OCD, do you think?'

'Could be, if the way he keeps his kitchen is anything to go by. One thing did interest me though.'

'What?'

'His golf bag had an empty compartment with a towel over the top... big enough to hide a rifle.'

54

EDINBURGH

'What do you think he's got?' Big Col Calhoun asked his solicitor as they were getting out of the car at Gayfield Square police station.

'The first thing you need to know is you have volunteered to attend. DI Aitken hasn't arrested you for any alleged offence so you can leave at any time.'

'So why did you say I should attend?'

'If you refused, he could arrest you and you would have no choice. Best to avoid arrest at this stage. Find out exactly what he has.'

'Did he give you any disclosure of evidence?'

'He's being a wee bit canny. As Aitken hasn't arrested you or charged you with anything, he's withheld details on the basis it might prejudice his investigation.'

'And this is to do with drugs and gun smuggling?'

'It is.'

'He's got nothing. Came to my club one night asking about Jenner Transport and said he was making enquiries. He had some notion someone had suggested I had links to Jenner.'

'And that's it?'

'He seemed to think Jenner had a hand in it. I guess he was probing to see if I did have any dealings with him. Didn't surprise me. Aitken's been trying to pin stuff on me for years. Bloody harassment if you ask me.'

'Don't let him rile you into saying something stupid.'

'No policeman ever has, and never will. I'm far too smart for them.'

'Then let's go in and see what he's got.'

'They're here,' DC Schultze said.

DI Aitken and DS Quigley were in Aitken's office drinking coffee. 'Stick them in interview room one,' Aitken said.

Schultze nodded and made to leave.

'Tell them we'll be down in a minute.'

'Okay.'

'Think he'll panic and slip up?' Quigley asked.

'He's a devious customer. Hasn't ever slipped up so far. He always seems one step ahead of the law,' Aitken said. 'Typical gangland boss. He rules by fear. No one seems willing to testify against him... until now.'

'I suppose Jenner has nothing to lose and thinks he has something to gain by spilling the beans. By the way, has young DC Schultze come up with anything yet on your old mate's plea for help in finding any record of this guy Upton?'

'He found a few people by that name on old electoral registers, but he hasn't been able to find an Oliver Upton who worked for an Edinburgh taxi firm yet.'

'How do you think you'll play this?' Quigley asked.

'I'll ask questions in a scattergun approach. See what comes out of it, then hit him with Jenner's statement.'

'Think he'll buckle and confess under pressure?'

'I doubt it. His solicitor will make sure he doesn't say anything stupid. But maybe I'll get him worried. Let him know we're getting closer to putting him behind bars at last.'

'We'd better not keep them waiting. He's liable to get up and go if he gets impatient.'

Five minutes later, the two detectives sat opposite Calhoun and his solicitor. Quigley switched on the digital recorder. Aitken read out the introductions, and stated the date time and place before cautioning Calhoun.

'I'm making enquiries into drugs and gun smuggling,' Aitken started. 'You have wide connections in the city. Ever hear anything from them about that?'

'I object,' the solicitor said. 'You are trying to imply my client's contacts are likely to be of, shall we say, dubious character.'

'Not at all,' Aitken retorted. 'Anyone can gossip. It's not restricted to people of ill repute.'

'Even so, I'd be grateful if you'd make your questions less suggestive.'

Aitken looked up from his notes and stared at Calhoun. 'You recently attended a black-tie dinner party.'

Calhoun smiled. 'And very enjoyable it was.'

'I understand a prominent councillor organised it. Is that the friend of yours you told me about at your club?'

'He is yes. What's that got to do with the case you're working on?'

Aitken ignored the question. 'You told me the assistant chief constable, Ramsay Irvin, was there. Is that correct?'

'Yes, he was there.'

'Did you speak to him?'

'No.'

'I guess he knew who you were and thought it best not to be associated with you, eh?'

'I object!' the solicitor blurted out. 'You are implying once again that my client is someone the police would not want to have anything to do with.'

'I'm not implying. It's a fact. I spoke to the assistant chief constable. He said he didn't know your client would be there. He said it was embarrassing for him to be at the same event, but could hardly leave under the circumstances.'

'What circumstances?' the solicitor asked.

'Because the councillor who organised the dinner happened to be friendly with the council chief executive.'

'I still don't see what point you're trying to make,' the solicitor said.

'I wanted to establish whether your client had any contact with Ramsay Irvin.' Looking at Calhoun. 'Have you ever had any contact or dealings with him?'

Calhoun shook his head. 'This is crazy. What the fuck's this got to do with anything?'

'Have you?' Aitken pressed.

'No.'

'When I saw you at your club you seemed to be gloating about the fact you'd been to a black-tie dinner where Irvin was present.'

'So?'

'Like you wanted to suggest you moved in the same circles.'

'Rubbish.'

'There is another explanation why Irvin wouldn't want anyone to see him speaking to you.'

'There is?'

'He wouldn't want anyone to think he had any dealings with you. *Has* he?'

'I've already told you, I don't have any dealings with him.'

Aitken changed the subject. 'Doug Jenner who owns Jenner Transport was there, was he not?'

'He was, yes.'

'Did you talk to him?'

'I may have done. I spoke to a lot of people.'

'What did you talk to Jenner about?'

'This and that. We both have our own business, so we were exchanging notes on how well things were going.'

'And how *is* your business doing?'

Calhoun shook his head again. 'I thought you were investigating drugs and gun smuggling. What's my business got to do with it?'

'Has your business got anything to do with it... or Jenner Transport?'

'No.'

Aitken decided to change tack again before pressing Calhoun further. 'You ever hear of a taxi driver in Edinburgh by the name of Oliver Upton?'

Calhoun stiffened and his eyes narrowed. 'What the hell has a taxi driver got to do with your investigation?'

'Just checking up on something. Thought you had a lot of contacts in Edinburgh and might've heard of him.'

'I haven't.'

'Doug Jenner met a man at his depot and a witness heard them talking about a consignment of drugs and guns. Was that man you?'

Calhoun looked uncertain for a second before answering. 'No. The witness must have been mistaken.'

'The witness didn't see the other man, but I know it was you.'

Calhoun smiled. 'If the witness didn't see who it was, how come you're so sure it was me?'

'Because Jenner said it was.' Aitken tapped the folder in front of him. 'I have in here a sworn statement from him. Seems he's willing to spill the beans in return for some leniency. He says you're the brains behind the drugs and gun smuggling operation.'

Calhoun's mouth dropped open.

Aitken continued. 'Claims you approached him some time ago to use his freight lorry to smuggle them in. You offered him a big cut of the proceeds in return.'

Calhoun looked as though he'd recovered from the shock that Jenner had shopped him. 'I know what's happening here. He knows you're looking for any excuse to put me away. The pair of you have concocted this ridiculous story so you can stitch me up in return for going easy on Jenner.'

'I think we're done here,' Calhoun's solicitor said, 'unless you think you have enough evidence to charge my client. All you have is the testimony of a criminal you've already arrested.'

'Fine,' Aitken said. 'You're free to go. Interview terminated at 10.30am.'

'He's right,' Aitken said after Calhoun and his solicitor had gone. 'Not enough concrete evidence to charge him... yet.'

55

OXFORD

Temple was on the phone when Fleming knocked and walked into her office. She waved him in and listened for a few more seconds. 'Okay, ma'am,' she said, and put the phone down.

'Chief constable?' Fleming asked.

'Yes. She wants to know what you found out from DI Gamez. Get anything useful?'

'Too early. The Met has issued an appeal for any witnesses to come forward, but no one has so far. Gamez seems to have come to the hasty conclusion that it must've been Kazan. She came up to question him and went through all the same stuff I asked him about when I questioned him over Upton. She didn't find anything other than no one could verify his whereabouts on the morning Jamila was shot. Said he was at home on his own.'

Temple sighed. 'So I've nothing to tell the chief constable?'

'I got DS Logan to run some checks. We can neither prove nor disprove Kazan was at home. But we know he didn't buy a train ticket for London, and CCTV cameras didn't pick up his car on the roads out of Oxford or on the M40.'

'No forensic evidence so far and nothing to prove he was at the scene. How can DI Gamez be so sure it was him?'

'Motive. That's about all. We searched his house to see if we could find anything to link him to Upton's murder, but Logan and I found nothing except...'

'What?'

'Nothing conclusive, just a thought.'

'Go on.'

'There was a golf bag in a downstairs cupboard. One compartment was empty. I wondered how the killer might have managed to disappear from the scene with a rifle and found out there's a nine-hole golf course on Clapham Common. It wouldn't have been open, but the killer could have turned up with a golf bag claiming he didn't know if anyone challenged him. A rifle could have fitted in the empty compartment in Kazan's golf bag.'

'Hardly evidence, and you can't put him at the scene of the crime anyway.'

'As I said... just a thought.'

'You questioned Kazan about it though?'

'Yes. He said he doesn't have a full set of clubs.'

'What about the taxi driver, Raj Syed. Has he been able to account for his whereabouts on the days Upton and Jamila Kazan were shot?'

'I have a witness who says Syed drove her home from Oxford train station around the time of Upton's murder. A colleague of Syed's confirms they were at a café before going on taxi duty on the morning someone shot Jamila.'

'Palmer?'

'On the film set.'

'Great. One by one your potential suspects are fading off the radar. Where the hell does that leave us?'

'I'm beginning to think we could be looking for a hitman.

Palmer may have had a motive to kill Upton, but not Jamila. Likewise, Syed. Maybe Kazan hired someone to kill them both.'

'Where do you go from here then?'

'Jamila's killer must have known she was staying with her sister in London. I need to find out who knew that, and who found out.'

'Be careful you don't encroach on DI Gamez's investigation. Don't forget, Jamila's murder is her case.'

'I know but we both may be looking for the same killer. I'll share any information.'

'Okay. How do you propose to find out who knew where Jamila was staying in London?'

'I'll speak to Jamila's sister. See if she knows who Jamila might have told, and track them all down. I'm going off with Logan and Anderson next to see if Jamila told any neighbours where she was going.'

'And make sure you keep DI Gamez informed.'

'You check the houses across the road,' Fleming told Anderson. He nodded to Logan. 'I'll take the ones to the right of Upton's place. You take the ones to the left.'

They'd come in a marked car and had parked up the street in the nearest available space. Fleming saw curtains twitch as he watched Anderson cross the road. 'Tongues will be wagging,' Logan said as he headed for his first house.

Fleming went through a metal gate leading to the house next door to Upton's and knocked on a heavy door knocker. No one came to the door. Fleming knocked again. Still no answer. He looked across the road to see Anderson coming away from her first house. She shook her head.

Logan shouted across to Fleming. 'No joy here. They didn't know where she'd gone.'

Fleming tried the next house. An elderly man, stooped and wearing baggy trousers, shirt and cardigan came to the door. He looked at Fleming through watery eyes. 'Yes?'

Fleming showed his warrant card. 'DCI Fleming from Thames Valley Police. I wanted to ask you about the woman who lives at number twenty-nine.'

'Don't know anything about her. See her coming and going. Never spoken to her apart from saying hello. As a matter of fact, I know nothing about her partner either. We had a uniformed officer knocking on all the doors asking about him a few weeks ago. Told him I didn't know anything.'

'I wondered if she told anyone where she'd gone to stay for a while. I don't suppose she told you?'

The old man shook his head. 'Why would she do that?'

'Sometimes people let their neighbours know when they're going away for a while.'

'She didn't tell me, or the missus.'

'Okay. Thank you for your time.'

'She may have told Betty next door,' the man said, pointing a thumb to his right. 'I often saw them talking together.'

'There's no one in. I don't suppose you know when she'll be back?'

'No idea.'

Fleming smiled. 'I'll try again later.'

He looked across the road again and received another shake of the head from Anderson.

Fleming had tried another two doors without any luck when he saw a middle-aged woman coming along the street carrying two shopping bags. He watched her push through the metal gate of the house next to Upton's. Fleming followed. 'Excuse me.'

The woman turned and gave Fleming a questioning look. 'Yes?'

Fleming showed his warrant card. 'DCI Fleming from Thames Valley Police. Have you got a minute?'

The woman put down her bags. 'Sure, but we've already had the police here asking about Mr Upton.'

'It's not him I want to ask about. I wondered if Jamila told you where she was going to stay for a while.'

The woman frowned. 'She did yes. Went to stay with her sister in London she told me. Why?'

'Did she say where in London? Give an address?'

'Yes. She gave me a key to the house here and asked me to forward any mail. Is there something wrong?'

'Someone shot Jamila dead on Clapham Common two days ago.'

'Oh my God!' the woman gasped. 'I... I don't believe it.'

'The thing is,' Fleming said, 'the killer knew where she was staying. Did you happen to tell anyone where she was?'

The woman went pale. 'Oh God!' she uttered again. 'Yes, I did. A man came round asking about her. He said he was an insurance agent and needed to contact her because she was the beneficiary of a life insurance policy Mr Upton had taken out. I rang Jamila to tell her.'

'Did the man leave a business card or say which company he was from?'

'No.'

'Had you seen him before?'

'No.'

'Did he give a name?'

'No.'

'What did he look like?'

'Oh, dear. Tall, well dressed in a flashy suit.'

'Hair?'

'Brownish, short.'

'Age?'

'Youngish, but not too young. Maybe thirties.'

'Build?'

'Not fat, but not skinny either. Well-built I suppose.' The woman's face reddened. 'Bit like you.'

'Anything else you can remember about him?'

'Yes... he had a Scottish accent.'

56

BALCORIE

Toby was sure the cleaner and fresher air in Balcorie was helping his asthma. He hadn't had an attack since being there. His relationship with Ailsa was blossoming into a close friendship. The relationship with his mother however was not improving. He'd phoned her the morning before Ailsa had taken him off on a long hike up into the hills. His mother had claimed she was feeling ill and couldn't cope. She'd begged him to come back to London. Toby had ended the call wondering if his mother would ever give up trying to get him to go back home.

The walk with Ailsa had lifted his spirits, and they'd enjoyed a fish and chip supper before setting off for the ceilidh in the village hall. It was a brick building covered in white render and had a slate roof. A single wooden door led into an outer hallway. Moira, the postmistress, sat behind a small table where she took entrance fees and sold raffle tickets.

Through double doors, there was a small area with a few tables and a kitchen area. Two more double doors led into the main rectangular hall. Tables and chairs lined the walls down each side. There was a raised platform at the far end where three musicians were busy tuning up.

Once everyone was in and seated, Pherson stood up on the stage and took a microphone in his hand. He tapped it a couple of times to test if it was working and began to speak. The chatter around the hall ceased.

'Good evening, everyone. Thank you all for coming and buying raffle tickets. We have loads of good prizes to give away later. There'll be the usual roll a pound coin to win a bottle of whisky for the person who gets the nearest coin to the bottle. All proceeds will be going to the village hall fund and the school.'

There was a round of applause.

'Tonight, we have our own resident Balcorie ceilidh band, The Highlanders. They'll be playing all your favourite barn dance tunes.'

Loud cheers and a banging of glasses on tables followed.

'We have Hamish on the fiddle, Moira on the accordion, and Bruce on the drums.'

More cheers and banging of glasses.

'And, of course,' Pherson continued, 'we have our very own professional caller, Finlay. He'll be making sure you get all the dance routines right, aided with his usual indomitable sense of humour.'

A round of clapping ensued.

'I hope you've all brought enough liquid refreshment because, as you know, we don't have a licence to sell alcohol.'

People raised their glasses to the air to show they had, indeed, brought their own drinks.

Toby had been a little nervous about meeting with a large group of people who all knew each other, but he soon overcame his coyness. Ailsa introduced him to so many people whose names he was not going to remember in one night. Men and women shook his hand and gave him the sort of welcome you'd expect from someone who had been absent for years.

Toby sat beside Ailsa with two other couples and Pherson's wife, enjoying the atmosphere already. Ailsa squeezed his hand as Pherson was about to speak again.

'And tonight, I have great pleasure in welcoming a newcomer to our village, the new school teacher, Toby Enderby!'

Toby reddened as the hall filled with applause. He felt overcome by the outburst of emotion. With a shaky hand, he took a swig of the whisky Ailsa had brought. 'Oh God,' he whispered to her, 'he's not going to ask me to speak, is he?'

'Don't worry, I told him not to.'

Toby smiled and returned the squeeze on Ailsa's hand. This was how life should be.

Pherson handed the microphone to Finlay and returned to the table, winking at Toby.

Finlay got straight down to business. 'Is everyone ready for the first dance of the evening? Let's have you all up on the floor.'

Toby looked at Ailsa. 'I've no idea what to do.'

Ailsa smiled. 'Don't worry. Most people only have a rough idea, but tend to forget the steps between ceilidhs. Getting it wrong is all part of the fun.'

Indeed, the first dance was a shambles. There were lots of animated hand signals and gesticulating. People turned the wrong way and resorted to fits of laughter. Finlay soldiered on through the chaos, trying to get things back on track. Eventually it all came together and the dance concluded with everyone more or less in step. Even Toby was getting the hang of it.

More dances followed. There were fewer scenes of chaos as Finlay cajoled everyone into shape. Toby soon got into the spirit of things and was enjoying himself. He was more and more intoxicated with the atmosphere and the whisky as the night wore on.

After several dances, Finlay announced a break for the band. 'We'll take fifteen minutes. If anyone wants to go out for some fresh air and enjoy the sunset, please feel free. See you all back here in fifteen for some more dancing!'

'Shall we?' Ailsa asked Toby. 'I mean, go out and see the sunset. It can be spectacular.'

Toby poured another drop of whisky into their glasses. 'Sure. Take these with us?'

Ailsa smiled. 'Why not.'

They took their drinks and followed a stream of other people who'd decided to do the same thing. The small crowd watched as the bright yellow ball of the sun began to sink below the horizon, casting a yellow hue across the sea on the skyline. The dark grey clouds in the sky became tinged in bright orange. 'Beautiful,' someone murmured. 'Who would want to be anywhere else?'

Toby heard the remark and raised his glass. 'I'll drink to that.' He clinked glasses with Ailsa. 'Thanks,' he said.

'What for?'

'Bringing me here. I don't just mean the ceilidh. I mean here in Balcorie. Best thing I ever did.'

Ailsa smiled. 'I'm glad you came. Shall we go back in before we get cold?'

A few minutes after returning to their table, things were soon underway again. Toby and Ailsa enjoyed taking part in several more dances before Finlay announced it was time to roll the pound coins for the bottle of whisky. Toby watched as one person after another got up and rolled their coins across the floor towards the whisky bottle.

'Technique... they've all got the wrong technique,' Toby said.

'You've played this before?' Ailsa asked.

'No... just observed. See how their coins go straight for a

while, then veer off to the left or right and get nowhere near the bottle.'

'What would *your* technique be?'

'Roll it fast at the bottle, hit it, and the coin should drop next to it.' Toby got a pound coin out of his pocket and showed it to Ailsa. 'Watch and learn.'

Ailsa laughed. 'You've had a few drams. Bet you miss.'

Toby winked at Ailsa and lined up to roll his coin. He pulled his arm back, swung it forwards and released the coin from his hand. It went in a straight line, but missed the bottle by inches. 'Good try,' Finlay said. 'Anyone else?'

The nearest coin was sitting about six inches from the bottle. 'No one's going to beat that,' someone said.

Toby produced another coin from his pocket. 'One more go.' He rolled again and the coin sped towards the bottle. It hit dead centre and bounced back a couple of inches before settling on the floor.

'We have a winner!' Finlay shouted. There were loud cheers and clapping as Toby accepted the bottle and returned to the table with Ailsa. Dancing resumed for another hour before Finlay announced it was time for the raffle and the end of the evening.

Toby and Ailsa didn't win anything and left the hall after saying goodbye to everyone. They were about to set off for Ailsa's flat when there was a loud bang. Ailsa jumped and grabbed Toby's arm.

Toby looked round. 'It's okay. Just a motorbike engine backfiring.'

Ailsa took a deep breath. 'Sorry... gave me a shock.'

Toby took Ailsa back to her flat before making his way to his cottage. He closed the front door behind him and frowned. *Why is she so jumpy?*

57

LONDON

Fleming had decided to drive down to London to see Jamila's sister. He'd checked with DI Gamez, but it seemed she had made no progress with her investigation. She was still waiting to see if any witnesses came forward. The SOCOs hadn't found any forensic evidence. He'd told her about the man claiming to be an insurance agent needing to find out where Jamila was staying. How his description didn't fit any of Fleming's suspects.

Before she'd asked, Fleming confirmed he hadn't found any record of an insurance policy amongst Upton's papers. Bearing in mind she had Atticus Kazan down as her number one suspect, Fleming had told her the search of his house had revealed nothing. Neither had he found anything to show he'd left Oxford on the day Jamila was shot.

Fleming found a parking space not far from Zaina Mwangi's house. A dog barked as soon as he rang the bell. A few seconds later, a chubby woman of medium height with short jet-black hair came to the door. The jeans and white shirt she wore seemed a bit on the tight side. Fleming guessed she was in her fifties.

'If you're a reporter, I have nothing to say to you,' she said.

Fleming showed his warrant card. 'DCI Fleming. You're expecting me.'

'Oh, sorry. Reporters have been pestering me. Like bloody vultures.'

Fleming smiled. 'I must admit they can be irritating.'

Winston had stopped barking and was wagging his tail as he tried to get to Fleming. Zaina pulled him back. 'Sorry, he gets excited when he sees someone new. He'll settle down in a minute. Come in.' Zaina turned to walk down the hallway into the sitting room. She pointed to a dog basket in a corner and Winston wandered across the room and slumped into it.

'Very obedient dog,' Fleming said.

'Yeah. We've trained him well. He was a bit traumatised when Jamila...'

Zaina's voice faltered. She pulled out a handkerchief to dab her eyes. 'Poor thing. They said he lay down beside Jamila and wouldn't leave her.'

'I'm sorry for your loss,' Fleming said. 'Are you up to answering a few questions?'

'Sure. Have a seat. Can I get you a drink?'

'I'm fine, thanks. Don't want to put you to any bother.'

Zaina sat opposite Fleming. 'I've already spoken to DI Gamez from the Met. Are you working with her on this?'

'Not so much working together. There's a connection between two separate cases we're looking at. I'm investigating the murder of Oliver Upton, Jamila is DI Gamez's case. Exchanging information would be more accurate.'

'I'm not sure I can tell you anything I haven't told her.'

'Jamila's murder is her case, but I'd like to get some background on Jamila. See if what happened here throws any light on my investigation into Oliver Upton's murder.'

'Of course.'

'Is your husband here?'

'No. He's had to go over to his mother's. She's ill.'

'I'm sorry to hear that. This must be a difficult time for you.'

'It is. First Oliver, then Jamila... Faraji's mother. What next?'

'Sure you're okay?'

Zaina nodded. 'Why would anyone want to kill Oliver and Jamila. I'm assuming it *is* the same person. It has to be, hasn't it?'

'I'm sure you're right. Seems too much of a coincidence otherwise. Apart from anything else, the killer used a rifle in both cases.'

Zaina shuddered. 'Dreadful business.'

'Jamila and her husband had been married for twenty-two years. Did you see much of him during that time?'

'Not a great deal, us being down here in London and Jamila and Atticus up in Oxford. Maybe a couple of times a year.'

'What did you think of him?'

'He was okay, I suppose. Bit dull, serious, very methodical. Could be ingratiating at times. Only thought of himself and his work.'

'Is that why Jamila left him, do you think?'

'I guess so. Jamila and I used to speak often on the phone. She'd started telling me how the marriage had gone stale. She reckoned Atticus was obsessed with his work and had lost interest in her.'

'Did Atticus strike you as a jealous man?'

'I had no reason to believe so, no.'

'Did you ever see him lose his temper?'

'Jamila said he had a bit of a temper, but nothing serious.'

'Did Jamila tell you she was leaving her husband to go and live with Oliver Upton?'

'She did, yes.'

'Did she say how Atticus had reacted?'

'Not well. He was angry.'

'Did Jamila tell you about the row they had when she went to the house to pick up some of her things? She reckoned he became agitated... angry. He frightened her.'

'She told me about it, yes.'

'Did Jamila have any communication with Atticus while she was here?'

'Not that I know of.'

'He didn't know she was here?'

'She didn't tell him, if that's what you mean.'

Someone outside shouted and Winston stood up and barked.

Fleming smiled. 'Good guard dog. Have there been any occasions since Jamila arrived when he started barking for no apparent reason?'

'No, not really. Oh my God! You're not thinking her killer was trying to get in, are you?'

Fleming pondered this for a second. 'Jamila had taken Winston out for a walk and no one would have known she was going to Clapham Common at that precise time. Her killer must have known she was here and was watching the house. He must have followed her there.'

'Are you thinking it was Atticus?'

'He's a person we're looking at as a potential suspect. Did Jamila talk to you about Oliver?'

'Oh, yes. She kept saying how happy she was after she'd left Atticus.'

'Did she tell you all about Oliver? How they met, his background, that sort of thing?'

Zaina frowned. 'Now you mention it, she never did tell me anything about his background. She would tell me what he looked like, how he drove taxis for Andy Cabs, what they did together, but she never said anything about his past.'

'You never met him?'

'No.'

'Did she ever say anything about him maybe seeming worried or anxious?'

'No.'

'He never received any threats?'

'She never said so, no.'

'How did Jamila seem when she arrived here?'

'Upset, confused... quieter than usual. Not surprising... someone had murdered her partner.'

'Did she get any phone calls while she was here?'

'Not on my landline, no. She could have taken a call on her mobile though.'

'Did she ever mention a life insurance policy Oliver had taken out with her as the beneficiary?'

Zaina shook her head. 'No.'

'I checked with Jamila's neighbours up in Oxford. One of them told me a man had called round saying he was from an insurance company. He wanted to know where he could find her.'

'No one came looking...'

Zaina trailed off as realisation dawned on her.

'I think it could have been the killer,' Fleming said.

Zaina gasped. 'Oh my God!'

'I have a description of the man. It wasn't Atticus.'

'So why'd you say he was a potential suspect?'

'He could have found someone to kill Oliver and Jamila for him.'

'You mean a professional hitman?'

'People do resort to that. Thing is, Oliver had a Scottish accent... so did this man. Did Jamila ever mention a Scottish connection?'

Another shake of the head. 'No.'

'Okay, Zaina. You've been very helpful. Thank you. Once again, I'm so sorry about your sister.'

On the drive back to Oxford, Fleming made a mental note to check with DI Aitken. It seemed the Scottish connection was all he had to go on for now.

58

EDINBURGH

'You said on the phone you had some information for me,' DS McCabe said, sitting opposite DI Aitken in the small meeting room at Gayfield Square.

'I do. Remember I told you Jenner had tried to kill his wife because she overheard a conversation between him and another man discussing a shipment of guns and drugs?'

'I remember. You said Jenner had gone on the run.'

'You haven't heard then?'

'What?'

'We've found him. He was holding a man hostage on a boat at Port Edgar Marina. I've charged him with assault, kidnapping, and drugs and gun smuggling.'

McCabe shook his head. 'Why only charge him with assault, I thought you said he tried to kill his wife?'

'Bit of bargaining.'

'Over what?'

'Testifying against Calhoun.'

McCabe hesitated. 'Over the drugs and gun smuggling?'

'Yes. Jenner's wife had gone round to her husband's depot to take him some lunch when she overheard him talking to another man about it.'

McCabe frowned. 'So why'd Jenner assault her?'

'Jenner and the other man were discussing a shipment of drugs and guns. The other man wanted Jenner to pick it up from the Netherlands. Jenner's wife tackled him about it after the other man had left. She told him he was stupid to get involved and she was going to go to the police.'

'Know who this other man is?'

'I'll come back to that. First, I want to ask you about DI Taylor's old investigation into Jenner.'

'What about it?'

'Remind me what it was about.'

'Sure. Taylor was still fishing for information about Calhoun and thought Jenner had links to him. Came to nothing and he ditched it. Closed the files. I think it was because he was coming up to retirement and didn't want to leave loose ends.'

Aitken sighed. 'Okay, can you pass the files over to me?'

'Sure, no problem. You were going to tell me about the other man and drugs and gun smuggling. What evidence have you got, apart from the wife's claim she overheard her husband talking to another man about a shipment?'

'A confession. That was the bargain I struck with Jenner. I suspected from the start that Calhoun was behind it all. Jenner spilled the beans hoping to get me to reduce a charge of attempted murder against his wife to assault. He's signed a statement saying Calhoun asked him to use his lorry for smuggling in drugs and guns in return for a cut of the proceeds. Calhoun was the other man he was talking to at the depot. Says he's prepared to testify against him.'

'Wow! A result! Have you arrested Calhoun?'

'No, not yet. The claims of a man who's already facing a

prison sentence aren't enough. A smart lawyer will say there's no concrete evidence. They'll say we obtained Jenner's confession because he thought he could bargain with the police.'

'What about his wife's claims?'

'Lawyer will say it's all lies. He'll say she wanted to get back at her husband for assaulting her.'

'You've questioned Calhoun though?'

'Yes. He has admitted he knew Jenner well enough to talk business with him when they met at the black-tie dinner.'

'But not that they were discussing drugs and gun shipments, I'll bet.'

'I doubt it.'

'And that's all you have? One meeting between Jenner and Calhoun, and two statements a lawyer could challenge? No other witnesses or forensic evidence?'

'No, just another little snippet of information.'

'Oh?'

'Jenner's wife said the man talking to her husband at the depot had a black car. Calhoun has a black car.'

McCabe shook his head. 'You haven't got a strong enough case to charge Calhoun, have you?'

'Not yet.'

'What are you going to do now?'

'Calhoun has another shipment of drugs and guns to pick up. He can't use Jenner, so he'll need to find someone else. We'll keep him under surveillance... see who he contacts.'

'And?'

'Pore over all your old files when you send them to me. Get forensic examination of Calhoun's and Jenner's accounts and get a check done on their bank statements. Calhoun must have found a way to pay Jenner for his services. And there must be large deposits from whoever Calhoun sold drugs and guns to.'

'Good luck with that,' McCabe said, getting up to leave. 'I'll get those files over to you, but I doubt you'll find anything useful.'

59

OXFORD

'I can't believe what's been happening,' Wanda Ingram, Jamila's manager, said, taking a seat behind her desk. She pulled off her black-framed spectacles and flicked a strand of short red hair from her eyes. 'First Jamila's partner and now poor old Jamila as well. It's beyond belief.' She pointed to a chair on the other side of her desk. 'Please, have a seat, Mr Fleming... or should I be addressing you as DCI Fleming?'

'Either is okay,' Fleming said, noting that Ingram's blouse and skirt matched the colour of her glasses. In contrast, large silver earrings dangled like chandeliers from her ears. Fleming reckoned she was in her early forties.

'I wanted to make sure. Some dons are a bit precious about people addressing them as professor rather than mister. Not all though. I am on first name terms with a few.'

Fleming smiled. 'Don't worry. I just wanted to ask a few questions about Jamila.'

'Of course.'

'Did you know she was going to stay with her sister?'

'Yes. She took a couple of weeks annual leave after Oliver's murder, but I told her to take as much time as she needed.'

'Did you happen to tell anyone else here she was going to London?'

'No. I didn't know she'd gone there. I only knew she was going to stay with her sister. Didn't realise where that was.'

'How long have you been Jamila's manager?'

'Since I came to work here, about five years ago.'

'What's your role exactly?'

'I act as the contact point for faculty members' funding applications, and work with the researchers in the faculty of history.'

'Jamila had been a researcher for about twenty-five years. Is that right?'

'I believe so, yes. They told me when I arrived here that she was good at what she did.'

'How well did you get to know her on a personal basis?'

Ingram furrowed her brow. 'Quite well, I suppose. We didn't socialise though, if that's what you mean.'

'You knew she was married to one of the lecturers at the university?'

'Atticus, yes.'

'Did Jamila ever talk about him? About their relationship?'

'Not at first. Only that they met at the university.'

'Did she speak about him more recently?'

Ingram hesitated. 'She did, yes.'

'Did she tell you her marriage was in trouble?'

'A few months ago I noticed a change in her. She'd become less gregarious, kept more to herself. Lost her smile. I asked her if something was bothering her. That's when she told me she'd met someone else and was thinking of leaving Atticus.'

'Did she tell you she'd moved in with Oliver Upton?'

'Later, yes.'

'And did she appear a bit more like her old self afterwards?'

Ingram smiled. 'Yes, she did, bless her.'

'Did she ever elaborate on what the problem was with her husband?'

Ingram shrugged. 'Not in great detail. She said he'd become dull and only thought about his work. Thought he'd lost interest in her.'

'Did you know Atticus well?'

'No. We spoke a couple of times at Christmas parties and other work events.'

'When Jamila said her marriage was more or less over, did she tell you how Atticus was reacting?'

'She told me he got angry when she left him.'

'Did she say he'd ever been violent towards her?'

'No... never.'

'Did Jamila tell you about the row she had with Atticus when she went back home to pick up some of her things?'

'Yes.' Ingram narrowed her eyes. 'Are you treating Atticus as a suspect?'

'We need to follow up on every lead which includes getting background information on victims and anyone associated with them.'

Ingram sighed. 'I understand that. Atticus would be angry with Jamila and Oliver Upton, but angry enough to kill them?'

'I've known people to kill for less.'

'You haven't arrested him though, have you?'

'No. As I said, we're just following up on every piece of information we get.'

'Of course.'

'Did you know Atticus had joined a rifle club?'

Ingram gasped. 'No, I didn't. Oh my God! You *do* think it was him behind both murders.'

'Mrs Ingram, I'd be grateful if you kept this conversation confidential. Wouldn't want idle gossip or rumours flying around. It could prejudice our investigation.

Mr Kazan is just someone we need to rule out as a potential suspect.'

'Don't worry. You should know though that there's speculation circling the university about who the killer could be. Atticus's name keeps cropping up.'

'Do you happen to know if any of Atticus's friends or colleagues are Scottish?'

'There are a few Scots around the university, but I wouldn't know if any of them are close to Atticus. Any particular reason you ask?'

'Just curious. Did you ever meet Oliver Upton?'

'Once... at a work party for Jamila's birthday.'

'Did you talk to him?'

'Yes but only to say hello.'

'Did Jamila ever talk to you about him?'

'No. I suppose it was a bit strange, now I think of it. I'd have thought it natural for Jamila to have said something about Oliver when she told me she'd moved in with him. All she said was he was a taxi driver. Nothing other than that.'

Fleming thanked Ingram for her time and left knowing he'd found out nothing new. He wondered about Upton and his mysterious past. Then there was the man with a Scottish accent claiming to be an insurance agent wanting to find Jamila.

Am I looking for a Scottish hitman?

60

BALCORIE

The day after the ceilidh, Ailsa had taken Toby for a long walk up into the hills behind Balcorie. It had rained earlier but had since cleared up enough to risk the walk.

'Beautiful view from here,' Toby said, looking out over the village down below to the sea.

'Yes, I love coming up here.'

'I enjoyed the ceilidh last night,' Toby said. 'Everyone was friendly and it was such good fun.'

'And you won a bottle of whisky.'

'Oh, yes. Tell you what, why don't I cook us dinner tonight and I'll treat you to a wee dram.'

Ailsa laughed. 'I can tell you're getting a taste for it. You had a few last night.'

'You'll come then?'

'I'd love to.'

'Great. Beans on toast it is.'

Ailsa laughed again and gave Toby a playful thump on the arm.

'Okay. I'll do a nice fish stir-fry with veg. Might even run to a bottle of white wine before we enjoy a tipple of whisky.'

'Can't wait!'

The pair sat in silence for a few minutes enjoying the view and breathing in the fresh air. Screaming seagulls soared overhead. They could still hear the sound of waves crashing against the cliffs in the distance.

Toby turned to Ailsa. 'Mind if I ask you something?'

'What's that?'

'Is there something you're worried about?'

Ailsa frowned. 'Why do you ask?'

'One or two things made me wonder.'

'Oh?'

'There was the man Pherson told you about... the man who was asking for you at the post office who said he was an old friend. You seemed concerned because you didn't recognise the description of the man the postmistress gave you.'

Ailsa didn't say anything.

Toby carried on. 'The day we went for a walk along the beach and some rocks fell... I thought I saw something on the clifftop.'

'What?'

'I'm not sure. It might have been a man.'

'Are you sure?'

'No. Just thought I caught a glimpse of something.'

'Falling rocks,' Ailsa suggested, nudging Toby.

'You seemed to get a real fright last night when the motorbike backfired.'

'Is that all?'

Toby hesitated. He wasn't sure whether he should raise this again. 'You were a little evasive about what brought you here and where you came from. Something *is* bothering you, isn't it?'

Ailsa looked as though she was about to say something, but then stopped.

'You said you'd tell me about it one day.'

Ailsa sighed. 'There is something. I owe you an explanation. I can trust you, can't I?'

'Of course. Goes without saying. What is it, Ailsa?'

'I was–'

The sharp ring of Toby's mobile cut in. He looked at the screen: *Quentin*. A sense of foreboding came over Toby. 'Hello, what's up?'

'It's Mother,' Quentin said.

'What's happened?'

'She's ill.'

'What's wrong with her?'

'I don't know. She wants you to come back to London.'

'Has she seen her doctor?'

'Yes.'

'What'd he say?'

'Told her to rest and take it easy.'

'And that's it. No diagnosis?'

'Not as far as I know.'

'She's putting it on... I know she is.'

'I don't know. She doesn't seem right. I think you should come home.'

'And do what?'

'Look after her. Do her shopping. I don't know.'

'Why can't *you* do that?'

'You know I'm always too busy.'

'So you expect me to drop everything and come back to see her... just when I'm getting settled in here?'

'You haven't started work yet. What's the problem?'

Toby was getting exasperated. 'Fucking Mother is the problem!' He ended the call.

Toby looked at Ailsa. 'Sorry about that. It's Mother again.'

'I caught the gist. She wants you to go home.'

'I hate her for this!'

'You should at least go and see her if she's ill.'

'Okay, I'll go. But if this is a sham, it'll be the last straw. She's a manipulative, domineering, selfish old woman. She's capable of doing anything to get me back to London.'

'Toby... she's your mother.'

Toby drew in a deep breath. 'If I find out she's not ill...'

61

EDINBURGH

Doug Jenner had spent two days in prison. DI Aitken had charged him and applied for remand in custody, pending trial. Jenner had been relieved that they'd sent him to a different prison than the one they'd incarcerated Big Col Calhoun's brother in. The last thing Jenner needed was to come face to face with him if he found out he was going to testify against his older brother.

Jenner had the benefit of a single cell and had kept himself pretty much to himself. 'Keep your head down and don't tell other inmates why you're there,' Aitken had advised him. Jenner wondered if he had done the right thing in plea bargaining. Naming Big Col as the brains behind the drugs and gun smuggling operation was dangerous. But then he weighed up that, without the possibility of more lenient sentencing, he'd be facing a likely life sentence.

As things stood, he might get away with ten to fourteen years concurrent sentences for taking a hostage and drug and gun smuggling. Up to five years for assault, compared to life for attempted murder. Aitken had told him the assault sentence would most likely be concurrent as well, so he was facing up to fourteen years in prison. With parole, he could be out in seven years. Five if he got away with concurrent ten-year sentences.

All in all, Jenner concluded he'd made the right decision. He was fifty-four and could be out before he was sixty. He had the proceeds from previous smuggling runs stashed away where no one could get at them. Enough to buy another lorry and start his haulage business up again.

He had three meals a day: breakfast, lunch, and dinner. The food was nothing to write home about, but it was passable. The evening meal was usually around 5pm. Afterwards, before lock-up time, there was a short period of association.

Jenner walked out of his cell to lean on the anti-climb railings which ran along the landing. He looked down to the ground floor. Prison officers had put up two table tennis tables. Eight inmates played games of doubles. Two others were playing on a mini pool table. Some sat at tables to read books from the library, talk or play chess and draughts. Jenner had decided not to mix. He preferred his own company.

'Not going down to join in then?' a voice said beside him.

Jenner turned to see a tall lanky man with a spotty face leaning on the barrier next to him.

'I'm going down for a bit,' the man said. 'Change of scene from the cell. Want to join me?'

'No, thanks. Just watching what's going on. Still trying to get a feel for things.'

'You only arrived a couple of days ago,' the man said. 'You're Doug Jenner, aren't you?'

'You're well informed.'

'Nah. Heard one of the officers call your name.'

'Right.'

'What did they get you for?'

Jenner looked at the man. 'Mistaken identity.'

'No way! You mean you're innocent?'

'Police have stitched me up for a robbery,' Jenner lied.

'Bastards. They'll pin anything on anyone they can, just to get their conviction rate up.'

'Yeah, I guess so.'

'Me... I'm guilty as hell. Keep reoffending to get back inside so I can get three square meals a day. No outgoings. No money worries. Opted out of the rat race.'

'What'd you do?'

'Burglaries. I either get away with it and I have money for food, or they catch me and here I am again.'

'You don't have a home then? No one outside?'

'Nobody who cares about me. What about you?'

Jenner hesitated. 'Wife. Marriage is on the rocks though. I guess this will be the final straw.'

'Right. You're not having a good time. Are you?'

'You could say that.'

The man slapped Jenner on the back. 'Hope things work out for you, mate. I'm off downstairs.'

Jenner watched him trudge down the metal staircase and join another inmate. Jenner was about to go back to his cell when an argument broke out between the two men playing pool. The exchange of words soon progressed into finger pointing. Three prison officers were about to intervene when one of the men hit the other with his cue. The other man flew into a rage and upturned the pool table. The balls rolled across the floor. The man who had been talking to Jenner picked one up and threw it at one of the officers who was trying to break up the fight. All hell broke loose and, within seconds, a riot had broken out.

Alarm bells went off and prison officers came running to the scene. Two officers who had been patrolling the landing where Jenner stood came rushing past to dash down to the ground floor. 'In your cell!' one of the officers shouted as he passed.

Jenner just about heard him over the noise of the riot down below and the harsh ringing of the alarm bells.

Thinking his cell was the safest place to be, Jenner retreated inside.

He turned when he heard his cell door close and saw two huge men who looked like heavyweight boxers standing inside the door. Both men were over six feet tall and had shaved heads. Tattoos covered their arms and necks.

'Been a naughty boy, Jenner,' one of the men said, arms folded to show biceps that looked as thick as Jenner's legs.

Jenner tried to say something, but the words wouldn't come out.

'Friend of ours suggested we come and say hello. Bit of a welcome to prison life.'

Jenner backed up against the far wall of his cell. He was finally able to speak. 'What's this about, mate? I don't know who you're talking about.'

'Oh, yes you do. See... you've agreed to testify against him in court.'

'No... no. You've got this all wrong. There's some mistake. I'm not testifying against anyone.'

The man doing the talking began to advance on Jenner. 'Only mistake is yours. Not a good idea to cross Big Col Calhoun.'

'Okay... I promise... I won't testify against him. I'll say I made it all up to try to get a lighter sentence.'

'Too late.'

'He can trust me!'

'I don't think so.'

Jenner panicked and tried to rush past the man. A punch hit him full in the face. He staggered back and crashed against the wall of the cell. The man moved fast towards Jenner. The other man stood guard by the door.

Jenner felt large hands grab his throat like a vice. He couldn't breathe. The man grinned as he squeezed.

'He won't be testifying against anyone,' the man said over his shoulder as Jenner's lifeless body slid to the floor.

Officers had at last controlled the staged riot on the ground floor as the two men walked away from Jenner's cell.

62

OXFORD

'This is driving me mad,' Logan complained on the way to Kazan's house.

'What?' Fleming asked.

'Trying to find anything on Upton's background. It's like he has no past. Might as well have arrived here from another planet.'

'Perhaps Naomi's theory about him being a retired spy isn't too far off the mark.'

Logan grinned. 'I'm beginning to think she could be right, even though she was joking.'

'Thing is... he reckoned he was in the army, but Naomi hasn't found any record of it. He also claimed he'd driven taxis in London, but we haven't been able to find any record of that either. Could be part of his legend,' Fleming added as a joke.

'His what?'

'Not heard of it, Harry?'

'Don't tell me, it's spy speak.'

Fleming laughed. 'It's a cover story.'

'Not a very good one,' Logan observed. 'We can't verify it.'

'Good point. By the way, I rang DI Aitken to see how he's

getting on with checking whether there's any record of Upton working for an Edinburgh taxi firm.'

'Any joy?'

'Not yet. I'm beginning to think we'll draw a blank there as well.'

'Except there does seem to be a Scottish connection,' Logan reminded Fleming. 'Is that why we're going to see Kazan again?'

'It's a long shot, but worth checking. You never know.'

'Maybe we should have seized his mobile phone and computer when we got the warrant to search his house.'

'The warrant didn't cover them. We only had authorisation to search for material relevant to the shootings. And, at the time, we were treating Kazan as the suspect, so we had no reason to be looking for possible Scottish contacts on his mobile or computer.'

'We could arrest him, and we'd have the right to search them now,' Logan suggested.

'If we arrest him, we could only keep him in custody for up to twenty-four hours. Then we'd either have to release or charge him. We don't have enough hard evidence yet to charge him as the killer, and even less with hiring one.'

'Guess you're right, boss. Even though I hate to admit it, he's a clever bastard. Smarmy git... but clever. If he did hire a hitman, there's no way he'd keep his contact details on his phone or computer.'

'True. He's also not going to admit to recognising the man in the facial composite we had made up from the description Upton's neighbour gave me.'

'The neighbour's seen the composite?'

'Yeah. She's confirmed it's a good likeness of the man claiming to be an insurance agent wanting to find Jamila.'

'This could be a complete waste of time then,' Logan said, parking the squad car outside Kazan's house.

'Maybe,' Fleming conceded. 'But at least we'll be able to see how he reacts when he sees the face. And, if he did hire a hitman, he's going to get worried we're getting close to him. He might panic.'

'Naomi might have more luck at the rifle club.'

'Let's hope so. I checked with the secretary. They have details of all their members on their computer, including head and shoulder photos. If Kazan hired someone from there, Naomi might find a match to the facial composite.'

Kazan took his time answering the door. When he finally opened it, he was less than happy. 'You again! This is bordering on harassment. How many times do you need to speak to me before you realise I had nothing to do with Oliver Upton's or Jamila's murders?'

'This won't take long,' Fleming said.

'You've already searched my house.' Kazan's irritating smarmy smile crossed his face. 'Have you come with another warrant? Think you missed something and you've come back for another search?'

'We don't need to come in,' Fleming said.

'Good, because I'm not inviting you.' Kazan's eyes narrowed. 'I've grown rather tired of your company, so please make it quick. I have dinner in the oven.'

'I just want to ask you one more thing.'

Kazan sighed. 'What?'

'Do you have any Scottish friends or colleagues?'

'I wouldn't call them friends, but I do know some Scottish colleagues. Why?'

Fleming ignored the question. 'What about the rifle club? Do you know any Scottish people there?'

'I believe there are some Scottish members. Look, what is this about?'

Fleming had been unable to detect any signs of alarm in

Kazan's face. He was either baffled by Fleming's questions or he was a good actor. Fleming pulled the facial composite out of his suit pocket and unfolded it.

'Ever seen this man before?' he asked, fixing Kazan with a steady gaze. He didn't notice any sign of recognition on Kazan's face.

Kazan shook his head. 'No. Who is he?'

'That's what we need to find out. Thank you for your time, Mr Kazan.'

Climbing back into the car, Logan asked Fleming, 'What'd you think?'

'I saw no flicker of recognition or alarm in his face. I'm not sure he does know the man.'

'Where does that leave us?'

'Waiting to see if Naomi has any more luck.'

Anderson was in Gavin Noble's office at the rifle club. She showed him the facial composite of the man who'd claimed to be an insurance agent.

'I believe you have head and shoulder photos of all your members on your computer. Mind if I check through to see if there's any match to this?'

'Doesn't look familiar to me, but please feel free to have a look.' Noble turned his computer screen round so Anderson could see. He clicked on a mouse a couple of times and the file holding the list of members came up on the screen.

Anderson watched as Noble scrolled through the whole membership list of photos. There wasn't a match with anyone who resembled the face in the composite.

63

EDINBURGH

It was late and DC Schultze sat at his desk staring at his computer screen while drinking from a steaming mug of coffee.

'Don't know how you can drink hot coffee after a sweltering day like this. Especially with no air conditioning on to cool the office down,' DI Aitken said, coming up behind Schultze.

'Helps keep me alert, sir.'

'Glad to hear it. Dare I ask if your heightened state of alertness has helped you find anything on this guy Oliver Upton?'

'Afraid not.'

'I think you need to change your drink, son.'

'What I mean is, I've finished checking and no one seems to have heard of a taxi driver called Upton.'

Aitken frowned. 'You've checked every taxi firm?'

'Yes, sir. Checked them all and no one had any record of him working for them from four to five years back.'

Aitken sighed. 'Okay. Thanks for trying.'

'So I asked them all to check their records further back... just in case.'

Aitken raised an eyebrow. 'Maybe your coffee is working after all. Find anything?'

''fraid not. No one of that name is on anyone's records going back up to six years.'

'All right. Call it a day.'

'What about the people I found on the electoral register? Want me to search to see if any of them moved to Oxford and see if I can find out anything about the Uptons who left Edinburgh?'

Aitken patted Schultze on the back. 'No. Can't spend any more time on a case that's nothing to do with us. You did your best. Well done, son. I'll let you get back to your other work.'

Aitken turned to go to his office and signalled for DS Quigley to come and join him.

'Something come up?' Quigley asked settling himself into a chair in front of Aitken's desk.

'I've been going through DI Taylor's old case files on Jenner and Calhoun,' Aitken said.

'Find anything interesting?'

'No, but it does seem like there was a hint of some superficial investigative work involved.'

'In what way?'

'Looks like some lines of enquiry weren't followed up.'

'As McCabe said, Taylor was only interested in retirement. Probably couldn't be arsed to follow things up and found it quicker and easier to close the files with a "no evidence" stamp on them.'

Aitken puffed out his cheeks. 'I think you might be right.'

'Changing the subject, did young Schultze come up with anything on the little task you set him?'

'No. Afraid I'll have to give my old pal Alex Fleming a call to say we can't find any record of his taxi driver.'

Quigley frowned. 'Something rings a bell in my head about taxis. Could be a coincidence.'

Aitken sat up in his chair. 'Go on.'

'I was looking through the old case files on the attempted jewellery shop robbery. There was mention of a taxi driver, but his name wasn't Upton.'

'Have another look. See what the files say.'

Quigley got up and made for the office door. 'Back in a tick.'

Five minutes later, Quigley was back holding a file. 'Found it in this one,' he said, tapping the folder with a finger. 'There was a guy who was the getaway driver. He identified and gave evidence against the other three men to get a lighter sentence. One of the other men was Calhoun's younger brother. The authorities agreed to drop charges against the driver and put him on witness protection.'

'Because he was at risk of serious harm or revenge attacks?'

'Yes.'

'Who was this guy?'

'Malcolm Munro. He was a taxi driver.'

'You're telling me Oliver Upton was him?'

'I don't know. There's nothing in the files except to say the Protected Persons Unit for Police Scotland took Munro under their wing. Files are silent on what happened next. As I said, could be a coincidence.'

Aitken rubbed his chin. 'I'd better have a word with them. You never know. Good wor–'

The shrill ringing of Aitken's phone cut him off. He snatched it up. 'DI Aitken.'

Aitken listened for a while with eyes glued on Quigley. He frowned, then spoke. 'Okay. Thank you. I'll get over there right away.'

'Problem?' Quigley asked.

'Someone's murdered Jenner in his cell.'

64

EDINBURGH

It was a drab, cold summer morning. DI Aitken chewed on the end of a pencil and watched droplets of rain trickle down his office window. It was first thing in the morning, the day after Jenner's murder. News hadn't yet broken out about what happened at the prison.

Aitken had gone there as soon as he got the call. He was sure Calhoun must have been behind it. Stood to reason since Calhoun knew Jenner was going to testify against him in court. Problem was, how was he going to prove it without a confession from Calhoun that he planned it? Unlikely, Aitken thought.

He'd arranged for the prison officers on duty and all the inmates to be questioned. It would take a few days but Aitken had already spoken to the two officers who'd been on the landing where Jenner had been standing when the riot started. One of them had told him he'd shouted for Jenner to get back in his cell but claimed they didn't see any other inmates on the landing. There had been one talking to Jenner but he'd gone down to the ground floor a few minutes before the riot started.

'They're not here yet,' DS Quigley said, coming into the office. 'You look deep in thought there, boss.'

'Been trying to work out if it's worth talking to Calhoun again. We only have Jenner's word that Calhoun was the man he was talking to about a shipment of drugs and guns. We have no proof Calhoun was behind it all.'

Quigley shrugged. 'Might be worth it just to keep pressure on him. He might crack. You never know.'

'We've checked his accounts and bank statements and found nothing. He must have devised a clever way of hiding illicit transactions. Surveillance hasn't come up with anything either.'

'Trouble is,' Quigley said, 'after interviewing him about Jenner and drugs and gun smuggling, he's going to be extra careful now he knows we're after him.'

'Man like him is always careful. It's how he's kept one step ahead of the law.'

DC Schultze appeared at the door. 'They've arrived. I've put them in interview room two.'

For once the interview room was cool. 'Need bloody heating on in this place on a cold summer's day,' Calhoun complained as Aitken and Quigley entered. They sat at the table opposite Calhoun and his solicitor.

'It's your age,' Aitken quipped.

'I answered all your questions the other day. What do you want now?'

Aitken nodded at Quigley who turned the digital recorder on. After going through the usual introductions and issuing Calhoun with a caution, Aitken answered the question with one of his own. 'You've no idea why I wanted to speak to you?'

Calhoun's eyes narrowed. 'I may be many things, DI Aitken, but I'm not a bloody clairvoyant.'

'Thought it might have been obvious.'

'Can we get to the point of this?' the solicitor interjected.

'Seen your brother lately?'

Calhoun frowned. 'No. Why?'

'Does he have contacts in the local prison?'

Aitken noticed a flicker of uncertainty cross Calhoun's eyes.

'How the hell would I know? I told you before, I only see him once in a while. We're not very close. Why would he tell me if he knew inmates in other prisons?'

'What about you? Do you know anyone in the local prison?'

'I know of a couple of people who your lot have put away, as does everyone else who reads the papers.'

'Know anyone close enough to call in a favour?'

'I don't know what the hell this is about, but I'm going to walk if you don't stop talking in riddles.'

'I told you Doug Jenner claimed you were the brains behind the drugs and gun smuggling operation. He was prepared to testify against you in court.'

The solicitor sat forwards in his chair. 'You said *was*. Has he changed his mind?'

'Not so much changed his mind as can't.'

The solicitor frowned. 'I'm not with you.'

Aitken fixed his eyes on Calhoun. 'You obviously haven't heard. Someone murdered Doug Jenner in his cell yesterday evening.'

The solicitor's mouth dropped open. There was no reaction from Calhoun.

'Thing is,' Aitken continued, looking at the solicitor, 'your client seems to have come by a remarkable piece of luck. A key witness is no longer able to appear in court to testify against him.'

'If you're suggesting my client had anything to do with that, you'd better tell me what proof you have.'

'None... so far. But once we finish interviewing inmates and find out who did it, they may be willing to say who got them to kill Jenner. Anything for a lighter sentence.'

'If you have no proof, you can hardly arrest my client,' the solicitor said. 'That being the case, we'll take our leave.'

Calhoun smiled at Aitken as he rose to go. 'There is one other thing you may wish to consider.'

'What?'

'I hear Jenner tried to kill his wife. Maybe you should be speaking to her. Could be she arranged it.'

65

LONDON

The journey down to London turned out to be a nightmare. Toby had decided to drive it in one day, setting off at eight in the morning. He'd estimated it could take a little under twelve hours and expected to arrive around eight at night. Road works, an accident, and slow traffic added another three hours to the trip. He arrived at his flat a few minutes after eleven.

Toby poured himself a large whisky and settled into an armchair, wondering how he was going to approach the next day. He would ring his brother first thing to see how things were, then call his mother to let her know he was back and would be round to see her.

He thought of the walk he'd enjoyed with Ailsa the day before. It already seemed a week ago. He'd tackled her about his concerns that something seemed to be worrying her. It was annoying that Quentin had phoned just as Ailsa had been about to tell him what was bothering her. The conversation had switched from Ailsa to Toby's mother. He hadn't pressed Ailsa to continue what she had been about to say. Likewise, Ailsa seemed relieved to change the subject.

Now, drinking his whisky, Toby dwelled on the issue again. It wasn't his imagination. There was definitely something bothering Ailsa. She *had* been about to tell him, hadn't she? Toby decided he had to ask her again when he returned to Scotland. Then a horrible thought struck him. *What if Mother is ill and I have to stay here?*

Toby drowned another glass of whisky and went to bed. It was either the whisky, or fatigue from the drive, but Toby had a restless night. He saw white lights and road markings rushing up to meet him in his dreams. Traffic lights turned into red eyes glaring at him. Then he saw his mother standing on a clifftop pointing something at Ailsa, laughing hysterically. Toby woke up with a start, bathed in sweat. He took several deep breaths and went to the kitchen to get a drink of water.

The second half of the night was better. Toby fell into a deep sleep and woke up at 8am. He looked at his alarm clock and climbed out of bed. There was enough time to ring Quentin before he disappeared out to work.

His brother answered after three rings. 'Hi, Toby. Only got a minute... dashing off.'

'I'm back in London. I wanted to give you a quick call to see how things are.'

'We're all fine, liste–'

'I mean with Mother,' Toby cut in.

There was a short hesitation. 'She's okay.'

'I thought you said she was ill.'

'Yes... well... she said she was. What I meant is, she hasn't got any worse. She wanted you to come home. I think it's just a bad cold.'

Toby was about to throw the phone across the room. 'A cold? You've both dragged me back here because she has a cold!'

'She did seem a bit distressed... not well at all.'

Toby ended the call and glared at the phone as though it was to blame for the deception. He dressed and had breakfast before ringing his mother, needing time to calm down before doing so.

It took a while for her to answer. 'Hello?'

Her voice sounded strained.

'It's me, Toby. I'm back in London. I'll call round to see you this morning. Is there anything you need?'

'Some painkillers,' she said, putting on a pathetic tone of voice.

An hour later, Toby parked his car outside his mother's house and let himself in. 'I'm here,' he shouted. 'It's Toby.'

There was no reply.

Toby pushed the sitting room door open and found his mother reading a magazine. A smouldering cigarette butt was in a full ashtray on the coffee table beside her.

'Quentin rang me the other day. He said you were ill and you wanted me to come home.'

'Yes, thank you for coming. I don't feel well at all.'

'You don't look ill to me... and you're smoking.'

'Too late to stop now.'

'What'd you mean?'

'Think I'm on my last legs. I need you here.'

'Quentin said you'd seen a doctor. What did he say was wrong with you?'

'Waste of time. All he said was to rest and take it easy.'

'He didn't diagnose anything?'

'Like I said... waste of time going.'

'Did he not even offer a clue about what he thought might be wrong with you?'

'No.'

'Might that be because there *is* nothing wrong with you?'

'Don't be silly, Toby. I'm suffering.'

'Suffering from delusions. You don't look unwell.'

'You're a doctor now, are you?'

'Did he take your temperature?'

'Yes.'

'And?'

'It was okay.'

'Blood pressure?'

'Yes.'

'And?'

'It was fine. Little high, but nothing to worry about.'

'He hasn't referred you to hospital for further tests?'

'No.'

'Know what? There's nothing wrong with you at all. You tried your best to stop me going for the job up in Scotland. Now you're making out you're ill to try to get me to come back here.'

'That's not true. Anyway... I always thought you wouldn't get the job.'

'People up there welcomed me with open arms. They're a friendly lot.'

'Wait till you start the job. It won't last long. You'll get bored, and you'll be back. You mark my words.'

'And you thought you'd pretend to be so ill that I'd come back. Is that it?'

'I *need* you here, Toby.'

'No, you don't. You've just got used to me being at your beck and call.'

'It's for your own good. You'll be much better off here.'

'You can't believe I'll stay after this. You've conned me into coming back thinking you might be ill. You've always tried to control my life. This is the last straw. Your duplicity is unforgivable.'

'Toby, please. You need to stay here.'

Toby slammed the painkillers on the coffee table next to the ashtray. 'I'm not sure you need these. I'm going back to Scotland tomorrow. Nothing you say or do will stop me.'

'Toby, please, I can't manage on my own.'

'Don't ever try to pull something like this again. I don't have to tell you what happens when people cry wolf too many times. After this, I'm unlikely to come back even if you do get ill.'

Toby left to his mother calling out after him. 'You'll be back!'

Later that evening Toby rang Ailsa. 'It was all a sham. There's nothing wrong with her. She was doing what she's always done... being manipulative, trying to control my life. I can't believe she thought I'd come back to London to live when I found out she deceived me.'

'Toby, I'm so sorry.'

'I'm coming back to Balcorie tomorrow.'

'I'm glad. Sorry about your mother, but I'm happy you're coming back.'

'For good this time.'

66

EDINBURGH

Hillary Vere was the manager in charge of the Protected Persons Unit. She got up from behind a clear desk to greet DI Aitken. She was a tall woman who exuded confidence and authority. Her handshake was firm. In her mid-forties, she had short black hair and wore black trousers and a white shirt.

Her office was small, but light and airy. A computer screen sat on one side of her desk. Three wire baskets stacked on top of each other sat on the other side. Aitken noted the out and pending baskets contained more than the in-tray. Vere flashed a smile at Aitken and led him to a small meeting table.

On the way to Vere's office, Aitken had reflected on the interview with Calhoun. It had gone more or less as he thought it would. Of course Calhoun was never going to admit to knowing anything about Jenner's murder, but maybe Aitken had said enough to worry him. He thought he'd noticed concern in Calhoun's eyes when he said inmates might be willing to share information in return for a few favours.

Aitken had studied the old case files on the jewellery shop robbery before coming to see Vere. He wanted to ensure he was well informed. There was nothing worse than barging in without having a grasp of all the facts.

Vere took a seat opposite Aitken at the meeting table. 'Can I get you tea or coffee?'

'No, thanks. I'm fine.'

'You said over the phone you wanted to ask me about an old case.'

'Yes. It was a jewellery shop robbery in Edinburgh... about five years ago.'

'Okay, but I'm afraid I won't be familiar with it. I only joined the unit three years ago.'

'No worries. I had to read through the files myself to get up to speed.'

'It wasn't your case then?'

'No. I happen to be working on another enquiry and the same man's name crops up.'

'Can you tell me who?'

'Guy known as Big Col Calhoun. He runs a nightclub in Edinburgh, but we're sure he's involved in organised crime. We haven't yet been able to find enough evidence to charge him with anything.'

'I've heard of him,' Vere confirmed. 'How can I help you?'

'Officers working on the old jewellery shop robbery had Big Col down as the brains behind it, but there wasn't enough evidence to link him to the crime. The only link was that Calhoun's younger brother had been the leader of the robbers. He and two other men went down for the robbery. The whole thing had turned out to be a bit of a shambles. It didn't go to plan. A cop on the beat tried to stop them and Calhoun junior shot him. The copper survived, but Calhoun still got life.'

'So where does the PPU come into it?'

'The getaway driver was a taxi driver called Malcolm Munro. He agreed to testify against the other three men. Problem was, if

Munro went to prison it would be as good as signing a death warrant. The odds of him coming to a gory end there were high if certain inmates found out he'd shopped Calhoun's brother.'

'So the authorities reached an agreement?'

'Yes. They decided Munro wasn't a key player. He was *only* the getaway driver. They agreed to drop all charges against him in return for his testimony. After testifying, they put him on witness protection.'

'I see. If you want to know where he is now, I'm not sure I can give you that information. You'll appreciate we have to deal with matters like this on a need-to-know basis. We try to limit the number of people who know where we've located protected persons.'

'I get that, but there is a possibility of a link to a case an old friend of mine is working on for Thames Valley Police.'

'May I ask what this possible link is?'

'My friend, DCI Fleming, is investigating a murder. Someone shot a man called Oliver Upton on a golf course near Oxford.'

Vere frowned. 'What has this got to do with Malcolm Munro?'

'Maybe nothing. Could be a coincidence.'

'Go on.'

'It seems Oliver Upton is a bit of an enigma. No one appears to know anything about his past. The only thing Fleming was able to find out about his background was that he may have driven taxis in Edinburgh about five years ago. Fleming asked if I could run a check for him with local taxi companies.'

'I think I see where this is going,' Vere said, nodding.

'I can't find any record of a man called Upton who drove taxis in Edinburgh five years ago. But a colleague of mine recalled Munro was a taxi driver who ended up on witness protection.'

'And you think there's a chance that DCI Fleming's Oliver Upton was Malcolm Munro?'

'Yes. Thing is, if it is him, it would provide a link to Big Col Calhoun. He might have wanted to exact revenge on the man who testified against his brother.'

Vere appeared to consider this for a second or two. 'If we did rename Munro as Upton and moved him to Oxford, there would be no further need for keeping the lid on it being as Upton is dead.'

'Quite. If Upton wasn't Munro, my theory goes out of the window and I don't need to know where Munro is now. If he did become Upton, Big Col becomes a suspect in arranging his demise.'

Vere got up from the table and sat behind her desk. She tapped something on her computer keyboard, waited for a second or two, then clicked and scrolled with the mouse. After a minute, Vere looked across at Aitken. 'Your theory was right. We renamed Munro to Upton and moved him to Oxford.'

'Wouldn't the PPU be concerned that Munro disappeared off your radar if regular checks on him were made?'

'We tend not to make too many checks. Maybe once a year. There's always the risk that a communication may be picked up by someone who shouldn't know about our interest. It's mainly the responsibility of individuals to contact us if they have any concerns.'

'I see.'

'Does this help with your current investigation?' Vere asked.

'Very much so. A man had agreed to testify against Big Col on the drugs and gun smuggling case I'm working on now. Someone murdered him in his prison cell. Bit of a pattern emerging here, which leads me on to something else.'

'Oh?'

'I saw on the files there was one other witness who testified against Calhoun's brother. A woman called Maisey Jackson. Someone found out about Upton. They could also have found out about her. I think she could be in mortal danger.'

The colour had drained from Vere's face.

'I need to find out where Maisey is now. We need to warn her,' Aitken pressed.

'I'll check and let you know.'

'It's urgent. Can't you do it now?'

Vere hesitated. 'I need to carry out some checks before I release any information, and it'll take a while. I promise I'll get back to you as soon as I can.'

67

OXFORD

It was Saturday evening and Fleming had decided to call it a day. It had been a hot one and Fleming had given a choice to Logan and Anderson. 'Incident room for a run-through where we are, or a change of scenery for a pint at the Trout Inn?' he'd asked.

Logan had answered first. 'Hard one, boss. But never say I can't make difficult decisions. Trout Inn.'

'Don't think it was too difficult for you, Sarge,' Anderson said with a laugh.

'I gave it a good deal of thought, but decided in the end that option two was far more sensible.'

'The Trout Inn it is then,' Fleming said.

Twenty minutes later, they were sitting at a table on the outside terrace of the Trout Inn. It was full of patrons enjoying the evening sunshine, but Fleming managed to find a table next to the wall by the river. A gentle breeze tugged at the white parasol they were sitting under and the sound of chatter and occasional burst of laughter drifted across the terrace. They sat in silence for a minute, watching a couple of boats going by.

Fleming ran a finger round the top of his beer glass. 'Chief constable and Temple are losing patience over the Upton case.'

'Just as well they can't see us here then,' Logan quipped.

'We are entitled to some time off,' Anderson said, taking a sip of her orange juice.

'Technically, we're having a working meeting,' Fleming reminded them. 'Though I'm not sure we'll achieve very much.'

Logan sipped at his beer and wiped some froth from his mouth. 'Thing is, out here in the sunshine having a relaxing drink can help focus the mind.'

'Didn't know you were into all that mindfulness stuff, Sarge,' Naomi said.

Logan wagged a finger. 'Clear the head and focus, Naomi.'

'You're beginning to sound like the old man in *The Karate Kid*. What's his name?'

'Mr Miyagi... and let's have less of the old man,' Logan pleaded.

Fleming smiled. 'In your new state of mindfulness, where do you think we are in the Upton case, Harry.'

'We've ruled out Earl Yates and Ian Hunter. Raj Syed was looking promising, but he has a cast-iron alibi for his whereabouts when both Upton and Jamila Kazan were shot.'

'Don't forget... Jamila Kazan isn't our case. DI Gamez in the Met is looking for her killer.'

'Only it seems likely we're both looking for the same man or woman,' Anderson reminded them.

'Agreed,' Fleming said.

'What about Will Palmer?' Logan asked.

'Case against him is weak. He didn't have the means to get a rifle off the film set, and he also has an alibi. He could have had time to get back to his trailer before the director called in on him though.'

'And,' Anderson said, 'if the same man... or woman... killed

Jamila Kazan, Palmer wouldn't appear to be a suspect. There's no motive we know of why he would want to kill Jamila.'

'Leaving Atticus Kazan,' Fleming said. 'But if it was the same person who killed Upton and Jamila, we can't put Atticus at the scene of the second murder. We also have no forensic evidence against him.'

'And,' Logan said, 'the description we have of the man saying he was an insurance agent doesn't match any of the suspects we had... including Atticus Kazan.'

'So there's someone out there we have no knowledge of. Maybe Kazan hired a hitman.'

'At which point,' Logan said, 'I think it's time for a snack and another drink.'

'Wondered how long it would be before you started to think about food,' Anderson teased.

Logan went to collect their empty glasses.

'I'll get them,' Fleming said.

'You got the first round, boss,' Logan reminded him.

'No worries. I'll leave you and Naomi to work out how we're going to find this bogus insurance man.'

Fleming was on his way to the bar when his mobile indicated an incoming call: *Gordon Aitken*.

'Hi, Gordon. Have you got news for me?'

'Yes and no.'

'Want to give me the no first?'

'We can't find any trace of your Oliver Upton as a taxi driver up here in Edinburgh five years ago.'

'Is the other news good news?'

'It is. I've found out that the Protected Persons Unit up here put a guy called Malcolm Munro on witness protection. They renamed him Oliver Upton and relocated him to Oxford.'

Fleming drew in a deep breath, unable to speak for a second.

'You still there, Alex?'

'Yeah. Trying to take in what you said.'

'I don't want to discuss it over the phone. Think you can get up here tomorrow and I'll fill you in?'

'Sure. I'll see if I can get a flight. I'll let you know when to expect me.'

'I'll come and pick you up from the airport if you text me the flight details.'

'Great. See you tomorrow.'

Fleming ended the call. He got the drinks and ordered three plates of chips before returning to join Logan and Anderson. He hadn't been feeling hungry, but his appetite had suddenly returned.

'Press release,' Logan said as Fleming put the drinks down on the table.

'Sorry?'

'Press release,' Logan said again. 'We find the phoney insurance man by issuing the artist's facial composite image in the papers. See if someone recognises him.'

'Right. Let's do it. Also, I just took a call from my mate up in Edinburgh.'

'News on Upton?' Logan asked.

'He's found out who Oliver Upton is.'

68

LONDON

After ringing Ailsa and having a bite to eat, Toby decided to call round on his brother before setting off the next day to go back to Balcorie. It was only a short walk from Toby's flat to the station at East Croydon and less than ten minutes on the train to Purley. Quentin's house was about five or six minutes on foot from Purley station, so Toby decided to leave his car at the flat.

Quentin's detached house was in a nice residential location. It had a white render finish, bay windows and an enclosed porch. Electronic gates led onto a large driveway of red block paving. It was late when Toby arrived. Quentin and Margo had eaten, and she and the two boys had gone to bed. Maybe as well, Toby thought. Things might get a little heated.

Quentin looked awkward when he opened the door. 'Hi, Toby. Good to see you. Come in.' He led the way through the porch and hallway into the sitting room. 'Get you a drink? Got a bottle of red wine open.'

'Sounds good,' Toby said, taking a seat.

'Hear about the shooting on Clapham Common the other week?' Quentin asked as he poured Toby's drink.

'No. Must have missed that in the news.'

'Maybe they didn't bother reporting it in the Scottish papers.'

Toby shrugged.

'They haven't found the killer yet. They reckon fewer people are walking their dogs there at the moment.'

'I suppose people will be a bit nervous,' Toby agreed, taking a sip of wine. 'Nice,' he said. 'What is it?'

'Rioja... 2016.'

'When did you go to see Mother?' Toby asked.

'Day before I rang you. Why?'

'You haven't been to see her since?'

'No. Work's been a nightmare. I've been too busy.'

Toby took another sip of wine. 'And yet you rang me to come back from Scotland because she was ill and couldn't cope.'

'Hang on there, Toby, I was only telling you what she told me. It was her asking you to come home, not me.'

'I seem to remember *you* saying you thought I should come home.'

'Did I?'

'Yes! Look after her, do her shopping, that's what you said.'

'Well... I–'

'Unbelievable! You think she's so ill and yet you can't find time to come round to see her.'

'I told you. I'm busy at work. They expect miracles.'

Toby snorted. 'You should change your job.'

'I can't. I have Margo and the boys to support.'

'You chose to buy a house which must be worth more than a million and run a fancy Alfa Romeo Giulietta.'

'It's a company car. They gave it to me when they promoted me to managing director.'

'It's your lifestyle. You make choices in life... as I did. All I'm saying is, I think you could make the effort to do more for Mother. I've done it for years.'

'Don't think I'm not grateful. It's just you had more time.'

'I saw her this morning. Sitting smoking and reading a magazine. There's nothing wrong with her.'

'She'd been to the doctor,' Quentin said, beginning to look chastised.

'Yes, and he didn't find anything wrong with her.'

'Okay... maybe she laid it on a bit thick... but she misses you and wanted you to come home.'

'She tricked me. Her duplicity is beyond belief. She's selfish and manipulative and I won't let her interfere in my life anymore. I've told her I'm going back to Scotland and not to try anything like this again.'

'Okay. I'll make the effort to see her once a week at least.'

'If she does need help, you have plenty of money. Get Margo to do an online shop for her. Hire a cleaner and a gardener. Worst comes to the worst... you have a spare room.'

Quentin held up his hands. 'Okay... okay! I'll do what I can, but taking her in... that's a step too far.'

Toby downed the last of his wine and smiled. 'At least you realise she can be difficult at the best of times.'

'When are you going back to Scotland?'

'Tomorrow.'

'I'm sorry I've not done more. Look, it's been good to see you again. Keep in touch and let me know how the new job goes when you start.'

'Sure.' Toby got up to leave. 'Say hello to Margo and the boys.'

It was late when Toby got back to his flat. Clearing the air with Quentin had been good. The last thing he needed was to leave with an ill feeling between them. Quentin meant well, but he used the pressures of his job as an excuse for not getting more involved in supporting his mother. Toby could see his point though... to a certain extent. Quentin did work long hours and had his own family to look after. Toby had more time off, longer holidays, and no wife or children, though he wondered how different his life could have been if he'd stood up to his mother long before now.

Toby poured himself a whisky and decided he didn't fancy an early morning rise for what might turn out to be another nightmare journey. He would call Ailsa in the morning to let her know he'd changed his plans. He didn't relish the thought of another fifteen-hour drive in one day if his journey down was anything to go by. An overnight break at Penrith seemed a much more sensible idea. After all, there was no rush to get back.

69

EDINBURGH

It was a bright summer's day with hardly a cloud in a blue sky. Logan had dropped Fleming off at Luton Airport early in the morning. The flight to Edinburgh had taken under an hour and a half and, as promised, Gordon Aitken was there to meet Fleming.

In a little over forty minutes, they were sitting in Aitken's office in Gayfield Square drinking coffee. 'So what's this case you're working on?' Aitken asked.

'A sniper shot this guy Upton on an Oxford golf course. The man you've now identified as Malcolm Munro. Despite all our efforts to find out about him, we couldn't get any information which could lead us to his killer. All we know is he worked for a local taxi company in Oxford, his wife divorced him, and he was Scottish. He had an affair with another man's wife who moved in with him. Then someone shot her as well.'

'All happening on your patch, eh?'

'It's been busy, yes.'

'Both killed at the same time?'

'No. Upton's partner was murdered later... on Clapham Common in London.'

'How come he was in Oxford and she was in London?'

'She went to stay with her sister for a while after Upton, as we knew him, was killed.'

'You said he was divorced. Have you spoken to his ex-wife?'

'Yes. Turns out she has a new partner who happened to be filming in Oxford at the time of Munro's murder.'

'You've questioned him?'

'Yes, and the husband of the woman who moved in with Upton. A couple of others as well.'

'But no arrests?'

'No. Not enough evidence against any of the suspects. It was a woman called Jamila Kazan who had the affair with Upton and moved in with him. Her husband is the prime suspect. The only problem is, he has an alibi to say he was elsewhere at the time of both murders. They're not watertight, but we're so far unable to prove he was at the scene of either murder.'

Aitken drew a deep breath. 'Could have got someone else to do it for him.'

'That's what I'm coming round to believing. There is a Scottish connection. We knew Upton... Munro... was Scottish, and we've found out a man with a Scottish accent was looking for Jamila. Her husband knows some Scottish people.'

'You've questioned them?'

'We will, but I wanted to follow up on your phone call first. Whatever it is you want to tell me may throw a completely new light on the case.'

'How come?'

'You said the PPU put Munro under witness protection and he's my Upton character. I could be looking for the people or person they were trying to protect him from. If so, it's not likely to be Jamila's husband.'

'Hmm.'

'You said you didn't want to go over details about Munro on the phone. What else was it you were going to tell me?'

'The chap you knew as Upton is the same man who testified against the younger brother of a man I'm investigating for drugs and gun smuggling... Big Col Calhoun.'

Fleming's eyes narrowed. 'So a hitman could be working for Big Col or his brother.'

'There was a jewellery shop robbery five years ago in Edinburgh. Big Col's younger brother got life for shooting a policeman. The copper survived, but Calhoun still got a life sentence. Munro gave evidence against him. That's why the Protected Persons Unit put him on witness protection.'

'Looking more and more like a revenge killing. Question is, why would the killer kill Jamila Kazan as well?'

'If Big Col was behind it, he could have been worried Munro had told Jamila his real identity. He could have told her about being on witness protection and why. There was always a chance she would tell you, and that would lead you to Calhoun.'

'I need to have a chat with this Calhoun,' Fleming said.

Aitken shook his head. 'I've done that. Questioned him about the drugs and gun smuggling operation... and another little matter.'

'Oh?'

'I have no hard evidence against Calhoun on the drugs and gun smuggling case. Just a man who was prepared to testify against him in court. Problem is, someone killed the man in his cell while he was on remand. Convenient, eh? Questioned Calhoun about that too, but apart from having a motive, I can't prove he was behind it.'

'Sounds like a man hard to catch.'

'Oh yes. He's always one step ahead of us. I think you'd have as much luck questioning him about Munro as I did about Doug Jenner.'

'The man who was going to testify against him?'

'Yes.'

Fleming sighed. 'But you have a written statement from Jenner?'

'Yes, but on its own, it's not enough. A statement from a man already charged with drugs and gun smuggling was never likely to help get a conviction. His attempt to plea bargain wouldn't help matters. A defence lawyer would claim Jenner made it up to give the police something they wanted in return for him getting a lighter sentence.'

'Sounds plausible.'

'You'd be wasting your time questioning Big Col at this stage. He could claim his brother may have told another prisoner about how Munro shopped him. Then got him to kill Munro and Jamila on release. Could explain why it took so long to kill them.'

'Or, if Big Col was behind it, maybe it took him this long to find Munro.'

'Either way, it would be advisable to see if you can get a bit more to go on before questioning Big Col.'

'The only thing I have is this,' Fleming said, getting the facial composite of the bogus insurance man out of his pocket. 'We managed to get a description of the man with the Scottish accent who was looking for Jamila.' He pushed it across the table to Aitken. 'Recognise him?'

Aitken gasped. 'I don't believe it!'

'What?'

'This,' Aitken said, pointing a finger at the image, 'looks like a detective sergeant I know.'

'You sure?'

Aitken shook his head in disbelief. 'It's a very close resemblance. I have to say. It can't be though.'

'Can you get in touch with your PPU contact and see if he made enquiries about Munro?'

'Sure, but the resemblance must be a coincidence.'

'A check will confirm one way or the other.'

'Right. There's something else. There was another witness who testified against Calhoun's brother. The PPU renamed and relocated her at the same time as Munro. I'm waiting for them to get back to me to tell me where she is so I can warn her.'

70

EDINBURGH

'This is not looking good for the PPU,' Hillary Vere said. She was facing Fleming and Aitken across the meeting table in her office. 'Someone found out where we relocated one of our subjects, killed him, and now you believe another is in extreme danger.'

'Have you made enquiries to find out who leaked the information?' Fleming asked.

'I spoke to the casework officer in charge of the Munro case, Pat Finn. She denies releasing any information about him and his new identity.'

'Did you tell her why you were asking?'

'No.'

'She doesn't know that someone murdered Upton?'

'Not as far as I know.'

'Is she on duty today?'

'Yes.'

Fleming looked at Aitken. 'You ought to take her in for questioning, but I'd rather we speak to her right now. You okay with that?'

Aitken thought for a moment. 'The leaked information is a

matter for Police Scotland, but I guess your murder enquiry takes precedence. I'm not arresting anyone and am here representing Police Scotland, so I'm content for you to take the lead. You are, after all, just having a quiet chat with a witness.'

'Thanks.' Fleming looked at Vere. 'You okay to bring her in so I can have a word? This is urgent.'

Vere bit her bottom lip. 'I suppose so. Maybe she'll be more likely to own up to it speaking to you when she finds out there's a murder involved.'

'Okay, let's have her in then.'

Five minutes later, Pat Finn sat opposite Fleming and Aitken. She looked to be in her thirties. Her face was pale, and she twisted a strand of her short auburn hair round a finger.

'These two police officers would like to have a chat with you, Pat,' Vere said.

Finn glanced from Fleming to Aitken and looked as though she was about to burst into tears.

Fleming decided the best approach was to go easy on her at first. 'You're not in any trouble. I just need to ask you a few questions. It's of the utmost importance to a case I'm working on.'

Finn looked at Vere who nodded encouragement.

'Okay,' she whispered.

'Mrs Vere has already asked you whether you may have divulged information on the whereabouts of Malcolm Munro.'

'Yes. I told her, I didn't.'

'She didn't tell you why she was asking you about it?'

'No.'

'I won't beat about the bush. Someone murdered Munro, who I knew as Oliver Upton, a few weeks ago.'

Finn gasped. 'Oh my God!'

'I need to know who found out where Munro was living and what his new name was.' Fleming decided it was time to apply a bit of pressure. 'You need to come clean and tell me if you did release any information. Not to do so could land you in serious trouble for obstructing a police murder enquiry and failing to provide vital information.'

Finn began to cry.

Fleming softened his tone. 'You can help us out here. I'm sure we could put an indiscretion down to an error of judgement rather than any ulterior motive. Could be you were just careless and let information slip out about his new identity and location.'

Finn wiped a tear from her cheek. 'It was a police officer. He asked to meet me in a pub. Said he was working undercover and didn't want to come into the office.'

'You believed him?'

'He showed me a warrant card. Said he was working on a case involving the brother of the man Malcolm Munro testified against. He said Munro was in danger because he believed certain people may have tracked him down.'

'You didn't think to tell Mrs Vere about this?'

Finn sobbed again. 'I've been so stupid. He was so convincing. Told me it was all top secret and no one else must know about it, not even my boss.'

'Why didn't you alert Munro?'

Finn looked at Vere with dread. 'I thought the police would do it.'

Fleming showed the facial composite of the bogus insurance agent to Finn. 'Was this the officer you spoke to?'

Finn nodded.

'And the name on the card he showed you?'

'Detective Sergeant Quigley.'

'That wasn't DS Quigley,' Aitken said.

'But I checked with Police Scotland. There *is* a DS Quigley in Edinburgh.'

'There is,' Aitken confirmed. 'But he's not the man you've just identified.'

'He had a warrant card.'

'Fake,' Aitken said. 'The man you spoke to is a DS McCabe.'

Finn looked with pleading eyes at Fleming and Aitken. 'I thought it was okay to tell him.' She looked at Vere. 'Will I get the sack?'

Fleming looked at Vere with a raised eyebrow. Vere shook her head. 'I don't think so. A policeman tricked you. You were foolish not to mention it though. I guess there'll be a disciplinary hearing and you'll get a written warning.'

'She may have identified a murderer or someone who recruited a murderer. That must count in her favour,' Fleming added.

'She's also identified a bent cop,' Aitken said. 'I always suspected someone was in Calhoun's pocket. Had a fleeting thought it might even have been the assistant chief constable, Ramsay Irvin.' He looked at Vere. 'You were going to let me know about Maisey Jackson, the other witness who testified against Big Col Calhoun's younger brother.'

Vere nodded at Finn.

'We renamed her Ailsa Brodie,' Finn said. 'She now lives in Balcorie up in the North West Highlands.'

Fleming put a hand over Finn's. 'You told McCabe where she is?'

Finn put her hands over her face and sobbed. 'Yes,' she whispered.

Back at Gayfield Square, Aitken had set things in motion to have McCabe pulled in for questioning. He'd also arranged local police protection for Ailsa. DS Quigley was checking where McCabe was at the time of Upton's and Jamila's murders.

Meanwhile, Fleming was on the phone with Logan. 'You can forget the press release of the facial composite, and questioning Kazan's Scottish acquaintances.'

'Why?'

'I know who the bogus insurance man is.'

'How come?'

'Long story. I'll tell you when I get back, but I could get delayed.'

'You sound as though you're onto something.'

'I think I may just have found out who killed Upton and Jamila.'

71

EDINBURGH

The next morning, Fleming and Aitken were back in Aitken's office at Gayfield Square. 'Be interesting to hear what McCabe has to say for himself,' Aitken said.

'It certainly looks like he's your bent cop. Assuming he is in Big Col Calhoun's pocket, that puts Big Col in the frame for arranging Upton and Jamila Kazan's murders.'

'Wins all round. If we get McCabe to admit he was working for Big Col, I finally get a chance to put Calhoun behind bars. All I need to do is prove he used McCabe to find the people who testified against his brother.'

'And I could find my murderer. Only question is, was it McCabe himself, or was he just the tool to find Upton and Jamila?'

'My guess is, given the evidence against him, he might confess to giving information about Upton to Calhoun. I very much doubt he'll own up to being the killer.'

Fleming scratched his chin. 'Are you sure you have enough evidence to put Calhoun away? You have a lot of circumstantial evidence, but nothing concrete.'

'True. All I have on the drugs and gun smuggling case is

Jenner's statement. He's dead, so they can't cross-examine him in court. A smart lawyer could claim Jenner was trying to stitch Calhoun up for some reason and his statement isn't reliable. They could also suggest the people who Jenner was supplying drugs to wanted him killed before he got to court.'

'I'm not faring much better,' Fleming said. 'Big Col had a motive for seeking revenge against Munro. But right now I'd find it difficult to prove he was the man behind his and Jamila's murders. As you said, Big Col could claim his brother may have told a friend in prison about Munro stitching him up. A lawyer could put it to the court that an ex-inmate could have carried out the murders for Calhoun junior.'

'In which case it would mean McCabe gave the info about Munro to this other inmate and not Big Col.'

'Except it's more likely McCabe is in Big Col's pocket and not his younger brother's,' Fleming pointed out.

Aitken looked crushed. 'It seems the only way we'll get a result is if we get confessions. As you say, all the evidence is circumstantial against Calhoun. It might be convincing but it's not quite enough. There's nothing in his business accounts or bank statements to point the finger at him and there isn't any forensic or DNA evidence.'

'We do know that McCabe tricked a case officer in the PPU to find out Munro's new identity and location.'

Aitken got up from his desk and went to a filing cabinet. He opened the top drawer and pulled out two glasses and a small bottle of whisky. 'For occasions like this,' he said, holding the glasses up between the fingers of one hand while waving the bottle in the other.

Fleming smiled. 'Too early in the morning, and not such a good idea if we intend to question McCabe.'

Aitken put the whisky and glasses back. 'I guess you're right. How about when we're off duty?'

'Sounds like a great idea. You never know, we may even be celebrating a result against McCabe and Calhoun.'

'I'll have a very large glass if Calhoun ends up behind bars for a long time.'

'Likewise. It'll keep my super and chief constable off my back if I get a result on the Upton murder enquiry.'

'And, don't forget, Jamila Kazan's as well.'

'That one's not my case. Her murder took place on Clapham Common in London. The Met's handling it.'

'Oh yes, you said. Still, you'll get some brownie points for solving it for them. No doubt your super and chief constable will get accolades from the Met for helping them out. They're bound to pass them on to you.'

'You're more confident than I am. Don't forget... I said *if* I get a result.'

Aitken was about to speak when a breathless DS Quigley knocked on the office door and burst in. 'Sorry to interrupt, boss. Got some news.'

Aitken sat forward in his chair. 'Yes?'

'I ran a check through the duty rosters and it appears McCabe was on leave ten days before Upton's... Munro's... murder.'

Aitken's eyes narrowed. 'And?'

'He was still on extended leave for a few days afterwards.'

'And what about Jamila Kazan?'

'He was off duty two days before, the day of the murder, and the day after.'

'They've pulled him in for questioning this morning?'

Quigley made a face. 'Afraid not. He went off duty last night and they couldn't find him. Didn't turn up for work this morning.'

'They tried his home address?'

'Yeah. Not at home either.'

Aitken slammed a hand down on his desk. 'He's either twigged the net is closing in on him and he's gone on the run. Or... he's on his way to Balcorie to kill Ailsa Brodie.'

'Fuck,' Quigley whispered.

'Better get his car details circulated to arrange an ANPR data search to find him.'

Quigley shook his head. 'No need, his car's still at his house.'

'He must have another vehicle then,' Aitken said. 'Get an all-points bulletin out for the police to detain him if he's sighted. Alert all units to approach him with caution. He's certain to be armed.'

'On it, boss.' Quigley turned to leave.

'Hang on. Get officers down to Waverley Station, and make sure an alert goes out to police at all ports and airports. Starting with Edinburgh Airport.'

'Right.'

'And,' Aitken added before Quigley could dash off, 'get patrol cars to check all roads leading north towards Balcorie. Best get local police up there to set up roadblocks into the village.'

'Right.' Quigley was about to go to arrange everything, but Fleming made another suggestion. 'Might be an idea while you're in touch with local police to get them to take Ailsa Brodie into protective custody until we find McCabe.'

Quigley, with a wry smile on his face, hovered with a hand on the office door knob. 'Sure that's everything?'

'It is,' Aitken confirmed.

Quigley pulled the door open and ran to his desk to start making calls.

McCabe was aware Aitken had gone to the PPU with a DCI from Thames Valley Police and realised the net was closing in on him. He'd gone off duty that afternoon to pay a visit to Big Col.

Early next morning, long before Quigley had started making his calls, McCabe was on his way north on a motorbike. Big Col had supplied it together with a Glock 17 pistol and a wad of cash, telling McCabe to kill Brodie and get out of the country.

After killing Brodie, McCabe was to bike back down to Aberdeen to catch a ferry to Lerwick. Once there, he would get a flight to Amsterdam. Calhoun had given him a false passport and details to find his drug dealer associate in the Netherlands. He'd told McCabe the contact would help him to disappear.

72

BALCORIE

Dawn had broken two hours before McCabe pulled the motorbike off the road at the top of the hill overlooking Balcorie. He wheeled the bike behind an outcrop of rocks. Grabbing binoculars out of his haversack, he climbed up onto the rocks so he had a good view of the village below.

The weather had been kind to him. Although still cool at seven in the morning, there was a clear blue sky apart from a few white clouds drifting inland from the sea. Screaming seagulls swooped and dived above the clifftops on his left.

McCabe removed his black helmet and placed it beside him. Lifting his binoculars to his eyes he scanned the village below. The only sign of life was an early morning milkman doing his rounds.

After an hour, there were more signs of activity. Early risers got into their cars and set off, heading south on the road towards Lochinver. McCabe guessed they were most likely going to work.

Half an hour later, the door to an old fisherman's cottage at the far end of the village opened. A young man appeared, hauling backpack straps over his shoulders. McCabe adjusted the binoculars and zoomed in on him. He was sure it was the man he'd seen walking with Brodie below the clifftops when he'd been spying on her.

Alert, McCabe trained his binoculars on the man and watched him walk up through the village. He stopped at the post office where McCabe had called in on the off-chance of finding out where Brodie lived.

McCabe saw the man glance at his watch before climbing some steps up the side of the post office to a door at the top. He knocked, but McCabe couldn't see the person who opened it as the man went in.

After fifteen minutes, the door opened again and the young man came out followed by Brodie who also wore a backpack. 'Result,' McCabe whispered to himself. *Going for a walk. Perfect.*

He trained his binoculars on them and watched as they made their way to the edge of the village. McCabe smiled. They were setting out at the foot of the coastal path coming in his direction.

Toby was thrilled to be back in Balcorie. He regretted the unhappy circumstances under which he'd left his mother, but felt better he'd made his peace with his brother. The time had come, Toby had resolved, to face up to his mother. It had been easier than he'd have thought possible, but that was due to her duplicity in trying to persuade him to go back to London.

On his return to Balcorie, they'd enjoyed a quiet evening at Ailsa's flat above the post office. They'd had a meal and a bottle of wine. Ailsa had said how relieved she was that Toby had come back and Toby relayed his encounter with his mother. It hadn't been too late before Toby went back to his cottage. Ailsa had suggested they go for a long walk the next day, so he'd decided to have an early night after his tiring trip.

Next day, Toby had a large cooked breakfast before setting off. It was half past eight when he left the cottage to walk up to Ailsa's flat. She was almost ready, only a few last things to cram into her backpack.

Fifteen minutes later, they were ready to go. 'Where are we going today?' Toby asked.

'Weather's supposed to hold all day, so I thought we'd head up the southern coastal path. The scenery up there is spectacular.'

'I've brought some light waterproofs... just in case,' Toby said.

'Me too,' Ailsa admitted, despite her confidence over the weather forecast.

On top of the hill, McCabe watched the pair make their way out of the village and up onto the coastal path. He lost sight of them at times, but had worked out where they would appear on the clifftops.

He grabbed his helmet and left it on the motorbike ready for a quick getaway. Making sure the bike was well out of sight of the road, he pulled the Glock out of the haversack and made off across the hillside towards the coastal path.

After walking for about an hour, Toby and Ailsa found a sheltered spot from the breeze coming off the sea and sat down to enjoy the view. A fishing boat bobbed up and down on the swell as it headed out to sea. Gulls dived towards them as though seeking titbits of food, then swooped away when they saw there was none.

They sat in silence for a minute or two, listening to the waves crashing against the rocks far below them. Toby decided to ask Ailsa again what was on her mind. 'You remember when I got the call from my brother when we were on our last walk?'

'Yes, why?'

'You were about to tell me what was worrying you. The long story you were going to tell me about one day. Feel like telling me now?'

Ailsa sighed. 'Okay. I guess you ought to know.'

'Go on.'

'Five years ago, there was a jewellery shop robbery in Edinburgh. It went wrong and I witnessed a man shooting a policeman while trying to escape. I identified him and testified against him in court. It was a man called Calhoun.'

'But he must be in prison. Why are you worried about him?'

'The police believe his elder brother is behind organised crime in Edinburgh. He's one of those gangsters no one seems able to touch. Uses other people to commit crimes and swears them to silence.'

'You think he's out to get you for testifying against his brother?'

'The police thought it would be a distinct possibility.'

'But it was five years ago.'

'The police thought me and another man who testified were at risk, and that the risk was so great the police decided to move us to different areas and give us new identities.'

Toby shook his head in disbelief. 'I don't know what to say. How awful. Do you know who the other witness is?'

'A man called Malcolm Munro.'

'Where is he now?'

'I've no idea. They didn't tell me.'

'So he doesn't know where you are and what your new identity is either?'

'I doubt it.'

Then it dawned on Toby. 'There was the man who asked about you in the post office and the day I thought I saw someone on the clifftop. You think someone is watching you, don't you?'

'I'm a bit jumpy yes. Call it a sixth sense. There's a chance this Calhoun guy may have found out where I am after all this time.'

The coastal path was less than a mile away across fields, McCabe guessed. He checked the Glock and set off once more, hoping he would meet up with Brodie and her companion before they turned back to the village. Pity, she had someone with her. He would have to die as well.

73

BALCORIE AND EDINBURGH

McCabe had left his hiding place by the side of the road at the top of the hill overlooking Balcorie. It was long before the police roadblocks had been set up and the all-points bulletin had been issued. He guessed the police would be on the lookout for him by now, but felt sure he'd gained a few hours.

The village wasn't in his line of vision as he made his way on foot across the hillside, heading for the coastal path. The going was tough across rough terrain. He'd decided to keep his motorbike leathers on which didn't make things any easier. Although sweating, he thought it was worth the discomfort. He needed to make a quick escape after he'd killed Brodie and her companion.

McCabe reckoned he would reach the coastal path in around half an hour. Maybe less. He was sure he would get there before the couple. Estimating the distance from the village to the point on the path he aimed to reach, he doubted they would be there before him. There was always the possibility they might turn back before they reached him, but McCabe thought it unlikely as they both had backpacks. A sign of a long day out.

~

Half an hour after Toby and Ailsa had left the flat to go on their walk, a police car pulled up outside the post office. A young uniformed officer climbed out of the car and went into the shop to find Moira, the postmistress, sitting behind the counter knitting.

'Not very busy then?' the officer said.

Moira squinted at the young man. 'It keeps me occupied when there're no customers.' She looped a length of wool round the end of a needle. 'Don't often see uniformed police calling in here. My guess is you haven't just popped in for some stamps.'

The officer smiled. 'No, I'm looking for an Ailsa Brodie. Small place. I suppose you know where she lives.'

'I do.'

The officer looked up at the ceiling. 'Where?'

'The flat upstairs. Steps are up the side of the post office.'

'Thanks,' the officer said, turning to leave the shop.

'But you won't find her in.'

The policeman sighed and turned round to face Moira again. 'I don't suppose you know where she's gone?'

'No. They went for a walk. Left about half an hour ago.'

'They?'

'Ailsa and her friend, Toby Enderby.'

'Which direction did they go?'

Moira shrugged. 'Don't know. There are lots of walks you can go on from here. Could have gone on any of them.'

The officer took in a deep breath. 'If they come back, can you ask Miss Brodie to call the police at Lochinver immediately?'

'Can do, but I think they could be gone for some time. They both had backpacks. It's forecast to be a nice day. I'd guess they might not be back till late afternoon.'

'Okay. You won't forget to tell her though, will you?'

Moira frowned. 'Of course not. Is there a problem?'

'She just needs to call us. It's urgent,' the officer said and left.

He got back in the car and turned to his companion. 'Missed them. The woman in the post office has no idea where they've gone. Better get on the radio.'

While DS Quigley was still making his telephone calls, Aitken had made two calls of his own. He put the phone down. 'Got a helicopter coming over from the air support unit in Glasgow... in case we need to get to Balcorie in a rush,' he told Fleming. 'It'll be here in about half an hour.'

'You're sure he's on his way to find Brodie and he's not done a runner?' Fleming queried. 'Bit of an expense getting a helicopter if it's not needed.'

'Budgets never bothered me, Alex. I just get on with the job and, if that means spending money, Police Scotland has to cough up.'

Fleming smiled. 'Man after my own heart. Doesn't mean you won't get a good bollocking for wasting money though.'

'Only if it's wasted. We might save a life. Make it all worthwhile, don't you think?'

'You don't need to convince me.'

'I've also arranged to get a couple of armed officers to come with us if we need to go.'

'Makes sense if we do find McCabe. In the meantime, I guess we can do no more than sit it out here waiting to see if we hear anything from Waverley. Too soon to get a result from the ABP or ports and airports.'

Fleming glanced out of the glass partition in Aitken's office and saw Quigley putting his phone down. Before he could pick it up again it rang. He watched as Quigley listened for a few seconds, said something, then ended the call.

Quigley got up from his desk and strode across to Aitken's office. He knocked and opened the door looking serious. 'Just had a call from Lochinver police station. Roadblocks have been set up on the roads into Balcorie, but there's no sign of McCabe so far. They sent a car there to find Brodie, but they missed her by half an hour. Sounds like she's gone off on a long walk with a male friend.'

Aitken made a quick decision. 'I don't like it. McCabe could have gone on the run, but I'm not taking any chances. I have a bad feeling about this. Get back onto Lochinver,' he told Quigley. 'Tell them to get as many officers as they can to start a search.'

Aitken looked at Fleming. 'We should get up there in the helicopter. We can be there in under an hour and a half.'

74

BALCORIE

M cCabe had been walking for about twenty minutes. He could see a slight dip in the field he was crossing, leading down to the coastal path. Glancing in both directions, he could see no sign of Brodie and her companion. Ten minutes and he would be on the path.

Over to his right, the path wound its way along the clifftop where it rose steeply then fell down to Balcorie. McCabe reckoned the village, still out of his line of vision, must be a good two miles away. It would be a steep climb up to the clifftops from the village. Brodie and the young man would be walking about twice the distance he had from where he'd left the motorbike. By McCabe's reckoning, he had to be on the path below him well before his victims arrived.

Time to search for the perfect spot.

On the path, McCabe looked up to his left. The path sloped upwards to what looked like the highest point, almost on the cliff edge. On the left of the path, which disappeared round a bend, there was a rocky outcrop.

Ideal. From there I'll be able to see them coming.

Seagulls swooped overhead as McCabe glanced down the

sheer drop of the cliff. The sea crashed against the rocks far below. Setting off again, he made the climb up to the rocky outcrop he'd seen.

After ten sweating minutes, he reached the bend in the path. The cliff edge was only three steps to the right. The cliff was about sixty feet higher than the point he'd left down in the dip. He turned the corner and found he could see the path some way ahead.

Climbing up onto the rocky outcrop, McCabe had a clear view of the path in both directions. He would be able to see if any other walkers were approaching when Brodie and her companion arrived.

'Have you told the police you're worried someone may have found out where you are?' Toby asked Ailsa.

'No, the local police don't know I'm on witness protection. Only the Protected Persons Unit know. They told me never to discuss it with anyone.'

Toby frowned. 'You told *me* about it.'

'I tried to avoid telling you, but we've become close and I trust you. There shouldn't be any secrets between us. You're a good man, Toby. If I'm in danger, it's only right you should know about it.'

Toby thought about this for a second, tilting his head to one side. 'You're not suggesting I shouldn't be your friend, are you? I mean... in case I get caught up in whatever danger you may be in.'

'Oh, God. No! I didn't mean that at all.' Ailsa put a hand on Toby's. 'That's the last thing I want. I just felt you ought to be aware of it, that's all.' She smiled. 'I was becoming worried you might find out and would think it wrong of me for keeping a secret from you.'

Toby saw the concern in Ailsa's eyes. He grinned. 'No worries. There's no way I'd want to stop seeing you.'

Ailsa smiled. 'Glad to hear it.'

'You could go to the local police and say you're worried someone is watching you. Tell them about the stranger asking where you lived, but don't tell them about the witness protection stuff.'

'I'm not sure it would be high on the priority list of local police. I mean... if I told them I was worried about a few instances where I thought I saw or heard something, and that someone came looking for me.'

'You could be right,' Toby conceded.

'The PPU did stress I wasn't to tell anyone. But... I may end up having to tell the police if they didn't think my concerns were anything to worry about. The fewer people who know, the less chance anyone could find me. If I go to the police, my whereabouts could leak out.'

'What about the PPU? Couldn't you have alerted them?'

'I thought about it, but then realised I don't have much I can tell them. It's only a feeling I have. Do you think I'm being a bit neurotic?'

'Of course not. What about the man asking about you in the post office?'

'That, I'm afraid, I can't explain. It's the one thing that does make me feel nervous. But is that enough to bother the PPU with?'

'I'd say so.'

'They'll most likely say people knew me as Ailsa Brodie for five years. It would be possible for an old acquaintance who knew me under that name to want to look me up if they were in the area.'

'I can see they might not want to take it seriously, but they have to look into it, don't you think?'

Ailsa sighed. 'You're right. I ought to give them a call. I'll do it tomorrow.'

Toby got to his feet and pulled Ailsa up. 'In the meantime...' He waved a hand along he coastal path. 'Let's carry on!'

McCabe had settled down to wait on top of the rocky outcrop. After almost forty-five minutes, he was beginning to panic. They'd either stopped somewhere for a rest, decided to go back down to the village, or headed off in the other direction.

The second and third options seemed unlikely. Carrying backpacks suggested a long day out. And... why would you decide to go back on yourself and go in the opposite direction? No, the most likely explanation was they'd stopped for a rest and a drink. *Be patient.*

He didn't have to wait much longer. He saw the young man's head first, then Brodie's as they came over the crest down below. A minute later they were in full view.

75

EDINBURGH AND BALCORIE

The squad car sped through Edinburgh with blue lights flashing and its siren wailing. It was on its way from Gayfield Square to Montgomery Street Park. In under four minutes, the car pulled up on the road beside the park. The black and yellow Airbus H135-T3 helicopter was waiting, parked near the roadside. People had gathered at the edge of the park to see what was going on as the aircraft had come in to land.

Fleming and Aitken got out of the car and ran across the grass towards the helicopter, ducking as they approached. The rotor blades wound up as the door opened and a man dressed in green zip-up overalls ushered them in. 'Welcome aboard. We'll be taking off right away. Take a seat and fasten your belts.'

The two detectives took the seats behind the pilot and the man next to him, and strapped themselves in. The officer who had welcomed them spoke again. 'I'm Jack, the rear air observer. Ewan is our pilot. Beside him is Glen, the front seat observer. We also have two armed officers sitting in the back. They arrived a few minutes ago.'

Ewan and Glen raised their hands over their heads by way of

greeting. The two men in the back, cradling Heckler and Koch carbines, gave a slight wave.

'DCI Fleming and DI Aitken,' Fleming said, completing the introductions.

They'd left Quigley in charge of things back at Gayfield Square. He needed to be on hand in case any news came in from the all-points bulletin, port or airports.

Ewan turned to check they all had their seat belts on before giving a thumbs up. Engine noise increased and the gentle swish of the rotor blades turned into a loud whine. Fleming felt a slight jolt as the helicopter lifted off the ground. The downdraught from the rotor blades flattened the grass beneath them as they rose into the air. Seconds later, Ewan swung the helicopter round to face west as it gained height to speed across Edinburgh.

It wasn't long before they were flying across the Forth, with the rail and road bridges sliding past below them. Jack touched Fleming on the shoulder and spoke over the rhythmic pulsing throb of the rotors. 'We'll be heading northwest. Our flight time will be about an hour and a half. I'll be in radio contact with DS Quigley in Gayfield Square and with officers on the ground at Balcorie.'

'Okay,' Fleming said.

'Glen will be keeping an eye out in the front as we near the village. He'll be using a thermal imaging camera,' Jack said. 'We have to have it on for evidential purposes... in case the armed officers have to use their weapons.'

'Got it,' Fleming said.

After about half an hour, Fleming could see the A9 and Pitlochry out of his right-hand window. It was then that Jack's radio crackled and he spoke into the mouthpiece. 'Eagle one, over.'

Fleming thought he could hear Quigley's garbled voice.

Jack listened for a few seconds, then said, 'Thanks for that. Out.'

'DS Quigley with an update,' Jack said. 'The APB hasn't come up with anything yet. No sign of the target. There haven't been any sightings at ports or airports. Neither have the roadblocks outside Balcorie been able to pick him up so far.'

Aitken turned to Fleming. 'Beginning to look like my hunch might pay off. I'm sure McCabe's on his way to Balcorie.' He rubbed his chin. 'Unless he's already there.'

'For Ailsa Brodie's sake, I hope not. But, with a bit of luck, we'll get to him before he gets to Ailsa.'

Jack had been on the radio again. 'I've been speaking to officers in Balcorie,' he said. 'Bit thin on the ground, but they've started to fan out from the village searching for McCabe or Brodie. No sign of either of them so far.'

Under an hour and a half after leaving Edinburgh, Fleming could see the sun glinting on the sea ahead. Ten minutes later, the helicopter dropped to a hundred feet, hovering over Balcorie. Fleming could see the thin line of officers down below, fanning out over the hill slopes behind the village. He guessed the local police must have taken a while to organise the search party. They hadn't gone far out of Balcorie yet.

'Take a sweep up the foothills behind the village first,' Glen suggested.

'Roger that,' Ewan said, and steered the helicopter away from Balcorie. It flew back and forth along the lower slopes first, then flew further out. Most of the slopes ahead were visible from the air. But there were lots of dips in the land where it would be difficult to see anyone unless hovering overhead. After a few minutes, it seemed a wasted exercise. They'd not spotted anyone.

'Try the path running along the top of the cliffs,' Fleming suggested.

Ewan gave a thumbs up and swung the helicopter round to cross back over Balcorie. Once at the seashore he veered off to the right to follow the coastal path going north.

Glen, Fleming and Aitken scanned the ground below for a few minutes, but there was no one in sight.

'Do you want us to keep going this way, or search the path going south away from the village?' Glen asked, turning to face Fleming and Aitken.

Fleming looked at Aitken.

'Go the other way?' Aitken queried.

'Okay,' Fleming said. 'Let's try the path to the south.'

76

BALCORIE

'Oh, no!' Toby exclaimed as he reached what he thought was the highest point of the coastal path.

'Forgot to tell you,' Ailsa said, coming up behind him. 'There's always another climb ahead just when you think you've reached the top of a hill round here.'

'Now you tell me. That was a steep climb up, and look... we go all the way down the dip then have to go up again.'

Ailsa laughed. 'I've been up here many a time. You'll be relieved to know that's the highest bit up there,' she said, pointing up to the rocky outcrop ahead.

Toby took in a deep breath of fresh air. 'Okay. We could have another rest and a drink when we get up there. Mind you,' he added, 'I have to say my asthma hasn't bothered me much since I moved to Balcorie.'

'It's good clean air up here. I read somewhere that central London can be one of the most polluted places in the UK. Traffic pollution, I guess. Can't have been doing your lungs any good.'

'You can say that again!'

'Be careful. You need to watch your footing when we get up there. The path goes quite near to the cliff edge and it's a sheer drop down to the rocks below. Wouldn't do you much good if you fell.'

Toby raised his eyebrows. 'Thanks for telling me. I'll try my best to stay on the path.'

Ailsa gave Toby a gentle nudge in the back. 'On you go then.'

McCabe watched as Brodie and her companion stopped at the top of the crest on the other side of the dip in the path. It looked as though they were having a quick word. He saw Brodie pointing up towards him and wondered if they were having second thoughts about going any further.

Fuck! That'll make things difficult if they do turn back.

He needn't have worried. As soon as the thought had crossed his mind, he saw Brodie nudge the young man in the back and they started down the path, heading to the dip below him.

McCabe watched the pair go down the path and then start the ascent up towards him. He felt a sense of relief. No other walkers appeared over the crest behind the couple. He looked behind him and couldn't see anyone coming the other way either.

Looking good.

A few minutes later, Toby reached the rocky outcrop first. He turned to hold Ailsa's hand as she took the last step up. Somewhere in the distance there was the gentle staccato throbbing of a helicopter engine getting closer.

'Time for that drink now?' Toby asked.

'You won't be needing a drink,' a man's droll voice came from behind.

McCabe stepped out from some rocks pointing his Glock at them.

Toby wheeled round in alarm. 'What the–'

Ailsa gasped and stared in horror at the gun aimed at them.

'Took a while to find you,' McCabe said. 'But nobody ever gets away with crossing Big Col Calhoun.'

'Wha... what do you mean?' Ailsa stammered.

'Maisey Jackson, isn't it?'

Ailsa shook her head. 'What?'

'You're Maisey Jackson, the woman who testified against the Big Col's younger brother five years ago. That right?'

'No... no, I'm Ailsa Brodie. You're mistaken.'

'No mistake,' McCabe said. 'I checked with the Protected Persons Unit. Big Col wanted to find the two people who were responsible for his kid brother getting a life sentence. That's why he recruited me to help. The only way to stand any chance of finding out where they were was by using a policeman.'

Toby was looking at the gun. His legs felt weak and his heart was thumping. He didn't know why, but felt he had to keep the man talking. As long as he was talking, he wasn't shooting. 'You're still in the police?'

'I am. Had to trick a young woman working in the PPU in the end to get the information. DS Liam McCabe... if you'd like to know. Don't mind if you do, being as neither of you will be alive to tell anyone.'

Toby was playing for time, trying to work out what to do. *Keep him talking.* 'You said two people. Who's the other person?'

'Was... got him first. The PPU renamed a man called Munro. They gave him the name Oliver Upton and moved him to Oxford. Bit unfortunate but he had a partner who I had to kill as well... just in case he'd told her about the witness protection thing. Could have led the police to think Big Col was behind it.'

'I don't know what you're talking about,' Ailsa said.

'Oh, yes you do. The woman in the PPU told me you were now known as Ailsa Brodie and you lived in Balcorie.'

Ailsa shook her head but said nothing.

Toby pointed at the Glock. He was trying to work out if he could rush McCabe, giving Ailsa a chance to run. 'That what you killed Upton and his partner with?'

McCabe looked at the gun. 'This... no. I used a rifle. Quite neat. I got Upton on a golf course and his partner on Clapham Common.'

Toby raised an eyebrow. He recalled his brother's words: *Hear about the shooting on Clapham Common the other week?*

'If you shoot us, someone may hear the shots,' Toby said, getting desperate. He couldn't keep McCabe talking much longer and would have to do something soon.

'Don't think I need this,' McCabe said looking at the gun. 'You're both going to jump... over there,' he said, waving the gun at the cliff edge. 'When someone finds the bodies, they'll think you fell.'

77

BALCORIE

Fleming looked past Ewan as the helicopter peeled away from the path, swung round to the left over the sea, then headed back towards Balcorie.

Ewan steered a course over the village before linking up with the coastal path going south. Hovering at a hundred feet, he flew the helicopter up the incline away from the village. Not long after, it rose above the first ridge to see the dip ahead and another ridge higher up.

'We have a visual! Three people up there on the next ridge,' Glen exclaimed.

Aitken craned his neck to look past Ewan and Glen. 'That's him! It's McCabe!'

Toby was starting to think there was nothing else he could do. He was about to launch himself at McCabe, but the sudden loud chopping of helicopter rotor blades made him stop. He glanced over his shoulder and saw it rising above the lower ridge like a giant metal insect.

McCabe growled as the helicopter swept towards them. It turned sideways on and hovered at an angle, thirty feet above the path. The downdraft from the rotor blades flattened the grass below and flapped at the clothing of the three people beneath.

A distorted, amplified voice boomed through a loudhailer over the pulsating throb of the helicopter engine. 'Armed police. Drop your weapon.'

Toby watched McCabe let his gun hand drop as though he was giving up, then drew in a sharp breath as McCabe lifted it with a sudden movement and aimed at the helicopter. He fired several rapid shots. Most of the bullets hit the underside of the fuselage, but one bullet thudded into the pilot's upper arm.

At the same time McCabe fired his gun, one of the armed officers let off a round with his Heckler and Koch carbine. A bullet tore into McCabe's shoulder. He tried to lift his gun arm again but Toby lunged towards McCabe and grabbed the Glock. He wrestled it out of his hand and threw it to the ground.

McCabe sank to his knees and toppled over onto his back.

Ailsa screamed and flung her arms round a shaking Toby.

Fleming watched Ewan as he struggled with the helicopter controls. Somehow, the pilot managed to lower the aircraft nearer to the ground.

'Jump out, now!' Jack shouted to the armed officers.

They needed no second bidding and were out and on the path beside McCabe in seconds.

338

One of the officers kicked the Glock out of McCabe's reach while the other felt for a pulse. He pulled his hand away from McCabe's neck and turned to signal to the helicopter but it had veered up in an erratic arc to head inland with a sudden loud whine of the engine. 'Fuck!' he shouted as the landing gear scraped the top of the rocky outcrop. 'It's going to go down!' he yelled as the helicopter disappeared over the ridge with its engine stuttering.

Inside the helicopter, Jack shouted to the pilot. 'Ewan! Can you land it?'

'Trying,' Ewan hissed through gritted teeth.

'Put it down in that field if you can,' Jack said, pointing ahead. Then, looking at Fleming and Aitken, 'Get ready for a rough landing and get out quick. Glen and I will see to Ewan.'

Aitken gave a weak smile and gripped his seat belt.

Fleming took a deep breath then yelled, 'Think he can do it?'

Jack had no time to answer. Ewan was wrestling with the controls and his head began to droop. The helicopter was about twenty feet from the ground when Ewan slumped over the controls and his feet slipped of the pedals. The helicopter dipped and spun out of control.

Back on the coastal path, the two officers stared at the top of the ridge and held their breath as they heard the helicopter engine splutter and die.

'Fuck!' one of the men exclaimed as there was a loud crash and a sickening screech of twisting metal. There followed a few seconds of deadly silence, then an explosion ripped through the air and a huge ball of flame leapt up into the sky.

78

EDINBURGH

It was four weeks after the incident on the clifftop. Aitken was talking to Logan outside interview room one at Gayfield Square.

'How's Alex?' he asked Logan.

'Thanks to you and the rear air observer... what was his name?'

'Jack.'

'Right. Thanks to you two, the boss is alive, but still in hospital with spinal injuries. Miracle you both managed to get him out before the helicopter went up in flames. And that the pair of you got out without serious injury.'

'I guess so. The pilot and the front seat observer, Glen, weren't so lucky. They both died.'

Logan grimaced. 'How about Ailsa and Toby? Must have been a shock for them. How are they doing?'

'Yeah. They had some mental health help. As far as I know, life seems to be back to as near to normal as possible for them.'

'Good.'

'I suggest I question McCabe first on the attempted murders of Ailsa and Toby, and his association with Calhoun,' Aitken said. 'It's then over to you to question him about the murders of Oliver Upton and Jamila Kazan.'

'Okay by me.'

'Right, let's go in.'

McCabe had survived. His life had been in the balance for a while, but he came through. Looking pale and gaunt, he sat beside the duty solicitor. Aitken and Logan entered the room and sat opposite them. Logan switched on the digital recorder and Aitken went through the usual protocols. He cautioned McCabe and looked across at the duty solicitor. 'Can you confirm your client is fit enough to answer questions?'

'I am,' McCabe answered for him. He winced and rubbed his shoulder. 'Never been better.'

Aitken looked at the solicitor and raised an eyebrow.

'As far as I know, there's no medical reason why you can't question him.'

Aitken turned to McCabe. 'You're facing some serious charges. It would be better for you if you told us everything.'

McCabe said nothing.

'Let's start with the murders of the two helicopter crew members. You have no defence. There were seven eye witnesses. I happen to be one of them.'

McCabe shrugged. 'No point in denying it.'

'You're already facing a life sentence so why not come clean about the attempted murders of Ailsa Brodie and Toby Enderby. Big Col Calhoun wanted you to find and kill Maisey Jackson who the PPU renamed Ailsa Brodie, didn't he? Wanted revenge for her testifying against his young brother.'

McCabe said nothing.

'You know he's going to point the finger at you when we question him,' Aitken said.

McCabe stared ahead and remained silent.

'We found the motorbike you went up to Balcorie on,' Aitken

continued. 'There was a haversack containing a wad of cash, a false passport, and the name and address of a man in the Netherlands. We know the man is Calhoun's drug dealing contact.'

McCabe stayed poker-faced.

'Thing is,' Aitken went on, 'police in Amsterdam arrested the man. He decided to co-operate. Came clean and admitted to arranging shipments of drugs and guns for Calhoun using Jenner Transport.'

'What's that got to do with me?'

'He claimed Calhoun had told him you would be getting in touch with him after carrying out a contract killing. Said you believed he would be helping you to disappear.'

'Is that a fact?'

'I suppose there was some degree of truth in that,' Aitken continued. 'Calhoun had told him to kill you. He couldn't take any chances the police might catch up with you.'

McCabe snorted. 'Bastard. Would have been better for me if I'd died from the bullet wound up there on the clifftop. No point in denying anything now, is there? Yeah, I was working for Calhoun and he wanted Brodie dead. Enderby just happened to be in the way.'

'Okay, let's take a break,' Aitken said. 'Interview suspended at ten thirty.'

Logan had taken over the questioning after a short coffee break.

'I want to cover the murders of Oliver Upton and Jamila Kazan,' Logan began. 'Kazan is really the Met's case but, under the circumstances, they've agreed I can question you on their behalf.'

'Good for them.'

'You've admitted that Calhoun got you to find and kill Ailsa Brodie because she testified against his brother. There was another witness, Malcolm Munro, who the PPU renamed Upton. He also testified against Calhoun's brother. Calhoun got you to find and kill him as well, didn't he?'

McCabe held his hands up. 'Okay. I've nothing to lose being as I'm already done for life. Maybe they'll release me eventually if I cooperate.'

Logan didn't comment.

'Can't deny it. Pat Finn in the PPU gave me his new name and location. Yeah, I killed him, and his partner Jamila Kazan. Calhoun didn't want to run the risk she might have known about him.'

Logan had the confession he wanted. 'Thank you. I have no further questions.'

'I'm fucked, aren't I?' McCabe said. 'Don't fancy my chances in prison as a convicted cop.'

79

EDINBURGH

Aitken and Logan had left Calhoun and his solicitor sweating in a hot and stuffy interview room two at Gayfield Square. Calhoun's solicitor had asked for a break for a drink of water and a chance to speak to his client. Aitken had agreed, and he and Logan left the room to get some fresh air outside.

After a ten-minute break, they were about to go back into the interview room. 'Okay if I carry on grilling Calhoun?' Aitken asked Logan. 'I want to pin him down over drugs and gun smuggling, and incitement to kill Ailsa Brodie and Jenner. I've already got the confession police in Amsterdam obtained from Calhoun's contact.'

'Fine by me,' Logan said. 'I've also got McCabe's confession about Upton and Jamila. You should have enough on Calhoun to put him away for a few years. If we get him for incitement to murder as well, it'll be the icing on the cake. He'll be facing a life sentence.'

'Okay,' Aitken said. 'Let's go and turn the screws on him.'

Aitken and Logan entered the room and took their seats

facing Calhoun and his solicitor again. Logan switched on the digital recorder.

'Interview resumed at 11am,' Aitken said.

Calhoun took a sip of water from a plastic beaker, eyeing Aitken over the rim with cold eyes.

Aitken met his gaze. 'Let's go back to the attempted murder of Ailsa Brodie and Toby Ender–'

'My client has already told you he had nothing to do with it,' Calhoun's solicitor cut in.

'I am aware of that. But there is evidence to show he had a motive to want Brodie killed. She testified against his brother and he got a life sentence.'

'Having a reason isn't proof of guilt. It's just a coincidence.'

Aitken ignored the remark and turned to face Calhoun again. 'We have a confession from Liam McCabe. He says he was working for you and admitted that you paid him to find and kill her.'

'One man's word against another.'

'There's enough evidence to convince a jury that you were behind the attempted murders of her and Toby Enderby.'

'You can't pin incitement to kill him on me as well,' Calhoun blurted out.

The solicitor put a restraining hand on Calhoun's arm to stop him from saying any more.

'He happened to be in the way!'

'I wasn't going to charge you with incitement to murder Toby Enderby. From what you just said though, it does sound like you did know McCabe was going to kill Brodie.'

Calhoun had recovered his self-control. He gave a weak smile. 'Only guessing that's what must have happened.'

'Let's move on to the drugs and gun smuggling operation,' Aitken said. 'Police in Amsterdam have a signed confession from a man who has confirmed he was helping you and Doug Jenner smuggle drugs and guns into Scotland.'

'He's lying.'

'Jenner's wife claims you were talking about it with her husband.'

'You told me she didn't see the man talking to her husband.'

'She saw a black car parked at Jenner's depot. You have a black car.'

'Yeah... me and thousands of others.'

'I also have a signed confession from Jenner.'

'Jenner's dead.'

Aitken glared at Calhoun. 'Convenient, eh?'

Calhoun's solicitor held up a hand. 'Hang on there, are you accusing my client of something?'

Aitken ignored the question and directed one of his own at Calhoun. 'Did you arrange for someone to kill Doug Jenner in prison?'

Calhoun let out a nervous laugh. 'You're joking... right?'

'You did, didn't you?'

'No!'

'Thing is, Jenner signed a statement confirming you were the boss of the drugs and gun smuggling operation. He was prepared to testify in court against you.'

'Seems everyone's lying to you,' Calhoun spat out.

'You knew the net was beginning to close in on you a while back. That's why you got Liam McCabe to persuade his old boss to shelve the case against Jenner and you.'

'Rubbish!'

'They've found out who the inmate was who killed Jenner. That worry you?'

Calhoun shook his head. 'Why would it?'

'Seems someone had it in for him and wanted to improve

their chances of getting parole. Decided to cough up and tell the police who the killer was.'

'Oh yeah?'

'Yes. There was forensic evidence as well. The man cracked and admitted it was him.'

Calhoun shrugged. 'People make enemies in prison.'

'They're also at risk if they've agreed to testify against a suspect.'

'Inspector,' Calhoun's solicitor said, 'are you suggesting my client had something to do with this?'

Aitken glared at him. 'The man who murdered Jenner has confirmed it was your client who wanted him killed.'

'He's lying. They're all bloody lying!' Calhoun shouted.

'I have no further questions,' Aitken said.

Logan cleared his throat and took over. 'My enquiry is connected to the charge that you tried to arrange the murder of Ailsa Brodie.'

'Look,' Calhoun's solicitor said, 'how many times do we need to go over this before you accept my client had nothing to do with that?'

'I said my enquiry happens to be *connected*,' Logan reminded him. 'It's a different case.'

Calhoun flashed a look at his solicitor.

'You paid Liam McCabe to kill Oliver Upton and Jamila Kazan, didn't you?' Logan said.

Calhoun shook his head.

'For the purposes of the DIR,' Logan said, 'the suspect is shaking his head. Do you deny Liam McCabe was a bent cop in your pocket?'

'Course I do. That's rubbish!'

'Why would he claim he was if he wasn't?'

'No comment.'

'DI Aitken has pointed out you had a good reason to want

Ailsa Brodie killed. Upton was the other witness. I repeat, you paid McCabe to kill him as well, didn't you?'

'No comment.'

'Was it your idea, or his, to shoot his partner Jamila Kazan as well?'

'No comment.'

Logan leaned across the interview table. 'McCabe has confessed to both killings. He says you got him to murder Upton and Jamila Kazan.'

'He's lying! I didn't ask him to kill Kazan as well!'

'As well? Meaning you do admit to getting him to kill Upton?'

Calhoun glared at Logan. 'No comment.'

Logan sat back in his chair. 'Interview terminated at five past twelve.'

80

OXFORD

Two weeks later, the chief constable put her hand on Temple's office door and turned as she was about to leave. 'Good job on the Upton case, Fleming,' she said. 'Afraid I must dash... another meeting to go to.' She paused for a second. 'Sorry you're having to leave us.' She pulled the door open and was gone.

'Good of her to find the time to pop in to thank me,' Fleming said. 'Regret about me leaving seemed a bit of an afterthought though. Didn't even ask how I was.'

'Unforgivable, I have to say,' Temple agreed. 'So how are you?'

'Lucky to be alive, I suppose. If it wasn't for Gordon Aitken and the helicopter crew man I wouldn't be here.'

Temple nodded. 'What's the long-term prognosis.'

'Spinal injuries take time to heal.' Fleming tapped the arms of his wheelchair. 'Stuck in this for now. Getting regular physiotherapy. Jury's out on whether I'll be able to walk again.'

'I'm so sorry.'

'Have you heard anything about Ailsa Brodie and Toby Enderby?' Fleming asked.

'They're fine. I gather there may be a hint of an engagement.'

Fleming smiled. 'That's great. I'm glad they're okay.'

'They have nothing more to worry about from McCabe or Calhoun,' Temple said. 'McCabe's certain to get a life sentence. If the court finds Calhoun guilty of incitement to murder Upton, Jamila Kazan and Ailsa, he'll get life as well. Then there's the drugs and gun smuggling charge and incitement to murder Jenner.'

'Glad it's all over.'

Temple sighed. 'You did a good job, Alex. Solved a murder case for the Met as well. They're very grateful, by the way.' She hesitated and Fleming thought he saw tears forming in her eyes. 'We'll miss you. Any plans?'

'Thanks, ma'am. Too early. No hasty decisions. I'll go and see Logan and Anderson on my way out.'

Logan was busy taking things off the whiteboard while Anderson was cataloguing documents for filing.

'How'd your meeting with the chief constable and the super go?' Logan asked.

'Very quick,' Fleming replied.

'Chief constable wasn't impressed? After all the fuss she made about lack of progress?'

'I don't think she's one for dishing out compliments.'

'Bet she was more concerned about getting a result than your health,' Logan said.

'That's a fair assessment.'

'Cold-hearted bitch.'

'Sarge! Someone might hear you,' Anderson warned.

'Don't care. Think I've had enough of policing. Now the boss is going, I'm thinking of applying for early retirement.'

'Maybe you should think on it for a while,' Fleming said. 'Don't do anything hasty.'

Logan smiled. 'I won't.'

'You hear any more about Earl Yates?' Fleming asked.

'He's doing okay. Still getting treatment.'

'You went to see Atticus Kazan, didn't you?' Fleming asked Logan.

'I did. Man's a pain, but it seemed the right thing to do since we had him down as the number one suspect.'

'How was he?'

'Bit smarmy as usual. Look of satisfaction we were wrong about him. To be fair though, he was grateful I'd taken the trouble to go and see him to tell him we'd found the killer. Said he was sorry to hear about the helicopter crash and your injuries.'

'Give him credit for that. What about the other main suspect we had, Palmer?'

'Went to see him as well. He was thankful I'd bothered to look him up. Relieved to find he was in the clear,' Logan said.

'Changing the subject,' Anderson said, 'did you get any thanks from the Met for solving Jamila Kazan's murder for them, sir?'

'Chief constable got a thank you, by all accounts.'

'You didn't get a mention then?' Logan asked.

'I don't know if I did, to be honest.'

Logan frowned. 'I should bloody well hope you did!'

'Super told me they were grateful.'

'Yeah,' Logan said with an edge to his voice. 'Bet the thank you was to the chief constable and not you, boss.'

Fleming shrugged. 'Doesn't matter. I spoke on the phone to DI Gamez. She gave me a grudging thank you. Got the impression she seemed a bit annoyed because it was me who caught Jamila's killer, and not her.'

'Unbelievable,' Logan muttered.

Anderson had a thought. 'Do you know what happened to the woman in the PPU. The one who passed information to McCabe about Upton and Brodie?' she asked Fleming.

'I gather they didn't give her too hard a time. She did, after all, identify the killer who was also a bent cop. There was a disciplinary hearing. She came out of it with a written warning and a directive to attend a training course.'

'I'm glad she managed to keep her job,' Anderson said.

Fleming turned his wheelchair round when he heard Temple's voice behind him. 'This just arrived from a very grateful DI in Police Scotland,' she said, handing over a wrapped box to Fleming. 'He wanted me to know how helpful you'd been and asked me to pass it on to you.'

Fleming raised an eyebrow. 'From Gordon Aitken?'

'Yes.'

'Going to open it now?' Logan asked.

Fleming undid the wrapping and pulled out a bottle of ten-year-old Laphroaig single malt whisky. There was a card attached to it. Fleming flicked it open and read it out. 'Just a little thank you for helping me put away Big Col Calhoun at last. Get better soon, mate. This is to make up for that drink we didn't get time for.'

THE END

A NOTE FROM THE PUBLISHER

Thank you for reading this book. If you enjoyed it please do consider leaving a review on Amazon to help others find it too.

We hate typos. All of our books have been rigorously edited and proofread, but sometimes mistakes do slip through. If you have spotted a typo, please do let us know and we can get it amended within hours.

info@bloodhoundbooks.com